X

AFG

D1436456

THE CLIMB

The terrible North Face of the Heide looms high above the Alpine village of Lundervald. Snow-lined and beautiful in the sun, its precipitous rocks have sent to their death all too many who have tried to climb them. Stories of disaster on its sheer slabs or hanging terraces have made world headlines; and the pressmen speak of it sometimes as the 'killer mountain'. Perils from avalanche, cold, stonefall and sudden storm make the North Face —often called the North Wall—the most dangerous climb in the Alps.

In this novel a group of people are approaching Lundervald. Why are they coming? Each has his secret business there. To Graeme Muir the North Face has been a loved obsession—and is now a place where the tangle of his own life, of love and remorse and fear, may be forgotten, or eased. To Hugh Ferris, who has climbed in many of the high places of the world, it is his last adventure, a chance to prove to himself that he is not yet too old for one of the great climbs. To the young Sean Randall it is a necessary excitement, an achievement that will make his name known to mountaineers everywhere, that will partner it with Whymper and Mallory and Irvine—because the Germans have climbed the North Wall, the French have climbed it, but never yet an Englishman.

But to Judith, Graeme's wife, this approach to the mountain brings to a head all the fear and jealousy from years of marriage; it marks the hour when the clock is about to strike, the point of no return.

The heart of the novel is the tremendous, even terrifying, story of these three men climbing; its end, in the clear quiet after violence, reveals the strange outcome. The climb has shaped and altered the lives of all who were concerned with it.

THE CLIMB

DIANA RAYMOND

CASSELL · LONDON

CASSELL & COMPANY LTD
35 Red Lion Square : London WC1
and at
MELBOURNE : SYDNEY : TORONTO : CAPE TOWN
JOHANNESBURG : AUCKLAND

Printed in Great Britain
by Ebenezer Baylis and Son, Ltd.
The Trinity Press, Worcester, and London
F. 462

For

NANCY

with much love

Author's Note

The North Face of the Heide is imaginary but owes much both in character and locale to the North Face of the Eiger. My thanks are due to a Vice President of the Climbers' Club who has most kindly read the typescript and offered valuable suggestions for its improvement; and to Heinrich Harrer's classic history of the Eiger's North Face, *The White Spider*.

D.R.

PART I

THE JOURNEY OUT

CHAPTER ONE

THEY were in Paris by six o'clock. The city was comfortably held in warm grey air; the tall mansard roofs showed dry and pale like sea-bleached stones against the darker sky.

The hotel bedroom, high up, contained the false dusty gloom of summer evening in a city. Judith went at once to the window, mastered a convolution of nuts, bolts and handles, opened it and looked out. The narrow street below sang its high, busy song, continuous, unregarding.

'Now it has begun,' was the thought in her mind, as she turned back to the room, but all she said was, 'I wonder if we shall sleep.'

Graeme was taking off his raincoat with the sweeping, purposeful movements of a man determined to make himself quickly at home. 'I don't see why not.'

'Noise?'

'Oh, Paris is always noisy.'

'At night this room is quiet like the tomb,' said the porter and went to fetch another suitcase.

'I doubt it,' said Graeme. 'But we can shut the window.'

Then the room will be too hot, Judith thought, but she did not say it. There had been enough arguments over the last days; this was no time to start another. As she had expected Graeme went out almost at once, head down, hands in pockets, muffled in thought. Such had been his habit over twenty years of marriage; no need to feel misgivings. She wondered what he did in the strange streets: stared in shop windows, perhaps, bought cigarettes, sniffed the place like a dog, trying to come to terms with it.

'Madame is quite comfortable?'

Graeme had gone without tipping the hotel porter: this

3

arose, Judith reflected, not from meanness but from a failure to grasp that life was punctuated by the irritating necessity to spend small sums of money at practically any hour of the day or night. She said she was comfortable and sought among the unfamiliar francs.

'*Merci, madame.*'

When he had shut the door she thought again, 'Now it has really begun.' Yet the room, containing the flat unalive anonymity of all transient places of lodging—as if no one had been able to love or suffer, rejoice or pray there long enough for it to become human—offered a safety margin of three days. In three days' time they would be stripping from the room the marks of their brief habitation, and the fear would be closer. Much closer.

She quickly opened a suitcase whose familiarity spoke oddly of home amid the alien corn. Sponge bag, a clean blouse, change of shoes . . . such things, she reflected, formed a handrail in times of anxiety. There would come a point, of course, when this handrail would give out, and she would be on her own. That was not yet.

A looking-glass. Not so much for reassurance as habit. She looked at herself with faint concern, as if at an acquaintance who was said to be feeling sick. Still, even at forty, something in the face of the girl who had played Robert Browning in a disastrous school production of *The Barretts of Wimpole Street*. Dark hair that lifted away from her face; a clean line of jaw; a look of challenge.

Not bad, she thought, turning away from the looking-glass. But not, it seemed, quite good enough.

Graeme soon returned, giving her a nod as if he were pleased but a little surprised to see her. Her mood, sprung from weariness and apprehension, looked with wonder on the structure of bone and blood and flesh which contained somehow, indefinably, the essence of Graeme: the outward symbol of the man with whom she had lived for twenty years and did not yet know. Yet if the flesh were broken and

4

destroyed, what would remain? (John Brown's body lies a'mouldering in his grave, but his——)

'It's damned awful hot,' said Graeme, filling a basin with cold water. 'Like a large fat woman sitting too close to you.'

'This is the wrong time of year for Paris.' Odd that all she said seemed to have the formal unreality of things spoken to cover an unmentioned embarrassment.

'That sounds as if we spent our lives travelling grandly about the Continent with a lot of pigskin luggage. Instead of sad shabby tigers like this.' He grinned and bent to unlock his suitcase.

(And I am still seeing him with a kind of double vision, she thought: aware of the flesh, and also of the unknown essence which makes the flesh somehow baffling and strange. . . . Curious, like hearing an echo.) She continued to look with interest: fairish, greying hair, plentiful and disarranged, large grey eyes that slanted downwards, a weakness of chin and a look of calm yet vulnerable intelligence. 'Some sort of medieval character,' Stella had said with a daughter's surprising detachment, 'whose mind has slipped aside from his illuminated manuscript to wonder if he isn't plotting in the wrong plot.' More reverent was the smooth voice of an American matron who had visited them in Oxford last summer: 'Why, Mrs. Muir, I think your husband has such a fine, thoughtful face. Ascetic. Kind of like a monk. After all, a don is quite like a monk, in a way, isn't he? A philosophy don, like Mr. Muir.' 'There are differences.' 'But you can't deny he's a very remarkable man. He has such courage!' 'Yes, he is brave.' 'I always say you can tell physical courage by the eyes. Even if I hadn't known about your husband, I'd have said he was a brave man. And you, of course—you have to be brave too.'

She said now before she could stop herself, 'I wish to God you weren't going to do it.'

'Oh'—he flicked shut the lid of the empty suitcase—'what kind of talk is that? Here we are in Paris—Hugh is

5

even now dashing purposefully across the Channel, bless him, equipment at the ready. Next stop, Lundervald. The thing's begun.'

'Yes. I just made a comment. Let it go.'

It had been a mistake, though; she realized that. Nothing now would do but the light formal sentences that they had so far exchanged, but all at once she doubted her power to keep them going. I must try, she told herself; usually I can make myself do anything. Judith has self-control and will-power they used to say; not especially lovable characteristics, perhaps, but useful at times, such as now.

He said, with the quick forgiving smile of a man whose wife has abandoned the argument before it has begun, 'We'll have a couple of leisurely baths. And then find some-where to eat. No rush. . . .' (The kind of soothing words, she thought, used by the dentist before he tears your nerves up with the drill.) 'We'd better,' he went on, 'as this card on the wall advises us, *sonnez la femme-de-chambre*. . . . Is your friend Joseph in Paris?'

She turned, one hand on the bell-push. 'What made you think of him?'

'Simply that an hotel bedroom without a bathroom attached is something, I imagine, Joseph hasn't known for twenty years. That . . . that was all.'

She noted the hesitation, aware that it marked something concealed. 'Yes, I suppose he's here. He usually is—more often than London or New York.'

'Why does it sound so grand to move from capital to capital? . . . And he was such a funny little man.'

'He still is. Funny little men get around.'

'Faster than light they do. Look at Hitler and Napoleon. It's a kind of compensation.' He stood up and stretched himself lazily, as if, she thought, to show that it was a compensation he had no need of.

She said, 'You're pleased with yourself.'

'Excited. Hopeful. I can't help it.'

6

When later they wandered out from the hotel, she thought there was about the pale city sky, traced with sunset, and the contrasting dazzle of neon lighting, something which answered his mood, which touched the nerves strangely and with excitement. Indeed, she was not quite free of it herself as she sat with him in the restaurant, whose wall-wide windows were open to the café tables on the Boulevard des Italiens. She read the large floppy menu covered with indecipherable arabesques of violet, and listened to the French voices going on about her. The small house in Oxford was suddenly far off, and she said, 'Yes, I'm enjoying this.'

His glance, a sudden lift of grey eyes to her face and a quick smile, was an acknowledgement, an expression of gratitude to a woman who was, according to custom, being civilized. They talked easily, not mentioning Lundervald. They were, she thought, a married couple, well behaved and well dressed, passably good looking, neither young: over them was the glaze of good manners, yet they were somehow weighted with years of knowledge, love, jealousy, happiness and pain: when she had drunk enough wine this became comforting, a perspective that diminished fear.

There was a young girl at another table, talking with enthusiasm alternately in French and heavily accented English to her two male companions. She wore a black sweater and black trousers, her face was pale, powdered even to the lips so that she looked like a pierrot in mourning, and her dark hair was awry.

Judith said, after looking at her, 'I shall go and see Stella tomorrow.'

Graeme also looked at the girl and said, 'I see the line of thought.'

'Shall you come with me?'

'No, I don't think so. Give her my love, and tell her that her father hopes to see her at dinner tomorrow night. Dressed, if possible, to look like something not out of the zoo.'

He smiled, turning the stem of his glass round with his fingers. 'Try to persuade her to come. I should like to see her before we leave.'

A little frightening, that. She said, 'I'll do my best.'

He smiled again and poured more wine into her glass; there was something friendly about the small action: she thought, Well, at least we are on good terms, we have a meeting place, a point where we can rest when we're tired of anger or constraint; some people haven't got that.

She said, reckless now with the wine, 'Graeme, please don't go to Lundervald. You can put it off.'

The girl in the black trousers was exclaiming loudly '*Ah, c'est formidable!*' He said, 'I do wish that girl would shut up. The thing is settled and decided. How can I make you believe that?'

'Nothing is so settled and decided that it can't be altered before it's happened. You can run away from the altar; you can *not* get into the plane you've got a ticket for——'

'A damned expensive pastime, what with breach of promise and the fare. I wonder whether to have cheese?'

After that they said little. There was some formal discussion about the bill and what francs were really worth; the kind of conversation, Judith reflected, that took place between tourists all over the world, intense and concentrated, while the Acropolis and the Arc de Triomphe, the Colosseum and the Grand Canal stood unregarded, growing cold.

She took his arm as they walked; the wide grey silent theatre of the Place Vendôme rang with their steps. All Paris seemed to Judith a comfortable harbour from which she must soon set out: danger was absent from the pavement cafés, crowded in the warm night, and the soft shifting brilliance of lamplit leaves. But not, she thought, from the gleaming traffic which skated through the dark: as they looked up the long distance of the Champs-Elysées from the Concorde she saw the red lights of the cars travelling,

8

massed and dangerous, without pause, towards and from the floodlit Arc de Triomphe. She said, 'I don't understand why they aren't all dead.'

'They say it's safer to drive fast.'

'To take risks?'

'Too much care can be dangerous.'

These words stayed in her mind when they were back in their room. By artificial light it came more sharply into focus; she saw that the wallpaper was oddly rural, showing a young woman hesitantly grooming a goat. This, illogically, pressed upon the fear.

In bed she tried to read, but bright images of the day obscured the page. Graeme wandered about the room for a long time, undressing, unpacking, thrusting home drawers which stuck, so that he swore. 'Sorry about all this,' he said, with a glance over his shoulder. 'Do you want to sleep?'

'No, not yet.'

The possibility that he would in the end make love to her could not be entirely ruled out; she did not know whether she wished for this or not. It would, perhaps, re-establish friendliness, create a brief warmth; it was, at least, a means of communication still open to them. On the other hand there was, and had been for some time, her own quietness and passivity, which it seemed was not in her power to change.

At last he said, 'Well, that's that; I don't see how I can do any more'; shut the last drawer home, patted her shoulder and climbed into his bed. Better so, she thought; yet there was at the same time the feeling of a distance widening between them. She could hear the lift, groaning its way upwards; voices of people on the stairs: Americans, having an early night for once and taking time off from Montmartre.

Then Graeme said into the dark, 'Did you know Martha was in Paris?'

'No. I don't see how I could know, if you haven't told me.'

'I telephoned her this evening, soon after we arrived.'

She was surprised more than anything else, having been certain he was merely wandering round the streets. How odd, she thought; and yet trust is still the best thing, after all, for had I spent that half-hour in suspicion it would have been unpleasant instead of peaceful, and the result would have been the same. 'Shall you see her tomorrow?'

'It's possible.'

'What is she doing in Paris?'

'She's on holiday, staying with her sister. The one who's married to the Embassy chap. You remember.'

Had there not been an occasion some years ago when she and Graeme had gone to dinner at an apartment in the Faubourg St. Honoré, with Martha and her sister and the chap from the Embassy, an evening a little too bright and too noisy, in some way not quite comprehensible, like a play the essential clue to whose plot one has missed? She said, 'Oh, I see,' noticing that the pang caused by Martha's name lasted only a few moments; she was in the mood to consider Martha a fine big girl who took herself too seriously, and this was the best mood to be in about Martha. Graeme seemed to be waiting for her to say more but nothing occurred to her, and the silence went on until she heard that Graeme slept.

She herself lay awake. Hands behind her head, eyes open, she looked into the dark, half-heard the noise and language of a strange city going on beneath the windows.

Martha here in Paris. Joseph too. She thought, So we're all here together. Strange, that. And the adventure ahead. . . . Voices on the stairs again; from the street the high-low bugle call of a police car. . . . Graeme breathing heavily, sunk in sleep, lost to her.

Martha. And Joseph. She and Graeme bound for Lundervald. . . . No, she wasn't going to sleep. There was a lot of time before morning, and the people and places were crowding in, playing out the story that had brought them so far. Weary yet wakeful, her brain went tracing it back.

CHAPTER TWO

First Joseph. With whom she had found herself in Paris for the first time, nineteen, virgin, a double room booked for them in an hotel near the Madeleine.

(One could, from this distance, see the cause clearly: not love for Joseph, nor a natural instinct to bed with young men for the price of a week-end in Paris, but a passage of arms with her father. Poor father; perhaps it was simpler for him in heaven. For he would, one imagined, be in heaven; his only sin was to lose a pretty and submissive wife too soon, so that with a nature both passionate and commanding, he loved an only daughter more than proved convenient.)

A smell of oil paint and turpentine; the large bare floors of the London art school; herself a first-year student, aware that Joseph, from the height of his third year, lingered to talk to her and watched her as she worked. Short and serious, with a broad, stubby face and sad Jewish eyes, he wasn't a conquest to boast of. 'Clearly,' said a young man languidly, squeezing paint on to his palette, 'one of the lost ten tribes was found on Ilkley Moor baht 'at.' Yet there was about him something curiously magnetic; she discovered beneath his shyness an unexpected arrogance, a drive and confidence that impressed her. He aroused, at the same time, a kind of pity, being aware that his north-country accent could prove a disadvantage. 'But Ah'm going to change all that.' The broad Yorkshire vowels were charged with resolution. 'It's a lot o' nonsense, but it's got to be done. Aye, it's got to be done.' Did his father, she asked him (thinking of fathers) object to Joseph's studying art? No, not at all; his father, Albert Sands, was a grand chap; in the clothing business up north; he didn't know a Fragonard from a fish

TC—B

and chip shop but he was all for culture for those who could take it, and Joseph apparently could. And his ambition, she asked him? To be a painter?

His sad Jewish eyes glanced over the territories of ambition. No, he wasn't good enough for that. His talent was limited. Wasn't all talent, she suggested? Aye, but he wanted to be the best or nothing. For a moment a Jewish flamboyance shone out, sudden as the flash of a scarlet cloak. No, he was going to be an art dealer. One of those chaps who travelled about Europe, smelling out great pictures and buying 'em up. Selling 'em too, sometimes. It was going to be a grand life.

Strange to remember, lying here in the hotel room, that she had doubted him. Too young then to recognize the power of an obsession. . . . The smell of that time came back; the days of uneasy peace in 'thirty-nine; the feeling in the air of the finality of things, of the dark coming closer and the bright day being done. Joseph speaking of the conquest of Europe by Hitler, explaining that he would in this event take poison, being a Jew. . . . The stubby, north-country face took on proportions of grandeur. . . .

The fumes of a noisy open sports car in a calm April evening; the smell of the sea. . . . On Brighton front, blue and empty with evening, they wandered together, arm in arm. The glitter of garish light made but small imprint on the vast pale transparency of dusk. Joseph leaned on the parapet and looked down at the sea. Far off, he said, perhaps the armies gathered. The fine career of art dealer might have to wait a year . . . perhaps two . . . perhaps for ever.

She took his arm again, impulsively. Their mood was melancholy, amorous, desperate. They stopped on the way home at a roadhouse, ate, drank and danced amidst a noise that all but shut out the memory of the dusky sea and the armies and the fear to come. She hung on him, let him kiss her, did not wish to leave him.

She arrived home at three in the morning, dishevelled, fairly drunk, and, rather to her surprise, still virgin, her head swimming with the sound of a waltz called 'Deep Purple' and the tramp of armies as they covered the world. All this was not without exaltation.

Her father waiting for her in the drawing-room. More apparent even than his anger was his satisfaction that she should arrive thus, and so late. She began to explain that she had been with Joseph. 'That dreadful little Sheeny,' exclaimed her father, 'I hope you're not fool enough to believe a word he says to you?' Youth and anger obscured for her the anxiety and dread behind the question. 'I'm in love with him!' she shouted, the words carrying the conviction of any untruth spoken in rage.

The rage lasted long enough for her to agree to go to Paris with Joseph for the week-end. On train and boat the rage diminished. For most of the time she was silent, trying to come to terms with the remarkable change in Joseph. He was now, in a cap and a rather distressing muffler, odd and alien. His air of calm, knowing certainty, and an occasional wink, did nothing to bring him closer. When had she decided to escape? Perhaps at the door of the hotel room when he turned to watch with deep interest the startling shape of a young woman going downstairs. . . .

The sharp taste of coffee; the scent of strong cigarettes; the swerving, melancholy song of an accordion. Where had the café been? Perhaps on the Boulevard de la Madeleine, not far from the hotel. . . . The sudden little plunge of panic, recoverable even now, when she found she'd left all her money in a wallet on the dressing-table. . . .

He was sitting a few tables away on her left, and he was nothing but a tall fair young man in a sweater. (Graeme, twenty years her husband: leaning back in his chair and quarrelling in icily civil terms with a history don from Merton; rather solemn-drunk at a party to welcome a visiting American professor; playing for an hour or more on all fours with the two-year-old Stella; happily lost in the charms of a tall blonde Swede called Elma. . . .) No; a young man in a sweater. Entirely unknown. Giving her a glance that was, in contrast to the glances from other parts of the café, merely one of passive amusement.

Encouraged, she went up to him and asked him to lend her five francs.

The Scottish inflection in his slow voice served to increase her trust. He smoked a pipe and was travelling, he said, on a bicycle. Yes, he travelled on a bicycle whenever possible: he hadn't much money; he was in his last year at Oxford, studying philosophy, and his mother was a widow with a small pension; a bicycle was the thing. No, he didn't mind when it rained; he disappeared inside a huge yellow mackintosh shaped like a tent which just left him room to see and breathe. All his belongings were in a rucksack on his back; this made him rather an odd shape under the yellow tent, but that wasn't really important. . . . Was she alone in Paris?

She said 'Yes. No, not exactly'; which he received without comment. And him? she asked.

'Yes. My companions have all gone home.'

She thought it sounded, with the flavour of his Scottish speech, sadly romantic, like something out of a ballad. 'Companions?'

'Chaps I've been climbing with. . . . Not the Eiffel Tower. In the Alps. A place called Lundervald.'

'You climb, then? Properly, I mean? With a rope, and everything?'

He grinned. 'Practically everything. From crampons to karabiners.'

'What is a karabiner?'

'A snap-link which should prevent you, if you use it right, from falling hundreds of feet to your death.'

She stared at him, Joseph forgotten. She knew nothing of climbing. She had seen pictures in magazines: once a short film which drew nervous gasps from the audience. Did this young man, his feet now firmly on the Boulevard de la Madeleine, at other times (when he was not on his bicycle)

14

hang by finger-tips and toes to a rock-face over an abyss? She said, 'Aren't you afraid?'

'Oh yes, sometimes. That's part of it.'

'To be frightened on purpose?'

'Not exactly. Just that fear happens to be around—it gives the whole thing a kind of bite. Makes everything else seem tame and dull and flat.'

She thought perhaps she was included in the things so dismissed. She became aware of a man possessed by a dream; there was something akin here to Joseph's ambition to travel the world, buying and selling great art.

How did it begin? she asked. Oh, with his father. (A pause; it seemed, a change of mood.) As a young man, his father had climbed with Winthrop Young and Mallory. He'd been killed in Skye: a fall from the Sgurr a'Greadaidh Traverse in the Coolins. . . . No, he had not been with his father when it happened; he had been . . . somewhere else. She noticed again a sudden shut-in look; it was as if he were listening to words he didn't want to hear.

And his mother, she asked? Didn't she find it hard to accept his climbing? 'No,' he said, 'she takes it very well. She never tries to stop me.' There went through her the recognition of inexorable purpose, wall-firm and frightening, and she felt a pang of sympathy for the Scottish widow who was patient while her son climbed. And I am nearer to her, she thought, than to any man, though I live with him till desire shall fail and the mourners go about the streets.

The gentle grey glance returned to her. 'When I asked you if you were alone in Paris, you gave me rather an equivocal answer.'

On an impulse she explained her position; he looked as if she had asked him the best way up the Matterhorn. 'I wonder what's best to do?' he said; and added, after thought, 'I'll go and see him.'

'See him? Joseph?'

'Why not? I could say you've been taken ill.' He seemed

15

to be making an effort to think of possible illnesses for young women. 'Indigestion perhaps, or a nose-bleed.'

'I think I'd rather have a migraine, or a touch of faintness on the Pont Neuf. . . . You're very kind. But I pay my own debts.'

He showed a gleam of interest; a sudden warm recognition. This, she found, pleased her; she watched him attentively for a few moments until, with a kind of explosion, Joseph was amongst them, sitting at the table, saying, 'That wasn't a very nice thing to do, was it? I've been looking for you everywhere. And I don't understand who this is.'

'My name's Graeme Muir——'

Judith said, 'He lent me five francs. I came out without any money.'

'I don't see why you had to go out at all.'

'I wanted to think.'

'She was obviously upset,' put in Graeme Muir.

'I wish you'd mind your own business.'

'Well, it is, up to a point——'

'Just because you lend a girl five francs——'

'It isn't a question of francs. She told me all about it——'

'Aye; I daresay; women always talk.' Joseph played morosely with a table mat.

'Anyone talks when they're in trouble——'

Joseph said in broadest Yorkshire, 'Oh, shut up.' And to Judith, 'I don't see why you had to pick up this chap.'

'I haven't picked him up; I tell you he lent me——'

'Five bloody francs,' said Joseph. 'There they are, and let's not hear any more about them.'

Graeme paid them no attention. 'All I wanted to do was to help if I could.'

'I tell you it's none of your damn' bloody business——'

She could see Joseph now, his face blunted and furious; Graeme calmly remote, as if his thoughts had returned to the Matterhorn. Harder to be Joseph, she thought, noisy and absurd with temper, deprived of his week-end. She began to be sorry for him, seeing him always as the loser. (And if Graeme had been in his place, would the week-end have ended differently? Perhaps.) Troubled by guilt, she let them argue on.

At some point, she remembered, they all got to their feet, Graeme making Joseph look stubbier than ever. There was some more barking from Joseph (perhaps because of this); from Graeme a polite but unconcerned farewell that left her stung with regret.

She hurried beside Joseph, who was walking fast and mumbling. '. . . made to look a fool. . . . All right, all right, you can have a whole bloody suite to yourself; I shan't worry you. . . . Only I'm damned if I'm going to any pension on any Left Bank; did you hear him offer us rooms? I want a place with class. . . . And who the hell was he, anyway?'

'A climber. On his way home from Switzerland. On a bicycle.'

'Climbing isn't a profession.'

'He's doing philosophy at Oxford.'

'Oh aye; university type; might have known.'

'You were terribly rude to him.'

'I daresay.'

'He was only trying to help.' (Unfair; behaving as though she didn't understand that Joseph, having travelled hopefully towards a double bed, was sunk in the gloomy anger of frustration. And perhaps also obscurely aware that Graeme had disturbed her peace of mind.)

He said, 'Riding round the Continent on a bicycle and climbing mountains. That isn't any way to make money.'

'Perhaps he doesn't want to make money.'

'Don't be daft; everyone wants to make money. Did you tell him your name?'

'Yes.'

'And where you live?'

'Yes.'

17

'Are you going to see him again?'

'No, I don't expect so.'

(In the bed beside her Graeme stirred, snored, still slept. A car's engine swept the silence away; let it fall again. Sudden voices in the street, stark in the night quiet, having about their gaiety a touch of loud alarm.)

Then Martha.

CHAPTER THREE

MARTHA was in Paris. Martha, Judith thought, had been everywhere for a long time. Oxford and Cumberland, Skye and Pen-y-Gwyrd. And now Paris. (Last week in Babylon; last night in Rome. . . .)

Asleep, perhaps? Dreaming of Bill—a sharp dream, too vivid for comfort? Hard to imagine that Martha slept; one saw her eternally awake, haunting the places where she had been. . . . Where first?

Pen-y-Gwyrd one spring, soon after the war. The young Martha had been, although thick and squarish, still voluptuous: something to do with skin, and the curve of the behind, emphasized by trousers. Fair hair pinned in a bun, blowing loose from it; the hair so fine and pretty that this also was attractive. A hint of the hockey field, quickly dispelled by a sensation of languor, warm winds and ripe fruit.

And Bill, of course. Martha's husband, a huge happy young man, whose talk was continually laced with obscenities, from which his affection and good humour extracted all offence. Bill was curiously vivid in the small room, conjured easily by a laugh which could split the air: anyone who had a bawdy joke ran with it to Bill all the way without stopping. He had also, she remembered, the restful quality of those who are not trying to get something or be something different from what they have or are. He would talk till two or three in the morning, smoking endless pipes and drinking beer; he showed impatience only when his companion took up a book: reading, he held, caused discontent; half the effing trouble in the world was caused by books; put the bloody thing down, lad, and come for a walk. He travelled, with Martha beside him, in an old open Ford; their luggage was tied with string, and they arrived always at the end of their journeys wind-blown, high-coloured and hilarious, drawing attention as large, light-hearted and handsome youth will always do. They were both good climbers; and over that first meeting there was no shadow at all.

With Graeme they were instantly friends. They came up to him, faithfully as dogs, anxious to learn from him, aware that they were welcome, even loved; and that they were inside the enclosure: they climbed and knew about climbing.

And myself? Judith thought. Where did I fit in? I wasn't one of the magic circle, but they were friendly enough—Bill especially; Martha a little on her best behaviour—'Are we boring you, Mrs. Muir? Do you know what a chockstone *is*, Mrs. Muir? . . . When I heard your husband had led Kipling Groove on Gimmer I was so *terribly* impressed. . . .' From here the solitary hours spent on the shallow slopes with sketch-book and sandwiches had a glow of independence. Mountain scenery came in useful for book jackets and illustration, and she was home sooner when it rained. . . .

Now she could feel on her hand the strong warmth of the fire, and see them as they returned from a climb—perhaps the menacingly termed Cemetery Gates—soaked and blown and muddied, Martha's hair entirely loosed from its bun so that it streamed incongruously on the shoulders of her climbing jacket: Graeme in a strange mud-coloured pullover with sleeves like a sieve, true to the tradition that the better the climber, the older and more ragged his clothes: there was about them the jovial comradely exhaustion of those who have shared adventure. Martha, her skin whipped into colour by the open weather, the rope slings, casually impressive, round her waist, was a young Amazon with greenish eyes which flew constantly to Graeme for applause and encouragement.

Now she could hear her own voice as she lay beside Graeme in his bed all those years ago, wakeful after his lovemaking: 'What d'you think of Martha?'

'Oh, a nice crazy girl.' Muffled, on the way down towards sleep.

'Is she? Crazy, I mean?'

'Well . . . sort of young and gay. . . . She'll make a climber.'

'Very good?'

'Fearless and careful. The best kind.'

'What is she like when she isn't climbing?'

After a pause: 'Don't know what you mean.'

'I mean has she ideas about anything; does she read?——'

It sounded prim and absurd. Another pause; then Graeme's voice, a little more wide-awake: 'Oh yes, under all that gay and crazy stuff she's quite serious-minded. She reads poetry.'

After a long time she said, 'Are you fond of her?' but Graeme slept—or at least, made no reply.

'I went twice more,' she said to herself. 'Twice more to the mountains. The last time, and the time before the last.' The two occasions in their violent contrast were linked together in her mind, and the shadow was on them both.

First, Cumberland. The day hot and fine (and even here, in the Paris bedroom, she could smell the warm earth and hear the wash of water over stones); Bill, who had strained a muscle the day before, waving them on their way with noises of encouragement. The three of them—Martha, Graeme and herself. 'We're going to take you up an Easy,' Graeme had said. 'Absolutely nothing to worry about.' Pride forbade her to argue.

Mountain summits nudged into the heat-washed sky; the stony path invited one, as paths in summer do, to go further. Clear now in the room were the voices ahead of her as the three of them walked up the fellside, Martha and Graeme together, Judith a yard or so behind, the rope round Graeme's shoulder a mute forewarning of unpleasantness to come, like a dentist's drill hanging motionless, as yet unused.

'I thought we might do Beacon's Slab,' Graeme was saying. 'It's an Easy.'

Oh yes, let's do Beacon's Slab, thought Judith. Every time.

'There's one pitch that might be called Moderate. Footholds a bit thin——'

Perhaps not.

'—But I think she could manage it——'

No. No.

'Oh Lord'—Martha's voice with its clear hockey-girl ring was contemptuous—'*Must* we? Beacon's Slab? It's so dull. If you're going to start anyone in climbing, they'd better *climb*. Surely? Not just walk up a lot of grass steps.'

Oh, I love Beacon's Slab with its grass steps; I love it more than life; I want to climb it like anything; let's do Beacon's Slab.

'Well, perhaps you're right,' Graeme was saying; Judith felt like a patient lying unconsulted while doctors discussed her prospects of life. 'What about the Cambridge Bastion?'

Martha pulled a tall blade of grass and flicked it in the air. 'Suppose we might do that. There's a Severe pitch at the top —the overhang, d'you remember?'

'Lord yes; so there is. No, that wouldn't do.'

You bet your sweet life it wouldn't do. *Over*hang. Gracious no.

'There's January Crack,' said Martha. 'Nothing really hard there, just a few tricky pitches to make it interesting.'

I hate January Crack. I think it's a silly name, and I don't want to go anywhere near it. Let's do Beacon's Slab: come on, let's all do Beacon's Slab: Mummy, I want to climb Beacon's Slab.

'What a good idea: January Crack. Clever girl. There's one awkward corner, if I remember, where you have to use a pressure hold, but we can get Judith round that——'

You can't. You can't. Over my dead body—and it will be, I shouldn't be at all surprised.

'We'll pull her round.'

I think I'll go back for my sketch-book. Or just sit here and enjoy the view. She said aloud, 'And where is January Crack?'

Graeme waved towards the horizon and said, 'That tall crag just below the summit of High Scarfe.'

This, she remembered, had left her where she was, not knowing which was High Scarfe. . . . Increasing heat and the ache at the back of her knees as they walked up the steep fellside to the base of the rock. . . . At this point, to her own mind, a good deal of nonsense about the rope. Could she tie a bowline? No, of course she couldn't; she wasn't a Boy Scout. Graeme would lead, Martha next, and Judith would be at the end of the rope. And of her tether, she made no doubt.

Graeme beginning the first pitch. . . . The climb melted away below him; it was like watching a man treading upwards, dream-like, in the air. Then Martha; her large khaki behind moving steadily on. Soon Graeme was out of sight; Martha discernible only by the toe of one boot. 'Come along, now!' called Martha; nothing to do but start. . . .

'I should have gone back for my sketch-book,' she muttered after some time of struggle with unmanageable rock. Apparently frozen for ever, like some prehistoric crab, on the rock-face, she solved the problem by levering herself up with one knee. Martha, seeing this from her vantage point, called, 'Mustn't use your knee, Judith. Might get on it and then not be able to get off.' (Here, as elsewhere, the pleasantest thing to do was ultimately disastrous.) Scratched and cross, she arrived on the ledge.

'The next bit,' Martha said, in a voice which conveyed nothing but a sensible, tennis-court friendliness, 'has the awkward bit we were telling you about.'

'Do remember,' called Graeme, 'when you come to it, that you're absolutely safe.'

After that, a good deal of waiting about: she was surprised that so much of the climb should consist not of climbing but of standing sadly alone, tied to the rock, and listening to people who were out of sight discussing unpleasant prospects ahead.

Martha had now come to the awkward bit. 'Do remember,'

she called back to Judith, 'that when you get here you're *absolutely safe*.' Unnecessary therefore to be sweating so freely from fear. Yet Martha herself seemed less confident, trying one handhold, then another; stretching out her foot, then bringing it back. Graeme, much higher up, sat holding the rope with an aloof patience that was impressive. (She could see him now, very clear, lonely on the higher ridge; remember thinking 'How small he looks, with all the sky and hills about him'; feeling a pang of baffled, angry affection, mixed with fear.)

Martha, with a fine thrust, over the awkward bit. 'Good,' said Graeme equably; no one got excited or cheered: the whole thing was taken with quiet seriousness, like chess.

The awkward bit. A gap in the rock, with the ground too far below, and a foothold beyond, narrow and slanting downwards. . . . 'St. Michael and all his angels,' she said, 'won't get me over there, rope or no rope. I was perfectly right never to climb: alone with one's sketch-book one at least has some dignity. What now?'

In the event it proved not at all difficult to get her off the climb, on to the easier grass; and after some varied argument, on her way back alone to the hotel, while Martha and Graeme finished the climb.

The walk back, herself booted and clumsy amongst the lonely sunny rocks; the flavour of defeat; the knowledge that Graeme climbed alone with Martha, freed of the hampering weight of her own incompetence. . . . All right, so he climbs with a pretty girl. You'll get nowhere minding about that: Martha's all tied up with Bill, anyway, and even if she wasn't, only Houdini could get up to any fun and games on those rocks. But you have to reckon with your own pride and jealousy: you've proved today—haven't you?—that you can't match Graeme's courage, or Martha's either; and you don't like proving that.

The hotel. Bill in a deck-chair on the lawn, drinking tea. She sat on the grass beside him. 'Dropped the other two overboard? That's my girl. Been lusting after you since for ever; come and sit close and madden me; oh shit, there goes my bun.'

She retrieved his cream cake from the grass and explained what had happened. Bill, wiping cream from his fingers with a large coloured handkerchief, said, 'Oh, I shouldn't mind *that*, chick. Climbing's a lot of balls, if you ask me. Takes your mind off sex, now and again. . . . Oh, well, I enjoy it, yes, but for those who don't it's a mug's game. Just go on drawing those splendid pictures; gets you further in the long run.'

She murmured something about defeat and failure and wounded pride.

'Oh, honestly, you don't want to think like that. You want to be like me: I don't worry about anything, not an effing thing. What's the good? It's all one to me whether I'm lying flat out here on the lawn, or stuck in the chimney on Heron's Nest . . . which I soon will be if I eat any more of these buns; got too much weight for a climber as it is. . . . Either way, you get back to your dinner in the end. Or not, of course, as the case may be. Honestly, chick, cheer up. Go on looking absolutely beautiful and driving me out of my mind with desire; who the hell cares about the rocks?' He turned to give her a smile of great sweetness.

Bill was very clear in her thought as she lay in the Paris room: the broad jovial face and the heavy body; the kindliness in the grey, merry eyes. Clear too in the dark, the sun of that long-vanished afternoon when he had comforted her; when he had come a step closer as a human being, and in the midst of her own defeat she had felt an affection and concern for him.

Then the last time. Wales, and the autumn and the mists that hung to the hedgerows, and the rain so continuous that it was like a tune played endlessly on the piano. And a fifth to the party: Sean Randall, a young cousin of Martha's, younger than any of them, not yet eighteen, and somehow at odds with them all. Stocky and fair, his blunt chin tilted confidently, he could be either boastful or inattentive; his goodwill when it came somehow lacked depth, like the goodwill of a shop assistant which is directed towards your buying something. When the others talked, he would sit, quietly smiling, lids drooping over his eyes, like a man who has superior knowledge which will make nonsense of all that is being said. He climbed with power and skill 'but somehow without friendliness', Graeme said to Judith; 'he is on the rope but not of it. And I'm tempted to say to him, "Excuse me, your ambition's showing." Never was anyone so mad keen to set his flag on the peaks. . . . Embarrassing. As I say, it shows. . . . Perhaps I'm being unfair. But something about the lad brings my nervous system out in spots.' 'He's very young. And I think . . .' She hesitated. 'Well?' 'I think he's fond of you. Of no one else, but of you.' 'Heaven forbid. And young or not, I can't help wishing he'd go home.' 'Is he afraid?' she asked, and he replied, 'No, never. Or seems not to be. Perhaps that's the trouble. I like people to be afraid. As I am myself.'

(And those last words one remembers, here in this room.)

Those days of rain, stretched nerves and argument; only Bill remaining equable, wandering about the hotel with a beer mug in his hand, talking happily and obscenely to anyone who offered him welcome. Judith did a sketch of Martha; the result was a Bacchante who played tennis for her school. 'Oh, I say, you are clever,' exclaimed Martha, viewing herself with surprised wonder. 'It is like me, you know, in a rather odd kind of way.' Bill said, 'Oh, well done, chick; bloody marvellous, but you've made her look sad; terribly out of character; Martha never looks sad unless she's got a pain, do you, ducks?' He smacked her behind. 'Gay's the word for Martha.' Yes, surprisingly, in the portrait the look of an Amazon who wept for some colleague slain. A mistake? . . . But Martha's face for a moment unguarded, and the droop of sorrow there. . . . Judith had, she remembered, been puzzled for a time.

And still the rain. Graeme turning savagely from the window: 'Who's for leaving it, and going home?' Martha answered quickly, 'No. Please not. We've a whole week more.' He glanced at her soberly; then went on, 'Well, we could try north of the border. Fort William. Or even Skye. Might be good there.' Bill said, 'Och, aye'; did a few steps of a Highland fling, sang some rude lines about Flora Macdonald, then dropped into a chair and said he wanted to stay where he was. 'You chicks gallop north if you like; I've unpacked and it'll take more than an effing braw bricht moonlicht nicht to make me pack up again.'

So they stayed.

And around her, coming closer, a feeling of depression and unease, so that when Graeme made love to her that night, she grasped him eagerly, seeking comfort as well as pleasure, trying to convey through her body a need and a love which could not form themselves in words. It seemed to her that in the strength and violence of his own body, some such things also were said, that he reassured her and loved her and told her that all was well. But as soon as it was done, and he lay apart from her, she felt the first touch of isolation, of uncertainty, and the unease returned, for his eyes were adrift and his face closed to her. After some moments he went to the window and thrust it open. She felt the cold mountain air, sword sharp, smelling of stones.

He said with excitement, leaning out, 'The rain's stopped. I think it's going to be fine tomorrow; the tops are clear, and you can see the stars.'

And the morning. The mist down again (and how useless now, all these years later, to wish that the mist had kept down, that the day, like the others, had been washed out, so that nothing came of it, and they were still bored and inactive, waiting for something better). But during breakfast the

27   TG—C

mist gradually cleared. The increasing light brought chatter from the guests. . . . It was going to be fine. The glass was going up. The weather forecast said bright periods for the west of England. Bright periods and what else? Well, cloud. Plenty of water coming off the tops; best to pick a sunny climb. . . .

Graeme's voice: 'We're going to do Curving Crack on Cloggy—special treat for Martha; she missed it last time.' Judith sat at the table, her head down, seeing the high steep cliffs of Clogwyn d'ur Arddu. A voice from another table, 'Curving Crack, eh? Going to be pretty damp in that chimney. Going to be a roaring waterfall.' Graeme smiled and said, 'We'll take an umbrella.'

She watched the four of them set out. She noticed that as he tied his bootlaces, Sean's fingers trembled with impatience to be gone. She spoke to him, but he didn't hear; he was in imagination already out on the rocks, triumphantly mastering the climb.

Shadows of the clouds slid over the rough hills at the wind's pace. 'Don't forget, chick,' said Bill, turning to her, 'you've got the best of it. At the end of this day you'll be bone-dry with a work of art; at the most we'll have wet pants, and piles. Give us a thought now and then and pray for those in peril on the rocks.' He smiled, hoisted the rope on to his shoulder, and waved to her. She watched them walk away.

She herself did not go far from the hotel, but sat and sketched within sight of Snowdon. She worked quickly, quite absorbed. She ate her lunch in sunlight, but already the clouds were coming up again, a grey tide streaming from the west, nearer and nearer to the sun. . . . Grey, all of it now, with a wind alive in the rough grass, and the first of the rain.

Back at the hotel she ate tea by a fire whose comfort was made marvellous by the jellied, rain-dissolved window and the premature storm-dusk that leaned close like a roof. Soon they would all return, soaked and exhausted and happy, Martha's fair hair on her shoulders, darkened by rain.

She worked further on her sketch of the mountains, but after a while she put it away. She could hear voices in the hall, loud in jovial protest against the false promise of the morning. . . . Now she was waiting and listening; useless to pretend otherwise.

Out into the hall. The front door gave on to an alcove which served as a filter for sodden climbers: on a stretch of coconut matting lay muddied climbing boots, soaked wind-jammers and coiled lengths of rope. John, the man from the hotel, was collecting these to take to some place of warmth and recovery. He smiled at her and said, 'Very disappointing, the day.' She nodded. Odd not to be able to say, 'They're late—is there any news?' The superstition that questions were unlucky had been with her for a long time. He went on, 'Tomorrow will be better'—(But tomorrow may be a day of unimaginable things)—'They say the wind's changing.'

Now she had the hall to herself. A pace or two up and down; a concentrated but unseeing look at the postcards for sale. And then the gritty sound of boots outside; and the door violently opened.

Sean. Drenched, very pale, and looking at her as if she had spoken to him in some language he didn't understand.

Then he said, water dripping from his hair and chin, 'I've got to get a stretcher party, and then an ambulance to go to Caernarvon.'

She put an anguished hand on his arm. His hair, plastered to his head by the rain, gave him a look of difference which stamped this moment as one of horror in her mind. He said, the telephone in his hand, 'Bill's had a fall. A bad one, I'm afraid. Martha? She's with him. Graeme too. They sent me for help because I'm the fastest. . . . Hullo? There's been an accident on Clogwyn d'ur Arddu. . . .'

Late that night Graeme and Sean returned from the hospital by car with Martha. When Graeme came into the bedroom Judith poured him a large drink of whisky and gave it

29

to him before she said anything. He slumped in a chair, took the drink, closed his eyes and drew his hand down his face. He said, 'He died just after we got him there. I didn't really expect anything else, but one has a kind of absurd hope, I suppose. . . .'

She felt cold, shocked and sick. 'But what happened?'

'He was leading in the chimney. I didn't want him to, but he was desperately keen, so I let him. . . . There was a bit of an argument with Sean, because *he* wanted to lead. I made Bill take a thread belay round a chockstone, but when he fell his weight pulled the stone out. I tried to hold him, but he went the length of the rope. . . .' Instinctively he looked down at his hands, torn and bloody from the savage run of the rope.

She said, 'Oh, God. . . . Bill. . . .'

'It looked nasty from the beginning. We talked about trying something else, but Bill was confident he could do it, and Sean was desperate to go on.' He stared down at his glass. 'What a bloody thing to happen. What a hellish, bloody day.'

'And Martha?'

'We brought her back here. She'll have to go into Caernarvon again tomorrow, but I thought it'd be better for her to be close to—to us tonight.' He turned the glass slowly round on his knee, not otherwise moving. 'She's been so terribly good.'

'I'll go and see her——'

'No; no, I'd leave her, I think. They gave her some dope at the hospital, and she's pretty sleepy. She's got sleeping stuff for the night, in case she wakes. I told her to come to our room if she wanted anything . . . felt ill, anything like that.'

'Of course.'

Strangeness, a sensation of disbelief: *Bill*—who had sat beside her on the lawn and comforted her; who had danced a Highland fling and sung songs about Flora Macdonald, now lying dead, and Martha, in her room at the end of the

30

corridor, a widow. These were words: only a feeling of cold hollowness persisted, turning the room harsh.

Bill. . . . 'He was leading . . . when he fell his weight pulled the stone out. . . .' Yes, you could see the fall: the skid of the boot, the handholds going, the cry, the violence, blood and pain——

She said quickly, 'One thing at least; let this mean the end of climbing. It must.'

He sat in silence. She would do better to leave it; he was saddened and exhausted, and in her heart she knew what the answer would be. But an hysterical impatience, a mixture of shock and grief and anger made her go on. 'Please answer me.'

He said at last, 'What happened today was . . .' she heard him sigh—'a terrible thing, a disaster . . . but part of it all.' He was speaking slowly and with difficulty, as a man speaks an uncomfortable truth. 'There are accidents. Men are killed sometimes——'

'But *Bill*—someone you cared about, someone not yet thirty—goes and smashes himself up at this filthy foolish game, and you're prepared to go on with it? You must be mad—really and truly mad—the whole thing's a kind of bloody circus, a means of throwing lives away. . . .' The words went on because she couldn't stop them; because all the time she saw Graeme, hand and foot slipping from their holds, falling as Bill had fallen; seeing an end come as quickly and savagely to her as it had to Martha.

He said, 'Oh, my dear, what good is it, talking like that? Bill is dead, and we're both of us shocked and tired and beyond reason—nothing we say can make sense. To-morrow——'

'Tomorrow you won't listen. Tomorrow everything'll begin to be the same as it was before. It's *now* I want you to think of it, with Bill only a few hours away from you; don't you see?'

He got up from his chair. She saw how all his body drooped with fatigue; she wished at the same time to comfort him, and to berate him because he would still risk his life. He said, 'I can't argue it now. Today has been . . . you know what today has been.' Abruptly he went out of the room. After that the house was silent. It was a long time before he returned.

It seemed to her, wakeful in the Paris room, that the division on the night of Bill's death had thereafter lain between them. She had not—till now—gone to the mountains again.

And Graeme? He had rarely spoken of Bill, but he hadn't gone again to Wales; nor had he for some time attempted the harsher climbs of Zermatt, Chamonix or the Oberland.

But then he met Hugh Ferris. (She heard Graeme's voice: 'Hugh is even now dashing purposefully across the Channel, bless him, equipment at the ready.') Graeme had met him first at a Climbers' Club dinner, and arrived home more drunk with the meeting than with wine. 'Quite extraordinarily nice, and monastic about climbing: I believe he says his prayers to a piton. . . . You know his name, surely? Heavens, he's at the very top: he was on the last Everest expedition, the nerve and brains of the whole outfit, but you'd never think it to look at him: (he's quite small with one of those squashed inarticulate army faces)—or to hear him talk: you'd think he was the last sherpa but one. . . . There's talk of our doing the Walker on the Grandes Jorasses. And perhaps the Triolet direct on the Argentières side.'

So gradually they came back, the great climbs of Switzerland, France and Austria: the long climbs that began in the small hours of the morning, after the night in the hut. Waking while it was still dark in the bedroom at home, she would think of him going through the cold mountain silence under the towering snows.

Hugh was now in Paris, happy at the prospect ahead. He would not, she imagined, be any more at ease with her than he had ever been: from the first his baffled friendliness had made his visits effortful: it was like entertaining a St.

Bernard—easy to feed him but hard to find subjects for discussion. He would stand awkwardly in the middle of the room, showing general goodwill, but without, it seemed, any powers of communication. Soon his kindliness emerged: if she was left out of the conversation he would determinedly praise the food, or her dress, or Stella; and, with an effort as of a man wrenching a ship's boom from right to left, try to talk about something other than climbing. She could remember him, alone with her in the drawing-room, moving his feet as if he were trying to get a stance on a difficult pitch, and saying that he hoped she didn't resent Graeme's climbing: chaps who liked climbing were a bit diseased—ha!—in a way, but Graeme was a terribly lucky chap to have such a charming wife, and he really did appreciate her, any chap could see that, even though sometimes . . . All this in half-sentences, sudden barks of embarrassed amusement, accompanied by a general wandering to different corners of the room as though he were looking for the way out.

Was it the summer after they first met that Graeme went with him to Skye? She thought so. . . . Clear in her mind was a picture of Graeme, the night before he left, wandering into the drawing-room of the Oxford house, folding his climbing jacket. When he had folded it and unfolded it twice, he said, 'Did I tell you that Martha was coming with us?'

This was, she thought, as she dug a needle unhappily into a school blouse of Stella's, a silly way to do it, since he knew as well as she did that he hadn't told her, and his not having told her was the only thing that made it odd. She untangled a thread of cotton and said 'No'. Various phrases like 'I shouldn't have thought she'd want to go near the rocks again'; or 'How strange: has she forgotten Bill so soon?' she laid aside as being those which give some relief at the time, but are afterwards regretted, since one does not mean them, but only the hurt behind them. She added, 'I thought she was staying with her parents in the country.' Graeme went to the window, as though Martha's movements were to be discerned somewhere at the end of the garden. 'Yes, but she wasn't happy; she went up to town and started looking for a job, but it isn't easy for her; she hasn't any real qualifications, except as a climber. And she isn't a town girl. . . .' So much learned seemed to suggest a meeting, or at least correspondence; she knew of neither. She said only, 'So what is she going to do?' 'She's got an idea of taking a job in a nursery garden—not far from here, as a matter of fact. But she wants a bit of a holiday first, so I suggested she should come to Skye.'

One remembered that because it was a beginning. Afterwards, whenever he went climbing, Martha was with him. Less and less possible to make any comment: Martha had climbed with him when Bill was alive; she still climbed with him. She had not lost, all these years after Bill's death, a look of dignified bewilderment; with Judith she was at once confident and defensive, as if she were about to say that for a young woman to see her husband killed before her eyes justified her in whatever she did. . . . Perhaps this was true.

A smudge of grey light round the window, scarcely diluting the darkness. Martha, now in Paris. More troubling to the mind than Hugh or Joseph, or even the memory of Bill. Because somewhere along the line Martha had changed from a sad friend who needed comfort, to Graeme's love; at some time, unknown, he had first made love to her, and the pattern for them all was changed because of it.

More certain light in the room, and the first voices in the street; the morning challenge, sharp after the wakeful night. Lundervald had come closer; she could see in a corner of the room the coiled rope and an ice-axe, incongruous in the plushy warmth, spelling certainty.

And this morning she would see Stella.

34

CHAPTER FOUR

THE room was small; morning sunlight intruded on its disorder, lighting the tangle of bedclothes and the unfinished picture of a rectangular fish in oils, propped against the wall. Stella, wearing a dressing-gown, said, 'In England it is unusual for gentlemen to visit young women in their bedrooms before the bed is made.'

André Tévernin, his head a little to one side, was watching her with lazy attention. He said, 'In Paris it is not so. It saves time and trouble for the bed not to be made, if you understand me.'

'Perfectly.' She began to brush her hair; she could see his reflection in the glass. His dark suit and bow tie were a little unbecoming; in the strong light his lean face looked sallow, and the skin below his eyes creased and faintly bruised. These things she noted carefully; they must be stored for the times of his absence, when he haunted her too vividly for comfort.

He went on, 'And you have told me that you are in love with me.'

'I am.'

'Then I do not understand what is the matter.'

'Last night my parents arrived in Paris——'

'And why we do not make use of the bed?'

'Because I have no trust in you whatsoever.'

'I have charm and intelligence; nothing else is of importance. Once you let me make love to you, you would be entirely happy——'

'I should be in hell,' said Stella, 'make no mistake. And I tell you, my parents are in Paris. They could be here at any moment.'

'Nonsense. You have explained to me that you quarrel

with your father. About mountain climbing, of all things.'

'Yes. It wouldn't necessarily stop him from coming to see me.'

André Tévernin shrugged and moved across the room, dipping his head to see himself in the glass. He appeared to call off, with a kind of automatic control, any further pleading. He said, his voice changed, 'I am interested in your father. His name is well known. I remember not so long ago that he did some very difficult and famous climb on the Grandes Jorasses—there were photographs in our paper. Why do you quarrel with him?'

'Because I think all this climbing stuff is a great big bore—kind of unreal, like a religion with no God. Part one. Part two, I don't want to be a female don, teaching history to a lot of bright girls.'

'Is there any reason why you should?'

'I used to come out top in all my history exams. Pa sees me as a terrible loss to Lady Margaret Hall.'

'I do not know who is Lady Margaret Hall.'

'It's a college. And not for me. Too much like sitting the same film round again. I want to have a bash at something new, something that's my own. Like painting.'

She was brushing her hair; he watched her, she thought, with a kind of amused, detached admiration; the look of a man who isn't going to waste time, lust and energy on a woman who says no. He said, 'You're far too pretty to be so serious. And certainly too pretty to teach anything to anyone —or anything on the curriculum of a college. Is that not clear to your father?'

'He's disappointed. Great big dreams (a) of climbing daughter and (b) of brilliant don daughter all gone up in smoke—or rather in the Ecole des Beaux Arts.'

'But he paid for you to go there?'

'I'm here by virtue of a legacy from a great-aunt.'

He frowned as if he were trying to work out the relationship of a great-aunt. 'What is he doing in Paris?'

36

'He's on his way to a climb.'

'What climb?'

'How should I know? Somewhere in Switzerland. Most of them are.'

'Would there be a story in it?'

'I don't know . . . how d'you mean, a story?'

He shrugged. 'As I have said, your father is well known. I think myself that climbing is a great deal of nonsense. But sometimes it is news.'

'No, I don't know anything about it. Only that he's going.' She put down her brush. He seemed to be on the point of leaving, but then he moved casually towards her and took her in his arms.

And this, thought Stella, is where the trouble starts; this is a one-way track leading to long wakeful nights, and *not* taking it leads to wakeful nights also. . . . Sort yourself out of that one.

He was saying, 'Now you do not feel at all like someone who is going to be a don; you feel like someone I could make love to now this minute, and who would like it very much. . . . You are a silly girl, but very, very nice, and I want you very much. . . . If I come back, will you have lunch with me?'

'Yes.'

'I believe you are in love with me. . . . And dinner?'

'Yes.'

'Not before have I paid so much attention to any girl who says no. You should be pleased.'

He kissed her, flicked at her newly brushed hair with one hand, and said, '*Au 'voir*.'

When he had gone Stella sat in front of the looking-glass and said, 'Damn' fool. Both those times ought to have been No.' (And if they had been? Quiet evening spent wondering where he is and with whom. . . . No one who pretends to be as intelligent and clear-sighted as you do should behave so much like a half-wit.)

She got up and walked to the window. The courtyard

below was cobbled, with green plants standing lonely in corners; a string of washing hung from window to window two floors down. A woman with a broom in her hand and a scarf round her head was talking in a flood of fast French to a nun who seemed to listen with courteous attention. . . . A smell of coffee, onions, Gauloises cigarettes. A foreign city: her chosen place of exile, the strong-point of her rebellion. Occasionally, as now, failing in magic; seeming no more than a place with a string of washing two floors down.

'Fair enough: that's the price of making a stand: from time to time the wind blows chill and home seems a long way off.'

'No one's fault but your own.'

'Oh, sure.'

'And retreat is easy.'

'Not for me.'

'Oh pooh; very grand and brave; who d'you think you are: Joan of Arc? And retreat or not, the parents are in Paris: one of them—if not both—will be here any minute now. You'd better tidy that bed.'

As she banged at the pillow-case, there came suddenly into her mind the picture of a man climbing a mountain. The mountain was large and the man very small. She felt, as the image persisted, a pulse of regret, the sensation of some task ill-performed, beyond retrieving now.

She abandoned the bed, and went back to the window. The nun had gone, but the woman with the scarf was still there, leaning on her broom and talking up to a window on the second floor.

The narrow roadway of the Rue Buonaparte was half in sunlight, half in shadow. Judith dawdled on the sunny side. Flaking plaster, curled like dry leaves in the sun; art shops, small art galleries, dusky and curtained, from which the paintings shone out, gaudy as tropical plants; doorways leading to courtyards where shadow and light divided the cobbles; loud white letters on the walls crying '*Algérie Libre!*' and '*Mort aux Fascists!*' Surprising to think that somewhere here was Stella.

Climbing a dark stairway on the farther side of one of the courtyards, she thought, 'I would like this to go well. But as one grows older one learns to pay less and less attention to that part of oneself that wants everything to go well.'

Stella's room was empty; Stella herself, wearing a dressing-gown, was talking on the telephone at the end of the corridor. 'Be with you in a minute!' she called, and went on talking in French which Judith tried not to think was affected, done on purpose, and—as she stood in the small chaos of the bedroom —going on too long. She turned her back on the unmade bed and looked out of the window. Washing, hung on a line, flapped from light to shadow; somehow it discouraged her.

Stella returned. 'Well, hi! Sorry about all that; an elderly follower who wants to set me up in luxury near the Etoile.' Judith didn't take this seriously, and decided to say nothing about the smear of oil-paint on the pillow-case. Stella moved a tray of half-eaten *petit déjeuner* from a chair to the dressing-table. 'Sorry about all the mess.' The dressing-gown blew open as she moved to show long slim bare legs. Judith was reminded of those legs running along the sands towards the sea; covered in cuts from a bicycle fall: now they were elegant, film-starish, seductive. This seemed to make conversation more difficult. Indeed, the early exchanges were formal: How did Stella enjoy Paris? Oh, very much. Was she a French beat or an existentialist? 'What—"I believe in Sartre, the Father Almighty"? No, not at all: I go my own way. I always have.'

Judith looked at her attentively. Any change in three months? Possibly a little thinner. And that, she thought, makes her look more like me, more grown-up, and a little sad.

'Sorry about this kind of dressing-gown life,' Stella was saying. 'Not so much Bohemianism as waiting for a bath.'

She was a little shaken, Judith thought; how did one

assure her of friendliness? Like trying to convince a nervous animal that one means it no harm. She said, 'I don't think I mind about dressing-gowns. I was hoping you'd have lunch with me.'

'Oh . . . lunch.' Stella pushed her dark fringe on end and looked as though lunch were a mathematical problem. 'I'm terribly sorry, I can't have lunch.' Her fringe fell back into place; she looked wide-eyed, prepared for battle.

Judith decided to play it mild. 'Very well. The important thing is that you should come to dinner.'

'Dinner,' said Stella. 'Well, you see, dinner——'

'Graeme wants you to come.'

More ruffling of the fringe. 'Does he? Does he really? After the skirmish? Well, that's charitable. Department of good behaviour. However. . .'

'He wants to see you before he goes.'

'Kind of off to the wars? . . . Well, but . . . no, I'm awfully sorry; no, I can't.'

'Can't?'

'I have a date. And anyway, it wouldn't really work.'

'Now don't be an ass.'

'No . . . no, it wouldn't. I can see what this dinner'll be like, full of Eve-of-the-Climb stuff—and it wouldn't do for me, it really wouldn't.'

'Why on earth not?'

'Because . . .' Stella seemed to be sorting desperately through a cupboard of clothes, and not finding what she wanted. 'Because I don't believe in it. All this climbing stuff, I mean.'

'Goodness, no one's asking you to believe in it. Just come and eat your dinner.'

'No, but sooner or later I'll say what I think. I always do. And then there'll be trouble.' Stella pulled open a drawer, spooned over the clothes and shut it again.

'He really does want to see you, you know. It'll make him unhappy if you don't come.'

40

Stella returned to the cupboard and pulled out a pair of slacks. 'Getting a bit late for a bath. . . . I don't think anything makes Pa unhappy except a chockstone falling out of a gully on the third pitch on the buttress. Or whatever.'

'He has . . . cared for you.'

'He's cared for getting to Cumberland and Skye and the Bernese Oberland and the Dolomites. He lost interest in me after that dreadful day in the Lake District. When he took me up some enormous wet hump in thick fog and was surprised when I wasn't pleased. Remember?'

Certainly she remembered. The twelve-year-old Stella, expertly equipped, had trudged silently on, making no comment at all on the wind, the rain or the absence of view. Near the summit Graeme had called back to his booted and plodding daughter, 'You're doing fine. Not cold? Or scared?'

'I'm everything,' Stella had replied, 'including bored.'

'You're being very silly,' said Judith. 'He was disappointed——'

'Because I didn't enjoy being wet and cold and utterly miserable?'

'It's a love,' Judith said. 'An obsession. These are always difficult to handle, and seem absurd to others who don't share them.'

The dark head went down. After a pause Stella said, 'Obsessions about people. Not about things.'

'So you won't come?'

'It just wouldn't be any good.'

Judith took a pace or two about the room, in so far as it was possible. She looked down from the window, seeing not the courtyard but the pretty chalets and the wood-carvings and the snow-split heights of Lundervald. She said after some moments, 'This is a very dangerous climb that he's going to do.'

'Dangerous?'

'Perhaps the most dangerous climb in the Alps.'

41

'Everything's always the most dangerous climb in the Alps.'

(No good getting angry.) 'This is different. They're climbing the Heide Nordwand. That means the North Wall—or the North Face—of the Heide.'

Stella said, 'I've heard of the Heide. I don't know anything about the North Wall.'

'It's only been climbed about a dozen times. . . . I think a dozen times. And there've been some pretty terrible accidents. Seventeen men have been killed.'

'Accidents?'

Judith was still looking into the courtyard. 'The kind of thing the Press get hold of and write up in purple and gold: "The killer Face of the Heide"; "The mountain of death". Not the sort of publicity Graeme wants, so keep it to yourself.'

Stella said after a moment's pause, 'Who's going with him?'

'Hugh Ferris.'

'Yes, I remember him. Army type; I remember the first time he came to the house. Pa said he was expecting a very great climber, and I sat up waiting for some sort of athletic Apollo, and in came this perfectly ordinary little man with a moustache. Didn't he write a terribly dull book that nobody could read, all about the Himalayas? About our splendid sherpas and the low temperature at Camp Five? Even Pa had to give it up.'

'Climbers aren't necessarily any good with words.' (But she remembered the book; a sad circumstance of unbought and withering copies that finally found their way on to the sixpenny shelves.)

'I thought Father said Hugh was getting a bit old for the big climbs?'

(Odd that Stella had remembered that.) 'He's got the experience.'

'Oh. . . . I think the whole thing's crazy. I honestly do. All this grand talk about climbing, as if there were something saintly about it. I'm sorry he's going, and I'm sort of sorry for you, having to go along with it. But I can't play it like that: if I don't believe in a thing I have to make a stand against it.'

'You could put your stand on one side, for Graeme's sake.'

'No, I'm sorry. It wouldn't be any good. It would go wrong, you know it would go wrong. Tell him I wish him well. And leave it there.'

'He truly wants—' Judith began, and then left it. She couldn't get it right with words: the confusion between Graeme and Stella needed something different to solve it; something physical and uncomplicated and violent. . . . She could not imagine what it might be.

She said, 'Very well, then.' Curious that there should be a pang in leaving the room, as if it were a place where she had been happy.

Stella said, 'Oh look . . . please meet me before you go . . . tomorrow. Please.'

Judith turned. Stella's face was suddenly vulnerable; she saw a child whose fears were different from her own, but valid and haunting. She said again, 'Very well——'

'At the Deux Magots. Round the corner in the Boulevard St. Germain. It's supposed to be full of Sartre and Simone de Beauvoir, but I've only seen a lot of people who look like me.'

'We shan't have very much time.'

Stella did not reply; her face looked sad and surprised and accepting, her smile uncertain. Judith went quickly down the long dark stairs, where she found herself suddenly face to face with a man who was already on the lower step.

'*Pardon, madame.*' He backed, allowing her to pass. He moved with a small flourish; she had the impression of dark hair, a bow tie, and a face whose lean intelligence aroused in her some unexplained distrust. She perceived his impatience that she lingered on the step, but this impatience was just held in check by a form of good manners that had no warmth in it.

As she walked through the courtyard she heard his

43   TG—D

footsteps going rapidly up the stairs. She said to herself, 'No, he wouldn't be going to see Stella; he was too old for her, nearly forty'. Nevertheless, her imagination placed him in the small untidy room which she had just left, with the unmade bed and the tray of *petit déjeuner* and the paint on the pillow-case. This aroused a feeling of discomfort; an indigestion of the mind.

'But I shall see her tomorrow,' she told herself.

On her way back to the hotel she walked slowly through the Tuileries. The sun was strong now and the stretches of blond dust harsh to the eye; the grey-white statues stared negligently over the heads of the bright-dressed children who threw their staccato French about them like corn.

The gritty sand was uncomfortable to her feet, and she sat down on an iron chair. A fountain played, sending its cool haze of water continually to the pool below. Something endearingly peaceful in the movement aroused the natural retort in her mind: 'I do hope you're not expecting peace for the next thirty or forty years? Peace! What an idea.'

'I don't see why not. One sees it lying around.'

'You know quite well why not. Graeme's climbing.'

'People say that a father who drinks is a problem, or a father who brings his women to the house: a father who climbs mountains isn't a problem; he can't be.'

'Well, he is. For after all, he loves mountains more than Martha; more than me; more than Stella. More, I suppose, than life.'

It occurred to her, sitting there on the iron chair, that men were ready, in the end, to throw all relationships away for things: for a gun, a bomb, a mountain not yet climbed, a place at the end of the world. For these they could shut the door; shake off all the compulsions and desires of loving, to be quite themselves, concerned only with what is next to be done, which rope to use, where the path goes. But for women the door was always open: the connexion with man, woman or child never quite broken: the mountain, the gun or the place in the snows would be, in the end, forsaken for the word at the corner of the street, for the half-hour over the dinner table, for the telephone call.

She shifted on her chair. A child went scampering past: his mother, some way behind, called '*Tais-toi, Michel; méfie-toi de l'eau!*' The child flung a smile back over his shoulder. The moment of communication was in some way touching; Judith saw more clearly that Graeme and Stella and herself were all of them separated from each other: scarcely at any time did they talk from the guts and heart— or when they did, it was in protest, not in understanding. 'We are,' she thought, 'like people shouting at each other across water. We are like——'

She rose from her chair, which was, in any case, now uncomfortable. This was the point to stop; one could go quite a long way towards melancholia, thinking they were like people shouting across water. Indeed the image, on further thought, became less apt, even hilarious: she saw them all with megaphones.

The cross-stitch pattern of the Eiffel Tower, blurred with haze and distance, kept her company as she walked: the trade-mark of a foreign city. Back at the hotel she found a message from Graeme: 'Waited for you till nearly one. Martha asked us to lunch: I've gone on ahead, the Restaurant d'Alsace. Do come; Martha's expecting you.' This seemed so improbable that she did not try to believe it. Nor did she go to the Alsace. She went to the restaurant that sits, incongruously, at the foot of the steps where Marie Antoinette climbed to the waiting tumbril, by the Palais de Justice. Here she watched the *avocats* in their gowns going up and down the broad steps, and decided that the day so far had offered little but defeat, and that something was necessary to restore her pride.

45

THE swing-doors of the Clarisse revealed a hazed and silky quiet. In the vestibule one or two men sat in relaxed expensive gloom, smoking cigars. Waiters moved with silent hurry; one felt that there was nothing, short of eternal life, which they could not instantly provide. Indeed, Judith thought, wealth had this in common with religious conviction: its temples conveyed an air of authority and untroubled quiet.

She turned, and saw her host coming towards her. He walked with his head down and one hand in his pocket; his stubby figure travelled through the hushed luxury of the Clarisse with the indifference of a man who has known it all too long to be aware of it.

She said, 'Hullo, Joseph.'

'Judith; it's grand to see you, love. Come along and have a drink.'

He put a hand at her back and pushed her towards the bar. Here in a quiet glow like an indoor Alpine sunset she sat at a small table, while the movements of the waiters troubled the ear as lightly as the movements of a nurse in a ward of the gravely ill.

She said, 'Every time I see you, I'm surprised because you haven't changed.'

He grinned and patted his stomach. 'Changed here all right, love: when people want to point me out to someone else, they say "that short fat Hebrew chap over there".'

'But you're the same person.'

'Oh, aye; well, I got what I wanted; that doesn't change people; it's not getting it that does, in my reckoning. I used to have ideas—didn't I?—about tarting up my accent and

46

turning myself into a gentleman : lot of nonsense ; I got by all right as I am.'

'Yes, you certainly did that.'

'Oh, I don't mean just all this.' He looked at the bar of the Clarisse as if someone had asked him whether he thought it had dry rot. 'This is a nice soft pink cushion for your arse when it needs it; no more, no less. But I can do what I want now, do things that interest me; have the kind of time I like, without pretending to be anything I'm not. Drink that drink up and have another; you look as though you need it.'

'Yes, I do.'

He sat back, chubbily comfortable ; his crumpled, familiar Jewish face not greatly changed from the face of the young man in the distressing cap on the journey to Paris. He said, 'You still look surprised.'

'When we came back from Paris all those years ago, I never expected to see you again. It's comforting to think that one piece of bad behaviour doesn't mean a final break; that people are harder to lose——'

'All that sounds a bit grand and fancy. I went on seeing you because I liked it—even though you up and married that great Scottish Don——'

'He isn't all that big.'

'I'm a little chap, and I didn't go to a university, and as for climbing, I once went up a hill near Minehead that damn' nearly killed me. So he seems big. You look pale, love. What are you doing in Paris?'

She told him.

'Lundervald? Oh, aye, I've been there.'

'You have?'

'There's a great big hotel there full of chaps like me: go as far as the railway goes and no farther. How long will you be there?'

She shrugged. 'Who can tell?'

He was watching her, the sad brown eyes disturbingly perceptive. 'You mean the climb, and the weather, and

47

waiting about down below—oh, aye; all these great enterprises are a question of waiting about for someone; is that why you telephoned me?'

'Partly. And because Graeme had lunch with Martha.'

'What, you mean that great big games mistress? That huge fair slut who follows him everywhere? You're a fool to put up with it.'

'Maybe. But more of a fool, perhaps, to make a fuss about something which doesn't really cause me any trouble.'

'Not?'

'No; I've got my own work, and it prospers: I'm doing a series of book jackets for Carter and Page.' She was surprised how unconvincing the words sounded. 'Not great art, perhaps, but it gives me my independence. And that's how I want it to be.'

'Is it?'

'You don't have to keep asking questions: yes it is.'

'Then why did you ring me up?'

'Oh, because there's always a bit left over; a margin of difference; a part of oneself that contradicts what all the rest says.'

'And I suppose because it gives your morale a boost to remember that you once turned me down: women!' He took a cigar, prepared it, and held a match to it as if he were trying to interest an animal in some strange food. 'You'd have done better with me.' He attended further to the cigar. 'And what's more, the offer's still open.'

So he must speak, she thought, over the desk in his office, seemingly casual, his eye alert for any nuance of reaction. He went on, 'No, don't smile like that; I mean it.'

She went on smiling; her second (or was it her third?) champagne cocktail made all this pleasant and unreal. 'This is a game we play; you ask me to leave Graeme and marry you and I say no, then we all go home and I don't see you for eight months or a year, and no one gives it another thought, least of all you.'

'No, you're wrong.' He blew out cigar smoke. 'You think just because I'm rather a vulgar chap with lots of brass, I haven't any deep feelings——'

'Not at all——'

'Well, I have.' (He spoke, she thought, as if he'd paid a lot for them.) 'About you, at any rate.'

'Perhaps because I behaved so badly all those years ago, and you've never yet made love to me.'

'Oh, aye, could be.' A frown, the look of a man undoing a difficult knot of string had quickly passed, leaving the comprehensive acknowledgement of one whose business opponent has made a valid point. 'You've got to give sex its due, like everything else.' He seemed to brood on this for a few moments. 'Of course, what I should have done was to make love to you all those years ago in Brighton. Women like you are apt to stay with the man they first sleep with.'

'I'll take that as a compliment.'

'Oh, it's meant for one. But as far as you're concerned getting into bed isn't all I want. The women I've known—well, nice girls: fine for a slap and tickle, but out for what they can get. Most of 'em. And if they weren't, they'd have hysterics in the bathroom when I'd got an urgent appointment somewhere else. . . . Well, maybe it was funny, but what I'm trying to tell you is that none of them were like you.'

'I can have hysterics with the best if I'm driven to it——'

'I dare say. But you're the only woman I've ever wanted to marry; take it or leave it.'

She looked across at him. He did not belong only to this moment here in the bar, he belonged to the past also, and the plumpness round his jaw-bone did not seem more substantial than the muffler he had worn on the boat train: she became aware again of the unchanging self, withheld and unknown, who wears so many different and confusing masks.

She said, 'Why haven't you married before?'

'Waiting for you.'

She shook her head. The movement made the bar spin

49

faster than it should. 'No. Because you've loved something more—pictures and money. Like Graeme and his climbing. There's not much, all said and done, to choose between you.'

'I dare say : business is business. But I want a wife as well.' His glance, meanwhile, travelling round the room, found a young woman who was letting a mink stole slide away from her shoulders as if it bored her : for a moment his expression changed, becoming that of the connoisseur.

She said, 'Would you be faithful to me?'

'Oh, aye ; within reason. And you'd have a nice time, you can't get away from it. I know you're not the flashy sort, but then no more am I, at heart : never have been. We could find a nice apartment in Paris, and another in London. All this hotel life can take itself off the high jump as far as I'm concerned : I only go in for it because it saves a lot of trouble, and I'm lonely. Maybe you think I'm trying to bribe you : well, I dare say I am : you can offer a woman worse things than a good time.'

'You sound as though you meant it.' (But surely no one, in the pale strawberry light of the hotel bar, meant anything : truth was for the shadowless daylight in the streets under the naked sky.)

'Yes, well, I do.'

'But why?'

He leaned back in his chair, flicked ash off his waistcoat, and made a face as a waiter jogged his elbow. These few gestures suddenly established him as a stranger ; how absurd, she thought, to be discussing marriage with him. He said, 'Because I'm damn' nearly fifty, love.' He gave the sleek and scented place about him a glance that was at once sour and amused and detached : he looked like a man who, well ahead in the race, hears the gaining stride of the runner who will outpace him. 'Because one gets older. All this playing around may be fine up till fifty—maybe longer. But after that you begin to feel the chill on the night air. Any road, it's not what I want. I'm bored with it. Like seeing the same bloody film

50

round all over again: time to put your coat on and call a taxi.' He smiled at her: a little of the sourness and detachment stayed on his face, so that he looked lined and sad, as well as smiling. 'That's the case for the defence.'

She looked around her. The luxurious honeycomb became for a moment insubstantial, only falsely secure like a well-lit room on a liner which is none the less sinking. 'Tell him to lay the cash a foot thick, to this favour must he come': one could rephrase it like that, of course. The whole thing, she reflected, would become more complicated if she was going to feel sorry for Joseph. (And still the impression that all the normal impulses of pity, love and affection were in this place of false lights and shrouded noise, suspect, not quite true.)

'The trouble is,' she said, 'that I'm not in love with you.'

'Who's talking about being in love? That's child's stuff. I don't know that I'm in love with you: I just want to marry you, and be with you and enjoy ourselves together. What's wrong with that?'

'I don't know.'

'Any road, it'd be better than all this nonsense about climbing, you can't deny that.'

' "Nonsense",' she repeated thoughtfully, looking into the murmurous haze of the bar.

'Well, of course it is. Going out of your way to be ice-cold and hungry and scared when you don't have to. Plain daft.'

'No . . . I don't agree.' (Rather a curious voice, like one heard over a faulty telephone wire.)

'Stone the crows, love; yes, you do. Sitting on a half-inch of ice when he could be warm and comfortable like me——'

'Of the two,' she heard herself say, 'I'll take climbing.'

Joseph was looking at her with the mild astonishment of a man who, expecting a musical comedy, has seen the curtain rise on the stark pillars of *Oedipus Rex*. 'Bit of a change round, eh, love?'

'No, I don't think so.' She seemed to be shivering which was odd, since it was warm in the bar. 'Climbing may be crazy, but it needs a whole sackful of guts, and I like the look of it more than travelling first-class in an air-conditioned room in the Clarisse.'

He seemed no longer surprised; his expression was again that of a man acknowledging an opponent's valid point. 'What you're trying to tell me is that you're all tangled up with this great climbing Don.'

'I dare say.' She felt reckless, drunk, starkly lonely and engulfed in self-pity, since she had no place here with Joseph in the Clarisse, nor anywhere else. 'Yes, I am. I always have been. And it should have been all right, because Graeme and I loved each other when we married, and we're a family which is what you're supposed to be; we're one flesh, and in health and in our right minds, as much as anyone is; but somewhere it's all gone wrong——'

'And no fault of yours——'

'We're strangers who argue over the bills or whether we should ask the Fowleys to dinner on Friday; all the mass of tiresome and trivial things that people spend the precious hours of their lives arguing about, under the threat of death.'

This outburst seemed to have sobered her. She said after a brief silence, 'I'm sorry. Judith's herself again. Or nearly.'

Joseph, she thought, was looking as though someone had outbid him. He hunched himself forward over the table and said at last, as she groped on the floor for her handbag, 'You'd do better to stay here with me.'

She shook her head and stood up. The monochrome murmur of the bar continued. This was no way to be quitting it, not quite sure of her way round the chairs. Curious that Joseph should have the means to crumble her defences and reveal someone who behaved absurdly. Disquieting; a problem for later, not now.

They were standing together, rather sooner than she expected, out in the street. The opaque golden cloud of the Clarisse stopped short of the daylight and the harsh traffic. She said again, 'I'm sorry. I was drunk.'

'I wouldn't say that. Just a bit carried away.' He was frowning, though whether in displeasure or at the change of light, she did not know. He wagged a plump hand at her. 'Now don't forget what I've told you. You'll be a great deal happier away from that huge climbing Don, whether you know it or not.'

She grinned at him; the words, blotted by the noise in the street, seemed like a casual facetiousness. He added, 'I'll see you again before long.'

She took this as a social insincerity. 'Yes, of course.'

He leaned towards her, conveying the scent of cigars, and kissed her cheek. 'You need to look after yourself, love.'

'Oh, sure.' (But she had found the small gesture oddly touching; perhaps this was merely the softened sentiment of champagne.) 'I'm all right.'

She refused his offer of a taxi, and walked away. Looking once over her shoulder, she was surprised to see him still standing there: a sturdy little man nearing fifty who had made a wreck of her self-control.

She walked on, scraps of the conversation sounding in her head like a ragged sound-track. And then, sharp and sudden, she saw the tall, snow-lined ridges above Lundervald. Frightened, she walked more quickly. There seemed now to be other words in her head: What will happen? You know quite well: Lundervald and the Heide and the climb; nothing will stop it now. . . . And to us? Him and me? Oh, that's over; there's nothing more there; Graeme is already far off, his mind and his love elsewhere. . . . I'm afraid of the mountains; I've always been afraid of them; what will happen? No one can tell you that. You have to go and see.

THE hotel bedroom, with Graeme tying his tie before the looking-glass, had the astringency of a cold flannel slapped in her face: to convey to him anything of her outpouring to Joseph or her fears for the climb would be as absurd as bursting into an aria from *Tristan* in front of a railway booking-clerk. He said, with a glance over his shoulder, 'I'm very nearly ready. . . . Where've you been? All this time with Stella?'

'No. I've been having a drink with Joseph.'

'Ah.' He slammed a drawer shut and looked at his reflection with the impatience of a man who resents having to dress up. He did not, as she expected, ask her at once about Stella, saying merely, 'I hope it went down on his expense account.'

The small show of jealousy was in some way heartening: she decided to say nothing about Martha. And indeed his face did not seem to show the softening of remembered delight: perhaps the lunch had not been a success? She kicked off her shoes and lay back on her bed.

He turned to her at once with the expression of a man whose mind, attentive to some recent problem, is short of sympathy for anyone who is going to present more. 'You really haven't time for that, you know.'

'Why not?'

'We're meeting them at half past seven instead of eight.'

'Them?'

'It's turned into a party, the way things do. Martha's coming.' (Last week in Babylon, last night in Rome. . . .) 'And also a Father Something—Père François . . . Mailleux, some name like that. And Sean.' Another bang of the drawer; a brief hesitation. 'You remember Sean, don't you?'

54

'Martha's cousin. . . . Yes, without any marked pleasure. What is Père François about?'

'He's a brother of Martha's sister's husband.'

She left this for another time when she should be feeling better, and said, 'So many people. . . . I'd rather stay here and go to sleep.'

'They must have been powerful drinks.'

'They were up to standard.' On his bed she could see maps and plans and photographs of the Heide; her eye rested on the familiar shape: the great soaring triangle with the swathes of snow.

He tidied them quickly together as if they were letters which must catch the post, glanced at his watch, then stood looking down at her. 'You really mean you'd rather not come?'

'No . . . no, I was only joking.'

He said, 'I want you to be there, you know.'

'Yes . . . yes . . . it would look odd without me, I suppose, wouldn't it?' She swung herself from the bed, ran water into the basin, and tried to disregard a slight humming noise which accompanied her as she moved.

He said, 'You ought to know by now that I don't care a damn whether things look odd or not. I simply meant . . .'

'Yes . . . yes, I know what you meant.' Rapidly she pulled clean underclothes from a drawer, turned off the tap, hunted for a pot of face cream. 'How long have I got?'

'About ten minutes.' He sat on his bed, idly turning over the maps and photographs of the Heide. At last he said, 'And Stella?'

She wiped her face clean, faced the naked, undisguised reflection, dark-eyed and pale-lipped. 'I'm afraid she isn't coming.'

In the glass she could see his head go down. 'You told her about the climb? That I wanted to see her before we left?'

She ripped a stocking on a finger-nail; began hunting impatiently for another. 'Yes, I tried to persuade her. I did all I could. She said she had a date, but of course . . .'

'You think that was an excuse?'

'I don't know.'

His head was still down and he was turning the map in his hands as though he were testing its weight. He said, 'I should have thought you could have got through to her. You've at least got an art in common.'

'Different kinds of an art. She hasn't much time for illustrations and book jackets. As far as I can make out, she spends her days at the Ecole des Beaux Arts painting pictures that look like the flags of foreign countries one doesn't know about. . . . There was a kind of square fish leaning up against the wall in her bedroom.'

He smiled faintly. 'It all sounds like an awful waste of a good brain.'

Stockings, hair, face, dinner frock. And Graeme wounded and sad: all this—including unaccountably a French curé at dinner—needed an effort that seemed beyond her. 'She said she wished you well.'

'Yet she's still angry?'

'Not angry exactly—making a stand, she calls it.'

'About climbing?'

'Yes.'

'Really it seems so absurd! And yet . . . well, never mind. Are you ready? Because it's late; I think we——'

'Yes, yes, I'm ready.' Aware of his disappointment, she grabbed coat and gloves, and tried to prepare herself for an evening that seemed already a little out of control.

The table, seating six, was near enough to the window to catch the sunlight, though the candles were already lit. A tangle of greetings and apologies, the appearance of Martha in a frock of crimson and gold peonies, the black-skirted figure of Père François, all seemed to Judith to exist inside a large bright echoing balloon. Perhaps those two aperitifs had been a mistake, though something had seemed necessary to increase her courage.

Somewhat to her surprise they were all sitting down, with Père François on her right, and Hugh Ferris on her left. Graeme was at the other end of the table; he seemed relaxed and lively, laughing with Hugh: nothing showed on his face of his disappointment.

'Judith dear, you look absolutely wonderful! I don't know how you keep so slim! Honestly, just look at my hips.'

This was Martha, sitting on Graeme's left, leaning across the table.

Judith said, 'Thank you. I use a scourge for twenty minutes every morning.'

Martha laughed a good deal at this, throwing her head back. There is, Judith reflected, more of Martha when she laughs than there is at other times; there is even, you might say, as far as I'm concerned, too much of Martha. Am I being uncharitable? Jealous, even? Both, I would say. This evening seems to have been going on for a very long time, though judging by the absence of anything on our plates, it hasn't even begun. . . .

'I beg your pardon, Father, I'm afraid I didn't hear what you said?'

Père François, on her right, was leaning towards her, smelling slightly of garlic. He was perhaps sixty, with a face that showed kindliness and an inward placid amusement. This seemed to arise from his being a little deaf, and filled in the intervals while he tried to work out what had been said to him.

'I ask, madame, if you climb these mountains also with your husband.'

She said No, she didn't climb at all. He leaned an ear closer to her, and she said more loudly and in French, that if she climbed she preferred to go by *ascenseur*, at which he laughed loudly and said, '*Moi aussi*,' meanwhile tearing at his bread as if he had not eaten for some time. Perhaps he hadn't, she thought; perhaps he was breaking a fast.

She said, 'Martha, of course, is a climber.'

Père François glanced to his right, where Martha was leaning across the table and discussing a gully with Hugh. 'Ah, yes. So tragic that she is a widow. We consider, in the family, that she should have married again.'

I'm afraid, Father, that had it not been for my husband, she most probably would have done. (No, I haven't said that aloud. Or if I did he hasn't heard.)

'And Sean—her cousin—the young man—he is also, I understand, a very fine climber.'

'Yes, indeed.' She considered Sean. Instantly aware of her glance he turned and gave her a small smile of recognition. The fair head was held very straight and high, as a woman holds her head to keep her double chin from showing. Though there were lines on his face, an alert youthfulness of eye made the Father's description—'the young man'—still apt. He was talking to Graeme; he used his hands as he talked, making small contemptuous movements, as if he despised the things he was saying. He seemed to be describing the clumsiness of a fellow-climber who had ruined a climb in North Wales. '. . . a really terrible fellow; he lay on the slab like a squashed meringue, shouting for help.' Graeme was happily listening; not a trace showed of his often-voiced distrust of Sean; they might have been friends for years.

Judith said, 'I don't understand why he's here at all. This evening is very strange'; adding, as the Father leaned his ear towards her, '*N'importe, mon père. Je parle à moi-même.*' He said '*Moi aussi*' again and smiled; she thought he seemed much friendlier towards her than anything she had said or done deserved.

She glanced towards Hugh Ferris on her left. He was sitting, unrelaxed, to a kind of sedentary attention, his good-mannered face ready to be talked to, but not, so far, up to saying anything first himself. To Judith's eye there seemed to travel behind him a moving backcloth of the Himalayas, with sherpas, high-altitude clothing and oxygen masks.

She said, 'I hear you've been doing some sailing.'

58

His face showed the embarrassment of a schoolboy spoken to by visiting royalty. 'Oh . . . well, yes, as a matter of fact. . . . One or two islands . . . mountains on them. . . .' He scratched his ear. 'Not, in the event, really worth climbing.'

'Graeme said you travelled thousands of miles.'

'Oh! Yes. Quite a distance, I suppose. Interesting. Took us about ten months.' He finished this off with a sudden bark of amusement, and ducked towards his soup.

In a silence, she heard Graeme's voice. He seemed relaxed, light-hearted, having about him that small quality of difference which someone deeply familiar takes on when he commands the talk at a dinner table. 'Now the interesting thing is that the North Face has been climbed by Germans and Frenchmen—mostly Germans—but never by us. The Germans were the first——'

'All the poor devils who went before them,' said Sean, 'could have had a much jollier time if they'd learned a little more about the weather on the Face, and the minimum weight of equipment——'

'Perhaps, perhaps.' Graeme did not sound irritated; merely anxious to get on, still smiling. 'But the point is that if we're the first to do it, there's to be no nonsense about the first *Englishmen*. As a Scotsman, I want to make that absolutely clear.' He crumbled his bread. 'On the other hand, it's so awkward to phrase. To say a mountain's been climbed by the British Isles suggests a beguiling geographical phenomenon, but hardly the truth.'

Hugh was still sitting to attention. 'Of course we've not climbed it yet, you know.'

'Yes but we will. The omens are all good——'

'What omens?' asked Sean.

'I've forgotten exactly: things like the wind blowing from the North when you put your left foot out of bed on Thursday——'

Sean smiled briefly and said, 'Personally, before I ever start on a serious climb I read every damn' word about it.

TC–E

By the time I begin there isn't a rock pitch or an ice wall that I haven't learned about. It takes time and trouble, of course, but that's the only way to do the job properly. I never under-estimate my mountain; if all climbers were the same there'd be fewer accidents.'

Hugh glanced at Sean; his face, Judith thought, betrayed a slight questioning, no more. He went on silently looking at Sean for some moments and then, as if a courteous and reasoned argument in his head had reached a climax that required speech, he said, 'I think we must admit that some of those chaps who were defeated by the North Face had fright-fully bad luck with the weather. When Goerz and Brandler started out everything looked set for a perfect three days. The storm on the evening of the first day was quite unexpected, and put a lot of loose snow over the ice on the Angel's Wing.'

It seemed to Judith as she listened that, within the en-closed light and warmth of the restaurant, rose the tall cold tower, sending its wind off the snows. (And how would Stella have taken all this?)

Hugh went on, 'Circumstances such as these—or the bliz-zard which kept Glissot and Torray on the ledge below the Cradle for thirteen hours——'

'Oh, yes indeed; one thing's clear: the North Face makes its own weather.' Sean was turned to Hugh at his side. 'I quote: "The clouds break on it in their fury and empty every-thing they've got." The only thing to expect is the unex-pected, and they had bad luck, those others. But luck, won't we all agree, goes to the chap who's taken care of everything? Equipment, now. They carried too much—if Goerz and Brandler had had less on their backs they might have been alive today——'

'All very well,' Graeme broke in, 'absolutely true; but it's a question of the devil and the steep, if you see what I mean; if you've got to bivouac for three or more nights, then you need a hell of a lot of stuff from the bargain basement——'

'I have always been so interested, madame——'

'I beg your pardon, Father?'

'I was saying that I have always been so interested in your English theatre.'

'In the ... ?'

'Yes, yes; I have always been greatly attracted by the theatre. As a young man I wish to become an actor. I dream of the theatre. I am *désolé* when my parents desire that I should enter the Church.'

She could still hear Graeme and Sean, arguing about equipment. She said, 'Of the two, Father, I should think the Church would offer greater peace of mind.'

'*Encore?*'

She said it again, and he gave her his friendly smile and agreed. 'But as a young man I see only the—the excitement and the applause. Once, when I am in England, it is perhaps thirty years, I go to the theatre. It is the Duke of York's. *Vous connaissez le* Duke of York's?'

Yes, she said. He nodded happily and drank more wine. Graeme was saying, with something of his lecture-to-students voice, that it would be impossible to cross the ice-field without crampons. . . . Judith said, 'I'm sorry, Father? Again?'

'I have no regrets, you understand; but the interest remains, a *nostalgie*. I read always the dramatic criticism in your *Sunday Times* and *Observer.*'

Sean was arguing against crampons. Hugh was listening with a frown and arranging the salt, pepper and a fork in the shape, possibly, Judith thought, of the first pitch. Martha and Graeme caught and held each other's glance. Their faces were serious. Martha lifted her glass and drank, still looking at him.

'Of course, it has been said, has it not, madame, that there is something in common between the theatre and the Church: that the actor is a preacher *manqué*. Or the other way about.'

Graeme was now frowning and looking at the tablecloth; Martha's eyes were cast down to her glass, but it seemed plain to Judith that some communication had passed between them, and that they were thinking of each other.

'Of course, madame, here in Paris the theatre is very fine, but there is something in my heart, a feeling for the English stage. I find there a warmth——'

Excuse me, Father, but I'm much troubled, for I fear that my husband is thinking of leaving me for the handsome woman at his side. (No, I haven't said that aloud; he is still talking about the theatre.)

'In my view'—this was Sean—'the deciding factor is determination—guts, if you like. That extra bit of plus effort. If Bern and Nordler had pushed their way over the Tightrope on the third evening——'

'I think we've got to remember'—Hugh's voice was quiet —'that none of us has been on the Face. It's one thing to sit here and talk about it—another to encounter the—er— difficulties at first hand.'

'Absolutely,' said Graeme. He was leaning with one elbow on the table, playing with a match box.

Sean pushed aside a small bowl of flowers as if it were an irrelevance. 'Yes, yes, of course. I'm not pretending to know more than either of you. But I think it *can* be done; we've only got to give it that extra inch of guts and energy——'

It seemed to Judith that this meal, which had so far failed to add up, was beginning to make a frightening kind of sense.

'It is a pity, madame, but I cannot hear what is being said at the other end of the table——'

Hugh, catching this, gave the Father a different kind of attention and said, 'I'm afraid we're talking climbing, Father; it's a terribly monopolizing subject as far as I'm concerned: if I belonged to your Church I'm afraid I'd have to confess to a distracting interest—if you do confess to things like that, ha, ha; as it is, I just hope the Almighty will take a lenient view, seeing that He put the mountains there in the first place, and I suppose, the desire in us to climb them.'

The Father nodded and smiled; Judith wondered how much of this he had heard, since Hugh, who had begun loudly as if he were giving a lecture, had ended up in the gruff mumble with which the sporting Englishman speaks of his God.

Hugh, his duty done, turned back to Graeme and Sean. The fear inside her, Judith thought, was more insistent.

'I always have the sensation,' the Father was saying, as Hugh turned away, 'that the Englishman holds *le bon Dieu* in high esteem but has not yet been introduced to him.'

'It is our national reserve, Father.'

'It is a pity.'

'Yes, I think so too.'

'Of course,' Sean was saying, 'there's the risk of stone-fall——'

'Now honestly'—Graeme was leaning back in his chair—'you don't have to explain that to Hugh. Or me either.'

'Sorry.' Sean turned the bright alert glance on Hugh. 'You'll just have to forgive me if I get carried away by this. It's something I've wanted to do for so long——'

The fear was now undeniable. She said, 'It seems to me, Father, that you're the one person here I envy.'

'*Encore?*'

She repeated it. He shrugged and smiled and ate a maroon-coloured creamy mess in a glass. 'You think I have no difficulties? No tedium, no doubt, no despair?'

She thought they had all drunk a lot: she said, 'No. But you have a place to stand on.'

He laid his spoon down beside the maroon-coloured mess, and passed a hand over his face. 'Yes. Yes, my child, I have that.'

Graeme's voice cut through: 'One thing is clear: there's no way out on to the Heiligen Ridge. Once you're on the Face you get to the top or—God help you—climb down again.'

'Oh yes,' said Sean. 'There isn't any doubt about that. And, for myself, I haven't any interest in climbing down. I like to get to the top.'

She said, 'Father, I am really very much afraid.' Yes, she said that aloud, for his face was turned towards her. The waiter slid in and out between them, removing the remains of the creamy mess. She saw that hers was uneaten.

'Afraid, my child?'

Cigar smoke and coffee. Martha leaning excitedly across the table, shoulder and arm and cheek visible to her, strangely clear and human, belonging to a person who was something other than human in her mind, a threat, a cause of bitterness and the absence of charity. . . . She said, 'Yes, Father. This climb they are going to do is very dangerous.'

'I know nothing about mountains. To me all climbs are dangerous.'

'This one is especially so. My husband was going to climb it with the gentleman on my left, Hugh Ferris, who is a famous climber.'

The Father's eyes went over Hugh's face with calm speculation. 'Ah, so.'

'But it has become clear to me that they are taking with them'—she seemed to have fallen into an odd foreign organization of speech—'Martha's cousin, Sean.'

'He is staying in the house with my brother. From what I have heard, this is so.'

'My husband has never been happy climbing with him. Their personalities clash; my husband'—she was getting tired of saying 'my husband'—'is—is calm, reserved; Sean is tough and aggressive, he likes to bang the big drum'—she saw the Father frown at this and then get it; he must be making a great effort to listen. 'My husband told me that they were at odds with each other, and that this was a bad thing in climbing.'

'Perhaps you exaggerate. I understand that Sean is a very experienced climber. May it not be better to have a third man with them? I am ignorant of these matters, but it seems to me a good thing.'

'I'm afraid it is more important that all those on the rope should be in sympathy. Without that, there can be grave trouble.'

'Yes, that I can understand.' The Father's face was serious, the lined jowl looked heavy.

'This climb is a terrible undertaking. There are many who say it is madness to attempt it. The presence of a man on the rope who . . .' Her words gave out, engulfed in dread, weariness, drink, a doubt whether the Father could still hear her.

But he turned to look at her, set down his brandy and said, 'I will pray for you, my child.'

She nodded. It was kindly but frightening: she said, 'I think you'd better pray for them, Father.'

'For all of you.'

Well, that summed it up: that was all you could do.

'It is of the greatest importance,' Hugh was saying, 'that the first bivouac should be as high as possible. Glissot and Torray let their pace slacken badly at the end of the second day——'

'What happened to them?' said Martha.

'They were never found,' said Hugh. He played with his glass; there was a silence over the table. 'They are believed to have fallen. And a fall on that almost vertical face of six thousand feet——'

'Glissot and Torray,' murmured the Father, 'are they talking of Glissot and Torray? . . . They were Frenchmen; yes, I remember having read about them.' He warmed his brandy and looked down at the tablecloth with compassion.

It was all, Judith thought, very strange: the tall shadow of the mountain and the smell of brandy and the licking petal of flame below a crêpe Suzette, the Father who would pray for them, and the three men who would shortly exchange their dark suits and the quiet-lighted ease of the restaurant for the shapeless protective clothes of the climber and the

65

steep terraces of the North Face, where the wind whipped its snow and did not expect to find men.

She heard Graeme say, 'Of course, the most unlucky of all were Bernz and Heindler'—and then she stood up. If they were going to discuss the accidents she wasn't going to listen; she would make for the *toilette des dames*. Martha said, 'Hey, wait for me; I'm coming with you.'

There was nothing, Judith reflected, like attending to the natural functions in close proximity for underlining one's common humanity; as they washed together she felt a pang of sympathy for Martha who, no more than herself, wished to hear about the accidents. Judith powdered her face and spoke to Martha's image in the glass which was not quite the same as the face she knew. 'What a very odd evening this has been.'

'I've enjoyed it. It's been marvellous.' She spoke without emphasis; so she must have spoken as a polite schoolgirl after a dull tea-party. Her voice seemed to lack some depth of maturity; it made everything she said sound uncomplicated, like a piece of music played within range of a few notes.

Judith said, 'What's all this about Sean going with them?'

'Yes; yes—it's a terribly good idea, isn't it?'

'I shouldn't have thought so.'

'Oh—don't you? Don't you honestly? But Sean's ten years younger than either of them. I thought you'd be pleased about it——'

'Graeme isn't. Or I imagine not, since he hasn't told me.'

'Oh, it was all terribly last minute. You see, Sean was going to do the climb solo. He likes climbing on his own. He's the kind who can——'

Yes, Judith thought, I can understand that; he's the sort of man whose confidence and vanity form a second self and are sufficient company.

Martha was leaning with both hands on the wash-basin.

'In fact . . . I mean, well it was I who persuaded him to join them. Honestly, Judith, I've talked to people—well, I've climbed myself, anyhow'—breathlessness made the light voice even thinner—'and the opinion is, what people say is, that neither of them—not Graeme or Hugh—is really young enough to do the North Wall. They've got the experience, but you need more than that. You've got to have—to be terribly tough.' All this was coming out fast. Judith listened, watching a tap drip. 'People—people have said that Graeme must have persuaded Hugh to go, and—and he shouldn't have done, because Hugh isn't really equal to it. So I thought that if Sean was with them——'

'And Sean? Does he want to go?'

'Sort of. Well, yes. I mean, he's disappointed about not doing it solo. But he's always admired Graeme, you know, as —as we all did. And he thinks it'll make a good story, with the three of them.'

'Graeme doesn't want a good story.'

Martha shrugged. 'Sean likes his applause. He always has. He doesn't believe in all this silent service stuff.'

Judith leant against the wall. The confusion of the wine seemed to have left her; she felt calm and far-seeing. Stage two, perhaps. She said, 'They will disagree.'

'Yes, but . . . they'll all be up against something, well, more important than that. On a serious climb, you bury your differences, you have to. I believe it's always been like that; I think that's how it'll work.'

She was now quite breathless, and sat down on a small prim chair. There was a smudge of powder on her skirt, and she brushed at it absently.

Judith said, 'In my view, Sean's being tougher won't help. It'll only mean that when Graeme and Hugh are exhausted, or even want to turn back, Sean will make them go on.'

'No, he won't do anything like that. I don't think he'd do a thing like that. This is right, Judith; don't try to make me feel it isn't.'

67

'I'm not trying to make you feel anything; I'm saying what I think.'

'No, but—I have got a kind of responsibility. I don't mean I made it happen, but I helped it to. And that makes you feel, well, anxious.' She glanced at Judith, who was still leaning against the wall. 'As a matter of fact, that's why I'm coming to Lundervald—I hope you don't mind.'

Judith was silent. This seemed now the natural ending to the evening, the final piece of knowledge. She said, 'Why should I mind?' but it seemed to her suddenly that they had stayed there long enough; she was tired of the wash-basins and of close intimacy with Martha.

Martha was saying, 'You know, Judith, I've always admired you so tremendously; I honestly always have.'

'Fine,' said Judith, discarding the other things she thought of saying. She seemed to be back at the point where she thought of Martha as a fine big girl who took herself too seriously. It would be ungenerous to offer this, she felt, as a return for Martha's compliment. She said, 'What's the drill? Do you and I take turns at the telescope?'

Martha sat on the small chair looking towards a gadget on the wall which claimed, if you put a franc in it, to cover you with scent. 'Oh, no, I hate those telescopes. I never see anything through them, only an inside part of the thing.'

She looked large and handsome and, Judith thought, disconcertingly sad. For a moment she saw her when they had all first met, when Bill was alive, and the two of them had filled the room with the noise and energy of their presence. Perhaps one should make an effort of the imagination, and try to think what it was like to be Martha? To have that memory of Bill? . . . But at the moment she had not the heart. She said, 'Shall we join the gentlemen?'

When they reached the table again she saw that the Father had moved up into Martha's chair and was sitting next to Graeme. The table looked untidy; the Father was talking in a mixture of French and English, the others listening with amused attention. There was a good deal of laughter, and the Father was laughing too, between the French and the English. She hoped he hadn't forgotten about praying for them, for it was the only good thing that had come out of the evening.

The bells of the church of St. Germain des Prés rang the quarter-hour. The café table on the pavement was in shadow though the Boulevard St. Germain flowed with continuous noise and light. All of this, since she must leave it that morning, seemed to Judith in some way closed to her, like a book which one will not have time to read to the end.

Stella was by now fifteen minutes late. Judith, who had arrived early, thought she was already a little tired of the roar of the boulevard, the purposeful ring of heels on the pavement, and the newspaper kiosk, with its magazines and newspapers wrapped round it like the leaves of an artichoke. The iron tables of the Deux Magots were mostly empty; some way distant two young men, negro students possibly, were in continuously cheerful conversation, showing white teeth; to her left a young woman sat cross-legged, frowning as she read a letter on thin paper, letting her coffee grow cold.

'I'm all for your seeing the child,' Graeme had said as she prepared to leave the hotel, 'but for the love of heaven, don't be late. You're running it pretty fine.'

His impatience, she thought, arose from excitement rather than irritation. Paris was over and done with; tomorrow they would be in Lundervald; he had the inattentiveness of a man who is keeping a number of important figures in his head. When she said, 'You never told me Sean was going with you?' he answered, rapidly moving a suitcase out into the corridor, 'I had no time, it was all arranged very quickly.' 'You want him to climb with you?' He was crouched over another suitcase, tying on a luggage label. 'Yes, I think it's a good thing. It was Martha's idea.' 'So she told me. She's coming to Lundervald?' He was still turned from her. 'Yes. With Sean.

69

They're travelling together.' He got to his feet, and said, 'Give Stella my love. Tell her I'll bring her back a cow-bell.' The small sour smile showed, she thought, in the midst of his abstraction, his enduring disappointment.

The thought of this was in her mind as she caught sight of Stella, coming from the direction of the Rue Buonaparte. Beside her was a lean dark man whom Judith recognized as the one who had stepped aside for her on the staircase the day before. 'He will, of course,' she told herself, 'go away as soon as they reach my table.' Stella was walking with her head down, listening; she looked concerned and remote, like a Prime Minister being given bad news at an airport.

'Hullo—sorry to be late.' Her smile was pleasant, if rather quickly gone. She sat down at the table, made a brief, curtailed gesture towards the man at her side, and said, 'This is André.'

And why, thought Judith, as he sat down too, was it necessary to bring him? The face of lean intelligence, now turned towards her with exaggerated attentiveness, confirmed her impression of mistrust. He slightly rose from his chair, bowed, sat down again and said, 'André Tévernin. *Bonjour, madame.* I am so glad to meet you; I have been a friend of your daughter's for a long time.'

'She has only been in Paris a few months.'

'Ah, yes; I mean relatively speaking.' His smile suggested that he had politely corrected her in some absurdity. 'And you, madame? Do you enjoy Paris?'

'I would, given more time. As it is, I have to leave in about half an hour.'

'Half an hour!'

'That is why——'

'Such a pity. But you must return; there is nowhere quite like Paris. Stella is so happy here.'

Stella, Judith thought, had something of Graeme's abstraction: her eyes were frequently on the streaming traffic; now and again she glanced quickly over her shoulder, as if expecting to be summoned.

70

Judith said, 'Stella darling, have you had any breakfast?'

She said, 'Yes,' with a quick smile, and went on looking down the boulevard.

'Stella always eats breakfast, madame; often I ask her, and she always tells me Yes; and she is a very truthful girl.'

And when I want, thought Judith, a conducted tour led by a complete stranger round Stella's habits, I'll ask for it.

'I think she's been working too hard, madame. At the Ecole des Beaux Arts the students, some of them, work very hard. I myself remember a young woman there'—Judith saw that this had made a small dent in Stella's abstraction—'and she works so hard, and is so *bouleversée* when she does not succeed that she has to go away for a long time and lie stretched out in the sun without anything in her mind at all.'

Stella let a silence follow this, then she turned to Judith and asked, 'How was the dinner?'

'Rather unexpected. Sean was there—Sean Randall. He's going with them——'

'On the climb?'

'Yes——'

'I am so interested, madame, to know that your husband is *Alpiniste*. Always I have been interested in climbing; it is in many ways, I think, a noble sport.'

Stella gave him a look which Judith found unreadable, and said, 'You did tell Father that I wish him well?'

'Yes, of course. He sent you his love.' Stella nodded; there was briefly on her face a sudden frown of unhappiness. 'Are you sure you're all right, darling?'

A quick smile, a glance in the direction of St. Germain des Prés. 'Yes, thank you.'

Judith glanced at her watch. A little nightmarish this, with the pressure of time, and André Tévernin whose good manners were not good enough to force him to go. She said, 'Here's our address in Lundervald. I'd like to know how you are——'

71

'I, too, would call myself a worker, madame. All my life I have worked hard; it is necessary, to get to the top, and I have always been ambitious.'

Judith was surprised that anyone could show so much enthusiasm in giving information which was received with so little interest. She wasn't even moved to ask in what direction he worked hard, and where his ambition lay.

'Stella here is the true artist. Her ambition is not for herself, but for the work.'

Stella gave him a weary smile. 'Oh, skip that. I'm not a true artist, and you know it.'

'My dear Stella, you have a splendid and original talent; you do not satisfy the vision in yourself, but that is simply a—a talisman of your stature.'

Stella said, 'I don't think talisman is the right word.'

'Quite possibly—I am afraid, madame, that my English is sometimes at fault.' His apology, Judith thought, was at odds with the note of satisfaction in his voice. 'I can go on for some while and then, crash, I come down like—like——'

'A wounded bird,' said Stella.

'I believe that is a cliché.'

'You're so right.'

I don't quite get the wave-length between them, Judith thought. It was curious that she should still receive from his face the impression of intelligence, since all that he said, surely, came under the heading of unmeaning social flatteries. Yet the look of intelligence remained; this, she found, confirmed her mistrust.

Stella was saying, 'I thought Father didn't like climbing with Sean.'

(Odd that Stella remembered these things: the small uncomfortable facts that had lodged in her own mind for so long.) She explained about Sean's comparative youth and strength, and Stella listened with her head bent, like a magistrate listening to a dubious witness.

'Then there will be three of them?' asked André Tévernin.

A little surprised, Judith said, 'Yes.'

'It is very perilous, this climbing. Myself, I have great admiration for those who perform it. . . . Your husband has long wanted to make this ascent, perhaps?'

She said again, 'Yes,' aware that Stella's abstraction had changed to restlessness; her hands played with the price-ticket beneath the coffee saucer, and her glance turned, not to the distances of the boulevard, but frequently to André Tévernin, who was saying, 'He has fears about this climb—yes?'

'Naturally.'

'Ah, yes. . . . I wonder, madame, if you can tell me . . .'

She lost his voice, catching sight of a clock in the distance. Its hands had the merciless look of those that leave you too little time to be with someone who means much to you.

'. . . such an enterprise as this naturally arouses opposition in those who feel it is wrong to risk lives for sport, is it not so?'

Vaguely she was aware, as she answered his questions abstractedly, of some smudge of anxiety, like a fingerprint, on her mind. And Stella, she thought, was now anxious for this to be done with; she had pushed back her chair and sat forward with her hands between her knees, the fingers beating restlessly together.

'I'm afraid,' said Judith, interrupting a further question from André Tévernin, 'that I've no more time——' She stood up, pulling the bill for the coffee towards her, but André Tévernin took it firmly with a slight bow and said, 'Permit me. I insist.' He shook her hand and bowed again. The idea that he had been in any way unwelcome seemed not to have occurred to him. '*Au 'voir, madame.* Please convey to your husband my best wishes for a successful ascent.'

She thanked him and walked between the tables, Stella following behind. They stood on the pavement, the roar from the boulevard's traffic giving to this moment a feeling of urgency; it was like talking in the midst of battle.

'Why did we have to have him?' said Judith, nodding

73

towards André Tévernin, who was sitting down once more looking sombrely at the legs of a young woman at a near-by table.

'Oh . . . André.' Stella frowned at the pavement. 'Yes, I'm sorry. He's a chap who hangs around rather.' This was all the explanation there was going to be. 'How will you go back?'

'I shall take the Métro.'

'You won't be late?'

'No. . . . You could come and see us off.'

Stella looked down the street, still frowning a little as if she saw coming towards her some friend she had wished to avoid. 'I think it'd be better not . . . all so last minute and sudden. I hate stations anyway; seeing people off on trains. Sorry about it. Tell Father that I wish him luck. . . . I really do.'

'I'll tell him. Good-bye, darling.' Judith kissed her cheek, and Stella slightly pressed her hand.

'I hope it goes O.K.'

She turned away with a smile of mingled friendliness and relief, the look of a child who has got through some threatening encounter better than she hoped for.

Judith hurried towards the Métro. She looked once over her shoulder, but Stella and André Tévernin had become quickly lost in the Parisian crowds.

'Now there—that huge one on your left—is the Wetterhorn. Yes, I'm sure it is; I remember two years ago a young man who was going climbing——'

'Excuse me: I do not think it is possible to see the Wetterhorn from the train carriage window at this point; it is on the other side of the valley——'

'Oh, really? I could have *sworn* . . . but then of course one can be mistaken; there are so many Horns, aren't there?'

'I think Josephine will see better from this side, George: let her stand here——'

'Of course, as the train turns round one sees the same mountain twice, which is so confusing——'

'I can always recognize the Jungfrau. Never Mont Blanc. Mont Blanc's a terribly nice mountain but it looks exactly like all the others.'

'You'll be able to get another breakfast, my dear, when we arrive.'

The wooden-seated mountain train climbed away from Interlaken. The angle was steep; sooner or later, Judith thought, one of these voices would exclaim that the Swiss were wonderful engineers. The long carriage was filled with morning sunlight, the blue-white dazzle of snows and an air of holiday.

In this, she thought, their company of five was not included. Graeme had his eye on the window with the calculating interest of a man who measures an adversary; Hugh sat silent, in the relaxed unoccupied calm of authority and quiet conscience; when he glanced at the mountains it was with the good-mannered acceptance of one saluting equals

TC—F

with whom he is familiar. Sean was sitting forward, one hand beating his knee, his lips seeming to hold back with difficulty an excited proclamation of what he was about to do. Every now and again he put his hand on the coiled rope and ice axe on the seat beside him, as a child stretches a hand from bed to touch a miraculous toy.

A German voice, suddenly loud: '*Da ist der Heide!*'

Judith turned her head. A man and woman were leaning close to the window.

'*Ach! Der Heide?*'

'*Ja; der Heide.*'

'Excuse me'—a large Englishman in tweeds leant across the gangway—'did you say that was the Heide?'

'*Ja*; in English the Pagan.'

Judith asked which was the Heide, and Graeme said, 'That far summit over there; the pointed one.' She looked from the window. The sky behind the mountains seemed somehow misted by the mass of snows; she could just see the pointed summit, its far shape unconnected with men. 'But you can't really see it properly from here,' he said; 'not till we get to Lundervald. Then you can see nothing else.'

I can wait, Judith thought. Her eyes burned with the wakeful night, when she had lain in the *wagon-lit*, seeing Stella at the café table; seeing also the highly organized bunch of red roses from Joseph, with the card saying 'To our next (early) meeting'. The card she had thrown away; the roses she had given to the chambermaid, for it was surely impossible to travel to the heart of the Bernese Oberland, and to her greatest fear, holding with difficulty a bunch of flowers from a man who wished her to leave her husband. . . .

Graeme and Hugh were discussing provisions. 'We'll buy them at different shops,' Graeme was saying. 'Otherwise the rumour will go round at once that we've got a big climb in view. And then there'll be a rush for the telescopes, and the Press boys'll get out their synonyms for "high up".'

'Sooner or later'—Hugh changed his position on the

76

wooden seat—'someone will say that we're only climbing the North Face because we *can* be seen through a telescope.'

'Let them say,' said Sean. 'And let them look.'

'Never could focus a telescope,' said Martha, who was half asleep. 'See it all blurred.'

The train climbed on. Judith's eyes closed; the voices drowned and spread. She seemed to be at once in the sunny train carriage, and with Joseph at the Clarisse; with Stella and André Tévernin at the Deux Magots; beside Père François at the restaurant—his face was close to her and he was saying again, 'I shall pray for you, my child; pray for you; pray for you. . . .' But then his words changed, and he was saying loudly, '*There is the mountain; it is behind you!*' and she was jarred awake as the train came to its final stop at Lundervald.

Her brain was still fogged, so that everything seemed to be happening too close and too suddenly. The station that was part of the street was covered with hot sunlight and luggage; a line of hotel porters waited like a musical comedy chorus: the loud, anxious sounds of tourists arriving in a foreign country overwhelmed all other sounds; when she turned her head, the sky seemed to be filled with dark rock and veined with snow. She could see the Heide, unmistakable now, hung high above the valley, the steep terraces of the North Wall spangled and innocent; and to the west, staining the Alpine sky, a wedge of blue-dark cloud as yet not near the sun.

The porters took the luggage and, unencumbered, the five of them walked up the street together. Judith walked in silence, savouring the ease of movement after the long hours in the train. Now Paris was far off, with the voices of Stella and Joseph and André Tévernin like voices on the wind; and Oxford was out of sight: this was it, on the hot pavement with the mountain close and the taste of snow somewhere on the warm air. Lundervald was as she had remembered it: the chalets and the wood-carvings and the geraniums, the heavy,

77

valley warmth, the Germans and Americans with cameras, and the English with walking-sticks; and all the time, like a menace of war unregarded, the soaring rock; the high places of beauty where men died. . . .

They were here already at their hotel, the Gletschergaten. Martha and Sean were staying at the Oberland, a little farther up the street. (She found this unexpected dispensation a little heartening.) Almost at once, as she, Graeme and Hugh entered the Gletschergaten, a tall blond young man rose from a chair shaped like a coolie hat, came forward and slightly bowed.

'I believe'—he began, as if about to state his faith—'Herr Ferris and Herr Muir and Frau Muir. My name is Helfer, and I am from the *Schweitzer-Zeiting*. I would like to welcome you to Lundervald, and to express the hope that you will have fine weather for your stay.'

Graeme and Hugh paused, looking wary; Judith leaned on the reception desk, and exchanged smiles with a sun-tanned young woman behind a typewriter who seemed to be trying to convey in dumb show that Herr Helfer was something regretfully outside her control. The young man went on, 'We would like to know if you are intending to climb during your stay in Lundervald?'

'Yes, naturally,' said Hugh with a crisp smile.

Graeme said, 'That's what we've come for, a certain amount of climbing. Now, if you'll excuse us; we've only just arrived from Paris, and——'

'Our readers would be so interested if you could tell them which climbs——'

Graeme gave the courteous smile of one who has been asked a question bordering on absurdity. 'That we've not yet decided.'

The young man swept a look over the luggage which displayed ice-axes, rope and helmets for protection against stone-fall. 'There has been a rumour, gentlemen, that you are planning a first British attempt upon the North Face of the Heide.'

What a pity, thought Judith, that Sean isn't here, because he would enjoy this, and he's the only one of the three who would.

Hugh gave a bark of amusement. 'Far too difficult for us.'

'Herr Ferris, for a man who has climbed in the Himalayas——'

'The Himalayas are the Himalayas,' said Hugh with a resonant sincerity as if he spoke his creed of life. 'The difficulties of the North Wall are unique.'

Graeme was browsing suspiciously amongst the luggage as if he had lost something. 'Rumours are a lot of hooey,' he said to the coils of rope. 'And any rumour about us must be of remarkably sudden growth, since we've only this moment arrived.'

The young man gave Graeme a rapid, hostile glance; his bland professional manner, when it was in place again, was not quite the same as it had been before. 'News is strange, Herr Muir; it has power to get through very small cracks, like smoke.'

'And like smoke it can be entirely insubstantial.' Graeme had not perhaps missed the young man's hostile glance; he turned to the girl behind the reception desk. 'These cases here are ours, and those belong to Mr. Ferris. Judith, I think if we get these unpacked first——'

'And of course'—there was a deliberate refusal to be snubbed; a loudness in the voice—'the North Wall is news, not only in Lundervald: when it is known that an attempt is to be made the telephone in our Office of Information rings from all over the world, from Rome, from London, from Paris.'

'We're quite aware,' said Hugh with guarded distaste, 'that a good deal of sensational stuff has been written about the Wall.'

'The Wall itself is sensational.' The words came quickly, the German inflexion giving an added edge to their belligerence. 'Six thousand feet of almost vertical rock and ice,

79

continually bombarded by falling stones'—a shrug, a movement with his pencil—'it is not surprising that the newspapers find this sensational.'

Graeme, Judith thought, was looking almost Chinese in his lack of response. Hugh said, 'Journalists will be journalists,' much as he had said, 'The Himalayas are the Himalayas.' 'I'm afraid we're not likely to give them any copy.' He said the last word in quotes.

The young man after a pause and a steady stare of blue eyes from one to the other of them, shrugged, bowed and retreated a step or two. He then turned to Judith and in the voice of a man who is out of temper speaking to someone with whom he has no quarrel, he asked her if she could tell his readers what it was like to be the wife of a climber. She said that it provided a life of continual interest, and this he wrote down.

'Good day, gentlemen. I trust you will have good fortune in whatever climb you undertake.' He bowed again and walked quickly out of the hotel.

'There goes one hostile witness,' said Graeme, turning back to the luggage.

Hugh was looking in a baffled way towards the entrance. 'I daresay we were a bit rude to the poor chap.'

'You can't be rude to journalists; they're unbreakable like toys for the very young. Now then. . . .'

Sunlight, which till now had stayed all over the vestibule, lending the encounter an ease and cheerfulness which it did not itself possess, was suddenly cut away. Judith wandered for a moment out on to the step. The cloud, vivid as the juice of some dark fruit, now spread over half the sky. On the Heide's face the mists had come down, leaving nothing but the lower rocks, and the more gradual slopes below the Wall.

After a storm on the first evening, the hot sunny weather returned.

80

'One or two practice climbs first,' said Graeme. . . . 'Which? Oh, well . . . the Scheidegg Face of the Wetterhorn, for one. . . . Something to get one into shape.' How long, she asked, before the curtain went up on the Heide? 'Oh, a few days. Perhaps a week.'

So there was to be a longer wait; the thing had not yet begun.

Martha said, 'While the boys are out playing the overture let's take the railway up to Alpiglen and walk back down to the valley. I'm not a tiger any more, I'm afraid: got too fat, or something.'

From Alpiglen, another six hundred feet above Lundervald, the Heide loomed close. The sloping meadows above the chalets gave way to the pine trees, and then the rocks and snow of the North Wall. 'Well, there it is,' said Martha, pushing back her hair and looking at the Heide with interest but without awe. 'You can see the first pitches of the climb; there, those tall buttresses of rock. They usually do that part unroped. It gets more difficult higher up.'

'Yes, indeed,' said Judith, feeling her heart beat as she glanced upwards to the high terraces. 'That one can see.'

But there was a fascination about coming so close to the North Face, and the next day she went up alone to Alpiglen, telling Martha that she was going to sketch. The train was full of cheerful Germans with light caps and cameras bound for the Jungfraujoch; she alone alighted at Alpiglen. The train drew off upwards, with a sound of gentle thunder, and she was soon alone with the vast sloping meadows, the few chalets, the velvet brilliance of gentians in the grass, and the Heide from whose dizzy rocks there seemed to come, even in this warmth, a taste of cold. As a ship leaves a wake in a placid sea, the summit snow feathered white into the blue burning sky.

She looked up and up, farther up. This was a shaking hands with fear, a steady eyeing of the possibilities which was in some way comforting. Better to know. She sat on the grass, making no attempt to draw, staring, lost. From time to time cloud passed slowly across the Face, baffling, like the train which plunges into darkness, and leaves one blinking and blinded, unable to read. The buzz of flies, the fall of water, the sad metallic 'bonk' of a cow-bell, the occasional hollow thunder of an avalanche. Cloud, rising and dissolving; the sun striking down the Face, its greater heat loosening the stones, so that their falling sounded like distant rifle shots. As the cloud slid off, the snowy ledges coming clear once more, high and terrible.

So this was it. Better to know.

On her return to the hotel, the girl at the reception desk said, 'Herr Klein is waiting to see you, Mrs. Muir'; and an old man rose, as the young reporter had done, from a chair shaped like a coolie hat.

'Frau Muir? You will not remember me: I am Ludwig Klein. I have often climbed in the past as guide with your husband. We met once here, you and I, it is many years ago.' He put one hand to his face. 'You must excuse me: I have toothache, it has been troubling me for some time.'

Weary from the day in the sun, anxious to wash and change, she made an effort and said, Yes, she remembered him; that she was sorry about the toothache; could she get him a brandy?

No; he didn't wish to trouble her; he only wanted a few minutes' conversation, if that was possible.

She led him through the hotel to the terrace which looked out on to the mountains. A brilliant orange sunblind threw an amber glow, bright as syrup, over the chairs and tables. Ludwig Klein lowered himself slowly into a chair; she could see on the eagle-shaped, sun-burned face the little flash of impatience that a man who had climbed with ease should now find it difficult to sit down. He must, she said, have a brandy; he was obviously in pain.

82

Yes, yes, well; it was very kind of her; perhaps a brandy. . . . No, not aspirin; such things he did not take. He leaned forward, clasping veined hands between his knees.

'There is talk in Lundervald,' he said. 'A rumour that your husband and his friends are going to make an attempt on the Heide Nordwand.' Faded blue eyes met hers, seeming to look at once into her face and beyond her; Graeme had said, she remembered, 'Klein believes in gods and spirits on the high places; going for a climb with him is like a tour through *Peer Gynt*.'

She hesitated, and Ludwig Klein again pressed one hand to his cheek. 'It is very bad, this; not before in my life have I had toothache.'

'Here's your brandy. . . . You must go to the dentist.'

'Yes, yes; but first we must get this clear.' She perceived that he had come to her at once, on first hearing the rumour, in spite of the pain in his tooth. He shrugged heavy shoulders. 'Naturally, he will not wish his plans to be known. In such things, a guide respects the wishes of his Herr. I shall betray nothing.'

'Very well—the rumour's quite right. I don't know when they start. It must be soon now.'

Ludwig sighed. The heavy white head nodded as if with its own weight. 'This I have feared. He should leave it to the madmen, to the young who wish their exploits to be observed—so.' He made the gesture of one looking through a telescope. 'Will you try to tell him, please——'

'Drink your brandy. . . . I'm afraid it's not the least good my trying to tell him anything.'

'The people of Lundervald have turned their backs on the Nordwand. . . . Do you understand me?'

She nodded.

'The guides also. If there is any chance of rescue, of course, they will set out; it is a religion with them. But on the Nordwand rescue is often impossible.'

Judith shivered, perhaps from a small wind that licked her

ankles like a dog. She said, 'He has set his heart on it.'

'I do not understand why he should so much wish to climb the Nordwand.'

'I don't know either.'

'You must tell him that I myself have bad feelings about the climb. I have lived all my life on the mountains; I know more about them than gentlemen from England who come with their fine rope. There is too much soft snow; it has not cleared away as it should. There will be danger from avalanches. Will you tell him this?'

'Yes. But he will go just the same.'

One hand held to his cheek, Ludwig Klein turned to look at the Heide. Mist blotted the summit; the lower slopes were clear. Slowly he shook his head. 'It does not go. Even if I were a young man I should leave it alone; too much plumber's work.'

'Plumber's?'

'Knocking in pitons. So and so and so. All the time; without pitons there is no climbing the Nordwand.' As he spoke the mist was crumpled and swept away like a dirty sheet gathered up for the laundry. The huge triangle of snow, ice and rock filled the eye. He pressed his cheek hard. 'I have a special affection for Herr Muir; he has courage combined with a gentleness of spirit. He has many climbs to be proud of—he has done the Eperon Walker on the Grandes Jorasses, and the Dru by the North Face. He has no need to attempt this.' The faded blue eyes, clouded with pain and a kind of shyness, looked into hers. 'Frau Muir, I do beg you to tell him not to go.'

After he had gone she stayed for some time on the terrace, occasionally turning his empty brandy glass in her hand. When Graeme, still wearing his climbing clothes, came towards the table she looked at him with unsmiling interest as if he were a stranger whose character it was necessary for her to judge. Indeed, sunburned, eyes and hair pale against the

84

darker skin, he was already changed, part of the world of rock and snow and ice.

He said, sitting down beside her, 'Well, that's the lot of playing snakes and ladders up all this other stuff. Tomorrow we go and camp above Alpiglen. We must camp there for a day or two to be sure of the weather. Then we start.'

She looked at him silently. Energy, happiness, a kind of controlled elation; any fear? If there was, he showed no sign of it. She said at last, 'Ludwig Klein came to see me.'

'Nice of the old boy. I ought to have called on him, but there's been all this tearing up and down rocks. How was he?'

'He had toothache.'

'Is that why he came?'

'No. He wanted to persuade you not to do the climb.'

'Ah . . . yes. Come to think of it, that's why I haven't been to see him. . . . Did he say the trolls had turned thumbs down, or something?'

'He said the weather was bad; that the soft snow hadn't cleared away——'

'Oh, poor Ludwig; whenever he wants to discourage you he tells you the soft snow hasn't cleared away. . . . If you mention the North Wall he shakes his head and looks like a doctor confronted with something inoperable. He's a dear old lad and I'm fond of him, but he's got a bee in his head about the Heide, and nothing will get it out.'

She still played with the brandy glass; it seemed to conjure Ludwig Klein, sitting there with toothache and expressing all his fears. 'He was very unhappy. He begged me to persuade you——'

'Oh, look, darling. Please see it straight. The whole of this business is organized to the hilt. Sean and Hugh talk of nothing else. Do you really believe I could step aside now and say: Well chaps, I'm not coming?'

'I should have thought——'

'Ludwig's a queer old boy; thoroughly good-hearted, but

85

full of omens and portents. Kind of Ancient Mariner. He always was.'

'I should have thought he was worth listening to. At the very least.'

He made a small gesture with his hands. 'If one listened to everyone! You have to come to your own decision; do what seems best to you. I can't change it now. Surely you told him that?'

'Yes, that is exactly what I told him.'

'Then really—what more is there to be said?'

She looked at him in silence, trying to see through the familiarity of his face the roots of this implacable certainty. She said at last, 'Why does it mean so much?'

He gave a smile of half-humorous irritation, as if to say What a time to ask that! 'I suppose because, when I'm on a climb, everything else is shut away—all one's guilt and fear——'

'But why should you feel these things?'

'Don't we all?'

'Perhaps . . . but we don't have to climb mountains to stop it.'

He shrugged. 'It's my kind of happiness, I'm afraid—to be so absorbed that nothing penetrates—so that even you yourself are lost.'

'Is that what you want?'

'It seems so. . . . I suppose, in the end, it's inexplicable. As any love is.'

'And worth even the risk of lives?'

'We all risk our lives, every day.'

Again she was silent. And in the silence a movement of despair shook her, the despair that comes with the certainty of change. For Graeme, in the world of his certainty and his love for Martha, was growing more distant, and after this it was impossible that things should be the same for them.

She looked towards the Heide. The great Wall was now clear, even tranquil, soaked by an amber and mushroom light. The snow was rich, stained with colour; the beauty fierce, overpowering, like too strong a scent. She saw that Graeme also looked towards the mountain. The printing of lines on his face showed that she had, for the moment, banished the lively happiness with which he had returned from his climb. Here there was strangely the sensation of having failed him, and she felt an impulse to put a hand on his arm and say, 'I'm sorry! You see, I love you and I'm afraid.' But the time for this had somehow passed; it would sound absurd.

She said, her voice now clean of all stress, 'Then what are your plans?'

Instantly eased, he said, 'We shall pitch the camp some time tomorrow afternoon. There may be a storm coming up, but it won't greatly matter. We shall wait until the snow has hardened. A day or two, perhaps. I hope not more.'

She nodded. Certain of change for them, she looked steadily towards the Heide. The Face seemed held in a vast silence, climbing upward and upward, and waiting.

'So they have gone,' said Ludwig Klein.

Judith stood with him in the sunny street. 'Yes. I've just been to the station.' She would, she thought, be glad to get away from him, but she stood where she was and asked about his toothache.

'It is better; the tooth has been removed. Did you tell Herr Muir all I have said?'

'Yes.'

'And he does not listen. He says, perhaps, that I am a crazy old man who talks of mountain spirits——'

She wanted to get back to the hotel; not to listen to Ludwig Klein. Unhappily Graeme's words about the Ancient Mariner returned to her. 'No, no; not at all.'

'Yes; it is so.' She saw on his face the childish bruised look of hurt affection. 'He does not think I am worth listening to——'

'Herr Klein, there's nothing in the world—no affection, or friendship or love that would have stopped him.'

'So.' But the hurt did not leave his face. 'It is a kind of madness. When does he start?'

'In two days, perhaps.'

He stared at the mountain, then shrugged heavy shoulders. 'Then there is nothing more to be done.'

On the second night after Graeme had gone, she woke abruptly. The room was filled with the heavy silence of the small hours. Ten past two. She went to the window and leaned out. Silence and cold and the smell of snow. She could not see the mountain; cloud or darkness covered it. Were they beginning now? Strapping on the heavy rucksacks; buttoning the windproof clothing; shouldering the coils of rope? Almost she could see them in their camp in the meadows above Alpiglen, where she had wandered alone over the sunny grass. But now it would be dark and silent and cold, and their only light would come from the lanterns clipped to their waists or to their helmets.

She looked longer into the muffling dark.

PART II

THE DAYS OF THE CLIMB

July 4th, midnight

The cold deepened. In two hours' time it would be colder still, and once on the Face colder—unimaginably colder—than that. Here at the start of the climb they were already eight thousand feet above the valley. Blanketed in his sleeping-bag, camped below the North Wall, Graeme lay measuring the cold. Beside him in the tent Hugh slept, giving every now and again short, commanding snores. Sean was encamped on his own.

And that, thought Graeme, just about sums it up. Because he's at odds with us; he's a go-getter, without reverence or poetry: ambition is all; he goes at the mountain as if he would rape it. Do I wish he weren't with us? No; I still think he is necessary. But there could be trouble between him and Hugh.

An argument began in his head:

'If you feel like that, you should pull out. Say what you feel, pack up and go back to Lundervald——'

'That's making too much of it.'

'Nothing's too much on the North Face.'

'We can't go back now.'

'Judith said—didn't she?—that nothing was so settled and decided that it couldn't be altered at the last moment. Hugh belongs to those climbers of the last century—Tyndall and Whymper and Hudson—who had a stately reverence for the hills, and wrote up their historic first ascents as if they were submitting a report to the House of Commons. Sean's a whole world away. You've seen the expression on Hugh's face after some of Sean's remarks: as if he'd seen someone coming on parade in his underpants——'

'Yes, but Hugh's a real climber. Once he's on the Face he'll put everything out of his mind except the safety of the three of us, the necessity to move as one.'

'You've got to allow for people being people. Hugh may control his feelings, but his feelings will be there——'

'Oh, be damned,' he said, tired of it.

Carefully, so as not to wake Hugh, he crawled from his sleeping-bag, and out of the tent. The air very cold; the snow on the dark looming rocks of the Face stained blue; no noise but the wind. After a moment or two Sean came out of his tent to relieve himself. He straddled, faced towards the mountain, and grinned.

'So much for the North Face!'

Hugh wouldn't have liked that either, thought Graeme. They stood together, looking up.

'Midnight,' said Sean. 'We could start in two hours.'

'All the same, we won't. We wait another day.'

'I'm damned if I can see why. The weather's fine.'

'There's a good deal of fresh snow still up there; it'll be avalanching.'

Sean shrugged. 'There'll always be avalanches on the Face.'

'All the more reason for taking care——'

'I still think we could start tonight.'

'We agreed on a policy of no risks. There isn't any other, you know, for that.'

'Risks,' said Sean, looking up. 'There are always risks. Over-caution can be dangerous too.'

Graeme lifted his head. An echo here that had nothing to do with this place of empty winds and tall rock: he heard himself saying much the same words to Judith in Paris. Here below the Wall the city seemed a bright improbable mirage, and the thought of Judith made a bruise on his mind from which he was glad to turn away.

Sean was saying, 'We could waste all the good weather, and then climb straight into storm.'

'Anything can happen. But one thing's clear: it'd be plain

92

silly to start in less than twenty-four hours. There's no question about that.' He made these words sound Scottish and severe, a useful trick which worked well with women who went on for a long time, and men like Sean.

'Very well. In twenty-four hours. . . . But as God loves us, not more. By then I shall have had my fill of playing Boy Scouts. I want to get on that Face and show all those rubbernecks at the telescope that the Germans and French aren't the only ones who can get to the top.' His glance went upwards, and Graeme's followed his. In starlight and dark, the Wall loomed immensely, as a thing looms in a dream, beyond reason and imagination.

In twenty-four hours. . . . His heart began to beat strongly. By day the necessity for planning—equipment, weather, route—kept the wheels of the brain turning: now in the dark these were stilled and the fears came up like smoke. In twenty-four hours. . . .

He turned to Sean, who made a slight grimace, as if he acknowledged that, in spite of his impatience and ambition, the thing ahead of them would need all their courage, might even prove beyond them, then grinned and said, 'A bastard, isn't he? The old Pagan. . . . They named him right; no Christian mercy on those rocks.' Graeme looked at him, there in the dark, seeing the face, lighted with starshine, of the man with whom he was to climb. Violent ambition, impatience . . . what else? He was aware of the things unknown in Sean: the stranger behind the words, who showed for a moment now in the cold silence.

Sean raised his hand, turned and crawled back into his tent. Graeme stayed a little longer, staring upward, and then the cold forced him back into his sleeping-bag. Hugh turned, and the rhythm of his breathing broke. He murmured a few shapeless words, and then said with the odd clarity of the half-asleep, 'Hullo, Lennox old boy, is that you?'

Graeme said nothing, and gradually the short parade-ground snores began again. Lennox, he remembered, had been Hugh's climbing companion long ago in the Kara-koram.

He lay longer awake.

July 6th, 02.00 hours

The air was cold but still. No sound of wind. The three of them were silent, preparing themselves with controlled speed. This strange activity below a mountain face in the early hours of the morning was the same as it had always been, Graeme thought; a performance of the body with the mind some distance off, cold, critical and uninspired. No colour anywhere, in the rocks, sky, or in one's head; one obeyed a time-table, the necessity to be well on in the climb before the sun was strong, making the most of the hours when the stones were bound hard to the rock by ice. Far off was a man burnt through with ambition and excitement, who saw this as the very top of challenge and adventure: now it was a dark and risky business, done in silence.

Everything ready? . . . He checked the contents of his bulging sack: food, Primus, fuel, pitons, hammer and cram-pons. . . . Good that they were going. The past day with its hot light had tightened their nerves: Sean was a restless animal, pacing about the meadows. 'That chap,' said Hugh, 'will drive me out of my mind if he doesn't sit down. What is he doing? Discovering perpetual motion?' Graeme looked up from the Primus stove where he was cooking sausages. 'He's anxious to get going.' Hugh gave a grunt. 'So are we all, but there's no need to behave like a *prima donna* before a first night.' 'He'll be fine once we start,' said Graeme, gently turning a sausage. Hugh gave another grunt, and went on reading from a rather shabby poetry book *The Ballad of the Revenge*.

Then there had been the reporters—two of them, out of breath from climbing up to the camp. Hugh and himself, Graeme thought, had been discouragingly non-committal, but Sean had come through with everything he'd got. 'Yes, of

94

course we're going to attempt it,' he said. 'And attempt's the wrong word: we're going to succeed. The first British party who has.' He expanded on his career as a climber, how he felt about the North Face, how he felt, indeed, about almost everything. When he had done he turned to Hugh and said, 'I was explaining that the North Face and I are just good friends.' Hugh made no comment, but turned a page of his poetry book and began to read 'Where are you going to, all you big steamers?' He looked, Graeme thought, like a dowager chaperone with a sexy young piece who keeps making eyes at the passing lads.

Yes, better that they were going.

In the cold dark they climbed unroped up the early rocks, lanterns clipped to their waists. Easy, Graeme thought, compared with what was to come, yet his skin pricked with excitement, and a voice in his head was saying, 'It's begun.' They were silent, each finding his own way. He felt at once the heaviness of his sack, and thought how good it would be to be climbing freely. But you didn't climb freely up a wall like this: you needed all that damned ironmongery to keep you from falling off, and the quilted clothing to keep you from freezing. . . .

He could see Sean and Hugh. They were climbing easily, yet differently: some of Sean's aggressiveness betrayed itself in his movements and the confident jut of his behind; Hugh went up more slowly, rhythmically, with the calm of a man performing some strenuous but non-dangerous job like hauling in a rope. He was at peace with the rocks; Sean, perhaps, at war with them.

Slowly the light changed, and the lanterns burned pale. What was featureless, grey, somehow uncreated, was now coming alive. The snow, till now without force, began to strengthen and gleam. The air, if anything, was colder. He could feel confidence and pleasure gaining with the light, as hands and feet found the small ledges, and his boots clung firmly to the dry rock. The Face stretched away above him,

95

seemingly almost vertical, a wall without end; the sky was showing streaks of bruised crimson which might mean storm; absurd to say one was not afraid, yet fear was swallowed up in a thirst of enjoyment and hope.

Full light was all about them, strangely and suddenly. They had climbed nearly a thousand feet; they had climbed the Lower Bastion and the Axe's Head with ease and comfort. But as he stood on a jutting edge of rock above the Axe's Head, he glanced upwards and thought, 'O.K., now the trouble starts. Now the Wall, as you might say, gets into its stride.' The rocks soared above them, smooth except for a long uneven crack, glazed with ice. The crack continued for perhaps a hundred feet—the pitch known as the Broken Finger. And up there they had to go. Rope now, and concentration and care.

As they roped up, the morning was streaming with light, though here on the North Face they were in shadow that seemed colder for the sun all about them. The sun was on the Lundervald valley with the toy red-roofed chalets, on the meadows of Alpiglen where the Heide itself threw a long whale's back of shadow; and on the mountain railway track, where the tourists travelled in the wooden-seated trains. None of this concerned them; they were on the Face; they were there for two or three days—or eternity; they were there till they'd climbed it, or failed.

Sean was smiling gently to himself. He said, 'The first taste of the real thing.'

Hugh shifted his rucksack on his shoulder, and wiped a little sweat from his face with his gloved hand. 'Some people have used slings on this pitch.'

'Let them,' said Sean. 'Nothing on that stretch beyond any one of us.'

'We've not climbed it yet,' said Graeme.

'No. But you can see.'

Graeme squinted upwards at the long perilous crack. 'And what you see encourages you?'

Sean shrugged. 'I just say, it'll go.'

Hugh had meanwhile taken out a small notebook. He consulted it as a man does before a lecture, holding it a little way from him as if he missed his glasses. 'Hockferrer,' he said, 'calls it Grade VI, Severe. The crack is followed by a gully which varies in severity according to conditions, but is equally severe when iced.' He put the notebook back in the pocket of his anorak and zipped it shut.

'Slings waste time,' said Sean. 'Fixing them, pulling them out. And time means everything: the longer we stay on the Face the less our chances of succeeding. At least we're agreed on that, aren't we?'

After a silence, Hugh said, 'Very well. If Graeme agrees, we take this one free.'

'Free,' said Graeme.

Belayed, as Sean was; tied to the Face by means of a piton driven into the rock, and a rope threaded through, Graeme watched Hugh begin the climb. Slowly Graeme paid out the rope, as Hugh moved upwards, finding foot and handholds in the crack. The rock fell away below him to a depth of a thousand feet; the holds were icy and small. If he slipped? He would fall the length of the rope, Graeme thought, however rapidly he took in the slack. Would Hugh then pull him off? Sean wouldn't be able to hold the two of them: the pitons went only a little way into the rock. . . .

Hugh was climbing less certainly now. At this point Graeme could see that the rock-face leaned outwards, as if it would push Hugh away from the Face. He made two, three tries at his next step, and failed. He said nothing; Hugh said little on a climb, Graeme recalled, except to swear vividly when he slipped, or to announce some long-thought-out decision.

Sean was watching, his face alert, interested, accurately summing up. He said, 'His pack's pulling him off balance.'

Hugh had gained no more height; Graeme could hear the

97

sound of his breathing. Then Hugh called abruptly, 'Sean's right. I shall have to climb down.'

Graeme watched him, holding the rope, as patiently and with care, Hugh moved down the vertical rock. Curious, Graeme thought, I'm always fond of him, but when I climb with him, when he leads and I watch him and pay out the rope, having, you might say, his life in my hands, I feel something like love for him. . . .

He was aware suddenly of Sean, who was not watching Hugh, but had his eyes on Graeme's face, with bright penetration, as though he read the thought.

At the foot of the climb, Hugh unslung his rucksack. 'You'll have to rope it up to me. Time-wasting, but there it is.'

With a crisp smile he was on his way up again. Now, thought Graeme, he climbed without hesitation: on this icy and dangerous pitch he made use of every lip and button of rock; he moved with quiet ease. Good. Let Sean see it, and let's not hear anything about Hugh being too old for the job.

Yes, there he goes. Foreshortened now, so that one sees the soles of his feet, his buttocks and his shoulders. High above us, getting to grips with the Wall, on his way, the first of us. . . .

Finally, his shout came down to them, that he was belayed and ready. Graeme picked up Hugh's rucksack, preparing to send it up to him by rope, but Sean said, 'Leave that to me. I'll bring it.'

'As well as your own? It weighs a good fifty pounds.'

'Never mind. There'll be two of you up there to watch over me, and I'll have the protection of the rope. Time's important.'

No arguing with that. Graeme nodded, and began the climb.

Yes, this was it. This was the Heide's North Face as legend described it. Earlier he had been conscious of the valley, of the vast stretches of rock winging away at his side, above and below him: now everything was given to the pitch he climbed.

Now the adventure was on, the wheels turning faster. The triumph of gaining difficult height! The air tasted of snow: shafts of the pure, unwarmed light struck across the cold shadow of the Face so that the rock glowed, rich and amber, and the snow cut the eye with brilliance.

He felt suddenly certain that they would succeed; that in three days—four at the most—they'd stand on the summit, with the North Face climbed. Then the easy descent, down the West Ridge, within a few hours, to Scheidegg, and the welcome and the warmth and the——

Almost as his right foot slipped, he felt the pull on the rope. With a sudden power more of concentration than of skilled climbing, he regained his balance. He paused for a moment while his heart slowed. Well, that was a lesson all right; splendid dreams of triumph must wait for the quiet hours in the bivouac sack: the Face demanded every second of your concentration, and rapped you quickly and hard when you failed to give it. . . . Sean must have seen that. Damn.

The gully at last gave on to a small but adequate ledge of rock, where Hugh stood, belayed. He gave a faint smile, and said only, 'My rucksack?'

'Sean's bringing it.'

Hugh nodded. All to the good; they would get on quicker. If he felt a pang of regret, he gave no sign. 'Watch him carefully. That's a devil of a weight to bring up.'

But, with the rope slung round his body, Graeme saw that Sean climbed as well as he himself had done, with double the weight. Well, he was ten years younger. And one wouldn't mind, thought Graeme, if one didn't feel that he was so pleased about it.

When at last he joined them on the ledge, he unslung the packs. Hugh took his with a nod and said, 'Splendid effort. Well done.'

Sean grinned. 'I had the rope.'

'You didn't need it.'

'Ah, but it makes all the difference.' He was, thought

Graeme, so pleased with his success that he could belittle it.

'Time we had something to eat,' said Hugh.

Sean was glancing up at the rock streaming into the sky above them. Far up, beyond sight, they could hear the swaddled thunder of a small avalanche. 'Shouldn't we climb farther? As far as we can before the sun gets hot and loosens the stones?'

Hugh said after a silence, 'The next pitch is the Angel's Wing Traverse. One of the hardest in the whole climb.'

Graeme looked ahead. The Traverse cut across the Face, diagonally and upward. He could see, on the early part of it, the hard gleam of ice. Almost vertical; below was space to a depth of two thousand feet. And above them further and further rocks. Yet the danger from falling stones was so great that the sooner the Traverse was behind them, the better. He was about to say so, when he caught a glance from Hugh, as he swung his head to look upwards.

He needs rest, thought Graeme. I don't know why I'm so sure of it, but I am. He said, 'For my part I vote for food. As far as this mountain is concerned, stonefall seems to be an almost continuous performance. And we'll climb better after food.'

'Yes, I agree,' said Hugh.

Sean looked as though he would protest; then shrugged, and was silent. As he hammered in a piton and tied himself to the rock, they could hear the sound of stonefall, far off, like the sounds from a coconut-shy at a fair.

08.00 hours

Dried fruit, biscuits, coffee, and the space hung below them and about them, rubbing against their shoulders, sliding away into light two thousand feet below their legs. . . .

Oh yes, this is it, thought Graeme; I'm on the North Face of the Heide, and there isn't anywhere else I want to be. Why can't I explain that to Judith?

Coffee out of the tin mug, better than any coffee anywhere. Judith? The name echoed, bringing unrest, impatience, a sense of failure. . . . (Mine or hers, I don't know which, but it's there.)

'Yet she begged you not to come on this climb. That must mean something.'

'A resentment of the whole thing. She's always been impatient of it; never tried really to understand——'

'Have you ever tried to make her understand?'

'I've said what I could.'

'Told her for instance about Sligachan and the quarrel?'

No, he hadn't told her that. The occasion, so long past and so painfully memorable, had not been told to anyone. He looked at it now.

He could see his father very clearly: the gentle, grey-eyed face, turned to look back at him as the nine-year-old Graeme climbed the mountain paths. He had climbed happily, buoyed and speeded by his father's praise: 'Verra guid, verra guid; we'll make a fine mountaineer of you, laddie; a wee bit more length on those limbs, and ye'll be one of the best.' The slow Scottish voice touched the ear now as if he could hear it, sitting tied to the North Wall.

He could hear his mother's voice too: 'Och,' she would say of her husband, 'he's no but a simpleton in his great boots.' His mother was impatient of men, of climbing, of everything that wasn't practical and hard-headed. Graeme scrambled off over the hills, glad to be free, clear where his loyalty lay.

And then at sixteen he had gone with his father to Cumberland. He himself had been moody, work had gone badly at school, and the headmaster had spoken before all the class of 'laziness, inattention and wilful misuse of talent'. At the hotel in Buttermere there had been a girl of fifteen, already practising with lipstick, silk stockings, and sliding glance across the dining-room. Graeme had passed quickly from speechlessness to infatuation; he spent his meals with his eyes dreamily on her while his food grew cold. She had, he discovered, no time for climbing; she thought it 'silly, boring and a waste of time'. Enslaved, he made no protest. In day after day of bright weather, he watched his father set out alone. His father did not reproach him, but the silences were longer between them.

At breakfast on the last day of the holiday, his father asked him to do the ridge walk over Red Pike, High Stile and High Crag. 'It's a perfect day; wonderful views up there, with Buttermere and Crummock below us a' the while.' Graeme could see the girl, sitting at her table, quiet-eyed but aware, still as a cat.

No, he said, he wasn't coming.

His father said, 'It was your favourite walk.'

And then Graeme found that pity and shame could fuse together to produce an explosion of words that had nothing to do with either. He said he didn't want any ridge walk; it was a fool's game, sweating up hills when one could have fun on the ground; it wasn't worth the trouble and he wasn't going to do any more of it.

Would he not come, his father asked quietly, to Sligachan in the spring? To Skye, which he had always loved?

No, he didn't want to come, ever again.

A sulky pride made him keep his word; in the spring he stayed with a school friend in Pitlochry. There a gradual but strengthening remorse, and a desire to be back on the climbs, made him impatient to see his father again and pour out his enthusiasm for the mountains and his regret for bad behaviour past. And there the letter had come, telling him of the fall from the Sgurr a'Greadaidh Traverse, of his father's death. So that all the words were unspoken then, speaking themselves often in his head as he climbed.

Then you should tell Judith.

It's the kind of thing she'd be impatient of. She's hard-headed and practical, as my mother was. She's tough, self-contained, dispassionate, standing firm on her own stance, independent of me. Different from Martha, who wouldn't know how to be alone.

And Stella? He saw the child far off, unconcerned with him. . . .

Somehow, in the thought of all this, was a sense of failure. Better to get on with the climb.

08.45 hours

Sean, they had decided, would lead on the Angel's Wing Traverse.

'Answers the description all right, doesn't it?' said Hugh, strapping on his rucksack and looking at the rocks which swept almost vertically down into sunlit space. 'And what's more the whole damn' thing's covered in ice. About as much help for your hands and feet as a looking-glass.'

'There's a fixed rope,' said Graeme. 'With love from the last ass who came this way.'

'We shall need it,' said Hugh.

Sean led off. Leaning outward from the traversing rope, keeping himself on the rock by a mixture of balance and the claws of his crampons, he moved with an awkward yet effective rapidity. As he watched him Hugh gave a grunt of admiration, and Graeme said with a grin, 'The Angel's Wing gavotte. Not quite Russian Ballet, perhaps, but damned effective.' He stood watching as Sean went farther from him, over towards the rim of the Wall. He no longer looked like Sean; he was any and every climber, in helmet and anorak, climbing breeches and boots, piton hammer slung from his wrist, ambition and vanity lost.

It was as he neared the end of the traverse that the first cloud came up. It slid neatly over the sun, as an eye-glass slips into a pocket-case. That was all, for the moment. A little wind blew suddenly, and there on the Face they were entirely in shadow, though the valley was still patched with light. Hugh let his glance sweep over the sky; made a face and said nothing. Graeme remembered the bruised crimson of the sunrise.

A call from Sean. He had made the upper end of the

Traverse; he stood now at the Owl's Nest, a ledge protected by an overhang of rock.

'And anyone who says I don't envy him,' thought Graeme, 'is crazy.'

' "In his master's steps he trod",' he said to Hugh, who gave a sympathetic grin; he knew, Graeme thought, that this was the kind of feeble joke one made when one's bowels weakened and one's heart beat. It was a help that he knew.

Graeme stepped out on to the icy rock. And knew himself at once strained to the utmost. Thank God for the traversing rope: there were no footholds, only by a kind of burning concentration did he seem to keep the claws of his crampons on to the glaze of ice. Air and space and icy rock; nothing else. Keep on and keep moving; better not to look down at the valley below your feet. He became aware that the cold was sharper, that there was a wind drawing strange sound from the rock like a weird song. Was the shadow in which he moved a little darker?

A shout, perhaps from Sean, perhaps his own as he pressed himself against the icy rock, while the stonefall rushed heavily in the air. He felt a blow on his shoulder, as though a man had banged him with a suitcase, taking it off the rack. Making a sudden movement with his head because of the pain, he felt the more savage blow on his jaw.

He didn't know if he cried out. He heard the stones smashing to pieces far below him. Though he felt dazed and sick, some part of his mind must be working for he had kept his balance, and his hand held firmly to the traversing rope. He saw the scarlet stain on his jacket with slow surprise. An urgency which till now had been with him seemed to have slipped away.

Voices. Needing to be answered; Sean asking if he could climb on and finish the Traverse or if he needed to go back. The cold was clearing his mind, and bringing a sharper pain to his jaw. He'd done about a third of the way. Easier, of course, to go back, take a drink, rest while Hugh bandaged the wound. Easier, and a murderous waste of time.

Even more of a waste of time to go on and then discover that he could go no farther——

'Shall I get down to you?' It seemed that Sean had shouted this more than once. 'Are you badly hurt? Graeme, are you badly hurt?'

He called clearly, 'No.' An astringent certainty seemed to take hold of him. It was, he thought, the kind of certainty Sean himself would have felt. 'I'm coming on.'

'Right.'

That's all the argument there was. Sean would trust him to make his own decision. The responsibility anyway was his. He began to climb on. . . .

How slowly was he moving? His sense of time seemed to have gone as it does in a dream: there's a train to catch, some desperate appointment, but one lingers, letting the hour go past.

Those who watched, he thought (for by now they must be watching through telescopes and binoculars) would comment on the sudden slackening of pace. He himself had read so often in the chronicles of failure, 'Their pace slackened dangerously on the second day.' A kind of feebleness in his limbs, new to him; a sharper awareness of cold; a sense that the great Wall was limitless; that he could climb and climb and find yet further rock. . . . Were they defeated already? So soon?

With an effort he climbed on.

His concentration was now feverish, so that his brain seemed to burn; the pain in his jaw dragged at his attention: important to disregard it, to have nothing clear in his mind but the next point on the icy rock where his foot must go.

The Traverse now nearly done. The Owl's Nest, with its ledge of rock and Sean standing there, within sight, his face strained with anxiety. Had he then taken so long? All idea of time seemed to have left him. There was a good deal of blood on his jacket; perhaps Sean thought him more badly hurt than he was. He tried to smile at Sean, but the pain of his jaw stopped him, and Sean called sharply, 'Watch how you go. Those last few steps are the devil.'

Ice-smooth rock became, if anything, smoother; the angle still more steep. A fury of concentration in his head, denying pain and feebleness, keeping him moving.

The ledge. The thing was done. He stood with the muscles of thighs and arms shuddering with release. Sean quickly banged in a piton and tied him to the rock; then began, with speed and care, to dress his wound.

Graeme leant against the Wall. His violently trembling limbs, the pain in his jaw and the weakness which had turned his body to sawdust, made the idea of climbing farther at this moment as impossible as taking flight over the valley.

He saw that Sean's fingers were trembling with haste as he took plaster from his pack. And suddenly he became aware of a darkness in the air; the blue-green darkness of oblivion. He bent his head, crouching on the ledge: he mustn't lose consciousness——

But the darkness wasn't in his head; it was all about him. Rags of cloud, paler than the storm colour behind them, were racing towards the Wall. The cold hardened; he felt the first scattering of snow on the heated throbbing of his face.

He glanced quickly at Sean. 'Trouble coming,' said Sean, unwinding a bandage. 'We must get Hugh across the Traverse as fast as we can. . . . I don't think you've broken anything but it's a hell of a bash. Needs stitches, but that's beyond me, I'm afraid.' He wound the bandage round Graeme's head like a nun's coif. As he did so Graeme looked into his face, seeing there with surprise a strange tenderness. This for a moment disconcerted him, and he said, as if to break off some unexplained communication, 'For God's sake bring Hugh over. Before the storm.'

Sean nodded, thrusting bandage, plaster and antiseptic into his sack. The little moment of communication was gone. The dark was suddenly more intense, as though someone had whipped out a black flag that covered all the sky; the rocks close at hand had a sombre clarity, as though within a green tent. The cold was sharper still.

Crouched on the ledge, Graeme watched as Sean wound the rope round his body, and waited for Hugh. The pain in his jaw did not seem now to exist on its own, it was merely part of the increasing darkness, the quickening snow, and his own anxiety lest the full storm should break before Hugh had made the Traverse. . . . Yes, he must do it. He will do it. Did I hold things up too long? Could I have gone faster? Useless to ask now. . . . But this is the responsibility which is inseparable from a climb; the sense that each life hangs on the other, that your own misjudgment can cause another man's death. It is a weight, and yet a happiness too: comradeship and the end of loneliness. (And it is here with Sean and Hugh, yet not with Judith and Stella, and I wish I knew how to bring it back.)

Now Hugh's figure was in sight on the Traverse. The snow was coming more quickly. Dwarfed by the unending rocks above him and the inky space below, he looked small and vulnerable. Graeme felt a sudden impulse of pride and fear and love.

Yes, he must make it. He would make it. He wasn't as young or as tough as Sean, but this was his job; he knew every inch of it; he knew all about bad mountain weather; he would allow for the new loose snow on the icy rock; he would know that the need to hurry mustn't make him careless; he'd be on top of it all the way. . . .

And after that?

Never mind after that.

Now the snow was coming so fast that his figure was a shadow seen dimly through it. The temperature was plunging. As he strained his eyes Graeme felt again the sudden, sawdust weakness in his limbs; the pain in his jaw seemed to have reached his temple. The clouds were on them now, wrapping the whole Face, so there was scarcely anything to be seen: only the wet snow-scattered rocks immediately close to them: beyond this cloud and storm, with the world the other side of it.

He thought of the world. He thought of the baffled telescopes and binoculars, the speculations and doubts, those who would be stimulated by the prospect of disaster, and those who would fear it. He thought of Judith, Stella and Martha, and felt again the touch of responsibility, this time a weight that troubled him, like the storm.

Now Hugh was close to them. Frozen snow lay on his brows and lashes; his cheeks were hollow with strain. He negotiated the last icy stretch of the Traverse, and as he climbed on to the ledge, he gave a faint, stiff smile. The storm was a blizzard now, the wind riding harder all the time, shouting tirelessly in their ears, so that they had to lift their voices above it. Water was pouring down the Face, bringing further avalanches of stones. From these the overhanging rock protected them.

'Got to tie on here,' Hugh shouted. 'Graeme must somehow lie across the ledge; Sean and I can sit on a couple of armchairs in front of him. Badly hurt, Graeme?'

Graeme shook his head. But the wind seemed to bang and shout and buffet him, like a rough woman in a temper, and he had no strength to answer.

'When this passes,' Hugh said, crouching on the ledge, 'we must see about getting farther.'

Sean wiped his face with his glove. His eyes were bleary like a drunken man's. 'Yes,' he shouted, the wind tearing at his words, 'we must be higher before nightfall.'

None of them said more. This weather could last the whole day—two days—even three. No use discussing that. Nothing to do now but wait.

The Bivouac

He lay, aware of the harsh pressure of the rock, of the protesting limbs that he could not straighten. The Face spoke and clanged like irons; the wind drew sounds like the cries of men from the high rocks. Pain and relief together muffled his brain. No further effort needed as long as the storm lasts. Sean and Hugh murmuring together, brewing coffee, preparing food. The air green-dark and seething with snow, but protection here from stonefall and from the most savage edge of the cold. Somewhere, far off, was the question of climbing farther, but this, like the damage done to their chances by the storm, did not seem yet to concern him.

'*I don't know how badly he's hurt.*'

These words were very clear, penetrating the fogged daze in his mind. Sean's voice? He thought so . . . but the words didn't belong to the ledge on the North Face; they belonged far back, and they were his own words, so vivid in memory because they were a lie.

('*Graeme! Graeme!*'

Martha, her voice desperate with panic and grief.

'Yes—yes. I'll get down to him. Sean can take your rope. I don't know how badly he's hurt.' But Bill lay below them, with blood all over his face, and it wasn't any good saying he didn't know.

'He isn't moving! Graeme, I think he's dead——' Her face colourless, anguished, the health and beauty wiped away as she stared at something she should never have seen. No, that he would always remember.)

He could see her very clearly. Now she was in her room, where he had found her that night, after his quarrel with Judith. . . .

(Still the noise of the wind; the train rattle of falling stones, the plumper dive of an avalanche. How long had he lain here, with the bloated throbbing of his jaw? It could be day or night; the rock where he lay seemed to belong to some place out of time.)

Martha's voice poured through his mind, through the noise of the wind; light, colourless voice, the words coming fast:

'*I suppose you ought to get back to Judith. It's better with you here. I don't like it when I'm alone. I never have been. At least it seems like that. There were always people. Family and brothers and then Bill. Yes, the others are still there, but one can't go back. I don't think I know how to be alone. . . . You see, I always had everything all right. I mean there were people who liked me, all the time; my parents had a big house in the country, not grand, I don't mean that; just big, and lots of friends; I suppose someone shut the front door at night but it never seemed to be shut, there were always people and dogs coming in or out of it. It was always untidy, and no one ever seemed to tell me not to do anything, I daresay they did, but I don't remember it, I just enjoyed everything, all the time.*'

(Strange to hear all this now: words far off in a woman's voice, having no place amongst the steep and lonely rocks. But the voice went on.)

'*I suppose marrying Bill made me grow up a bit. Or something like that, I don't know, anyway, it suddenly seemed to me that I'd had everything my own way always, and no one could go on doing that, it was just all too good, and I began to get it into my head that I'd be punished, and I have been, no I don't mean by Bill's death—that's a terrible thing to say isn't it? But you see I married Bill when I was seventeen, he was like all the people I knew, the people I'd grown up with; it seemed the obvious thing to do. But it was wrong, I only knew how wrong when we met you and Judith here for the first time; this is awful to tell you this now but I can't help it; someone will have to forgive me, because I found I wasn't really in love with Bill (someone will forgive me, won't they?) I was in love with you.*'

(There was still the wind, and the slime-green colour of the storm. The rush and hiss of water down the Face, as though a hundred taps were turned full on. Perhaps he had slept; his cheek and jaw still throbbed heavily. Sean and Hugh were talking, but the words slid away before he could grasp them. He told himself, 'I am on the North Face of the Heide,' but he did not quite believe it. More clear than the icy ledges was the sun-warmed rock of Pinnacle Ridge on Sgurr-nan-Gilean, two years after Bill's death.)

The two of them on the rock. In ease and comfort: odd that he could create it in his mind while the cold explored his body with its merciless instruments. Martha and himself together: where was Hugh? (Here on the North Face . . . no, he was thinking of a time long past.) He couldn't remember where Hugh had been; the effort brought a swing of nausea and sharpened the pain in his jaw. He could see the strange hot April weather of Skye—Skye, where his father had been killed. That had been April too, and the weather fine. The oppressive heat of the valley; the burn where Martha bathed. In her underclothes, with a kind of animal innocence that he had not quite trusted, thinking, 'Women can mean two different things at the same time. . . .' Menace over the valley; a smudge of cloud over Loch Scavaig; it had been (hadn't it?) the last day of the fine weather. And the last day of inno- cence, the time before the beginning of trouble.

(Cramp grasped his limbs; he tried to move them, but there was no room. Sean and Hugh, huddled together, crouched on the lip of space. . . .)

Martha in his arms, and then his own voice: 'If we stay here long enough, Hugh'll send out a search party.'

'It's all a kind of joke to you.'

'No, it's not a joke. I'm terribly fond of you and I want you very much.'

'That sounds matter of fact. Not what I want to hear.'

'I'm sorry. It's the truth.'

'You talk as if the whole thing could be measured, summed up; it isn't like that for women, all cut and dried: there's a terrible loneliness coming in all the time and one's afraid; I've been afraid for so long, ever since Bill died.'

And himself, that evening, pacing his room, waiting for Hugh on the other side of the wall to stop bumping about and gurgling with the water-pipes of his basin and get into bed. . . . (But Hugh was here, with him now, stoically seated there through the cold hours, his close companion.) At last, after a long pause, the creak of Hugh's bed. He could remember wondering about the pause : perhaps Hugh said his prayers. At odds with piety and innocence he had gone along the corridor to Martha's room, stepping at once into a different world of passion, remorse and fear.

July 7th, 01.00 hours

He moved his head. There was a silence about the mountain like the silence when a train stops by a grass bank : the sounds of iron movement so suddenly quenched continuing in the mind, gradually diminished by the waves of quiet. He could see Sean and Hugh still huddled there, shapeless, attentive, like guardians. The air beyond them seemed dark, but with a difference. . . . Had the snow stopped? The cold was sharper, and his bandaged jaw felt huge, like a throbbing melon. The cold seemed to have built itself into his body, to be part of his bones. He said, 'What time is it?'

One of the muffled figures turned. Hugh. 'Hullo. Feeling better?'

'Yes. How do we stand?'

'One o'clock and a fine morning, thank God. We should be able to start again in a few hours. But it's up to you.'

05.00 hours

The Face in the grey light was transformed with the sudden blooming of snow. The mists had gone, the storm silent, and they were climbing again. But climbing, Graeme thought, with a difference, having moved into a new dimension of cold. Cold seemed to lie on his skin like a suit of icy armour, so that his limbs moved stiffly and slow ; it was impossible to imagine that there had been at any time anything but this cold. The pain in his jaw was numbed and lost in the cold. Exaltation and excitement had gone ; he was on the Face ; he would climb it if he could. The challenge remained, but its colours had darkened ; there was something of enmiyt in it now.

At the Owl's Nest they had left ropes and food, in case they should be forced to retreat. He didn't want to retreat, he wanted to climb the damn' thing now he was on it . . . but every now and again the thought of the supplies at the Owl's Nest touched his mind with a little signal of comfort.

Below them were gulfs of blue mist. The grey light was changing, flushed with colour. He wondered how far they could climb before a second storm broke. He thought of the people in the valley, early awake, looking from their windows, saying, 'They've had bad luck with the weather.'

And ahead of them was the Ice-Field.

Somehow, he was afraid of the Ice-Field. In the days when they planned the climb, he had dreamt of it more than once. In his dream it had climbed for ever, streaming dizzily upwards, muffled by the thick shadow that seemed in some way part of his own fear. He always fell from it; that sudden, abandoned dream fall which seems half accident, half desire, and which brought him awake, sweating and trembling. 'Anxiety,' a psychiatrist friend had said, 'a feeling that some situation in your life is too much for you, is going to end in disaster.' Well, perhaps it was Martha after all, and nothing to do with the climb. But still the threat stayed.

Now he could see it ahead of them. He knew its pattern from the photographs: a compact white shape, like an outspread wing, lying on the Face. It wasn't like that at all: it was an expanse of dirty ice, pitted like a smallpox skin with falling stones, sweeping upward at an angle of fifty-five degrees. It could take five?—six?—hours to cross. Perhaps more.

'The drill for this,' Hugh was saying, 'is that I'll lead off, cut a good stance in the ice, bring Graeme along; lead off again; wait while Sean comes up. And so on. Agreed?'

Sean said, 'Unless you'd like me to lead.'

It was odd, thought Graeme, that in such conditions one could be aware of the small hurt silence before Hugh said, 'I think this is a job for me, old son,' and bent to strap on his crampons. They looked insect-like, somehow sinister, and

Graeme saw suddenly the restaurant in Paris, with Martha and Judith and the French priest, heard his own voice and Hugh's over the food and wine, discussing crampons. So many miles, ages ago; part of another world.

Once on the Ice-Field his dream kept him company. It was long, slow, difficult work, with a layer of snow to be cleared away to get at the ice underneath, frequent stonefall, and the aeroplane view of the valley below his feet. But most of all, the place was ugly: a great lake of scarred and dirty ice set on end and stretching to the sky. Hugh's figure, his own and Sean's too, were dwarfed by the great expanse, were made of no account, no larger than grubs on a vast frozen sea.

He felt oppressed, lonely, disheartened. He remembered Scott's words of the South Pole: 'Great God, this is an awful place!' Here they were not at the ends of the earth, they were within sight of the valley, yet he felt isolated from the world of human exchanges, separated even from his companions, who moved slowly and silently, as if the spell of the Ice-Field had turned them into automata.

Ice. And more ice. And this odd oppression at his heart, as if at a remembered failure, or cruelty. Words went through his mind. 'If we' e killed on this Face—and we may be: weather and time are the two arch-enemies, and we don't stand too well with either—I shan't see any of them—Judith, Stella or Martha again.' He was aware of failure, of too many words unsaid. Better to get on with the climb. . . .

The cold strengthening, as if cold were the element of which these towering rocks were made; a grinding ache in his ankles from the strain of his crampons; a sense of ill luck, of the odds turning. . . . So long on the Ice-Field, so little ground gained.

And he thought, as he scraped away the new snow with his axe, 'If I come through this, it'll be my last big climb.' He'd said that before in moments of danger, but this was different; this was a cold decision, made between one step and the next. Something about the Ice-Field oppressed his heart; he was stretched to his limit and beyond it, and after this he couldn't want any more.

('Can you do this?'

'I don't know. Perhaps.'

'Do you want to do it?'

'I want to win the fight. And I want to see them all again.'

'All?'

'Yes; yes, all of them.')

Morning was well up; the depths of sky and space that hung about them were washed through with light. Were there mornings when one woke between sheets to a smell of coffee, to a steady, comfortable and peopled world? There seemed nothing but this slow and discomfortable movement over the pitted ice.

'Good stance here,' said Hugh. His voice sounded deliberately cheerful; his face showed marks of strain. 'I've banged in that piton as far as it'll go. And that isn't very far; the ice is hard. But with luck it'll hold. Tie yourself on to it while I have a bash at the next stretch.' He gave his small, crisp smile. 'Enjoying it?'

'Like a dose of double pneumonia.'

'Can't get a Face like this without ice-fields.'

'Does it have to go on for so long?'

'Always rather tedious work. Crampons, and all that. Well, now for the——'

It was Sean's voice that cut in as he called, 'Hadn't we better hurry? This seems to be taking us a hell of a time. If we're not careful we shall get the worst of the stonefall.'

Graeme saw the jerk of Hugh's head, as if he had felt a sting on his face. Then after a brief pause Hugh called, 'We're going as fast as we can. Safety's important too, you know.'

Silence from Sean. Graeme, holding Hugh's rope, watched him as he led off once more on to the Ice-Field. His movements were skilled and rhythmic; he scraped away the new snow, from time to time pausing to chip out small steps for the points of his crampons. Since Sean's words, was Hugh going a little faster? It seemed so.

The stones were coming now. He saw Hugh press himself against the ice, as they whipped through the air, singing and plunging, to break and smash far down. 'The worst of the stonefall . . .' By all the rules it shouldn't come yet; not till the sun was higher, but this damned Face made its own rules.

Perhaps that savage fall of stones ruffled Hugh. He was moving now, Graeme saw, even faster, chipping out the ice with rapid impatient movements of his arm. He was climbing towards a bulge in the Ice-Field. From where Graeme stood, the bulge made a great profile of ice.

Now Hugh was fixed on it, a figure against the sky.

Then there was suddenly the treble crack and splinter of ice, the shrieking skid of crampons, as the step broke under him, and Hugh fell.

There were no thoughts, Graeme found, only a bracing of his body for the savage pull on the rope, and a knowledge, deeper than thought, that this was it; their attempt was ending, briefly and bloodily, for only by a miracle could the piton hold against this sudden weight.

Then he was standing there, aware of the stampeding of his heart, with the rope taut in his blood-stained hands. Standing in an ice step a few inches deep, four thousand feet up on the Wall, and safe because Hugh had banged in that piton just hard enough, so that against all the laws of probability, it held.

He called, 'Hugh! Are you all right?'

His voice came up clearly. 'Yes. Bugger it.'

'Can you climb back?'

'Yes.'

After that, nothing more, only the slow effort as Hugh dug his crampons into the ice, the sound of his breathing as he climbed nearer, chipping out more steps. Graeme watched him with a kind of loving, anxious attention: how much had the fall shaken him? You might have said not at all, yet when at last Hugh stood beside him on the step, he heard the rasp of his breathing, and saw the shadows under his eyes and his cheekbones.

'Idiot business,' said Hugh. 'Sorry.' He gave a glance and a tired smile at the piton. 'God and all His angels must have been with me when I knocked that in. Now for the same bit all over again. Bloody tiresome.'

'Are you sure you're ready to do it?'

'Oh Lord yes. Absolutely. That was just a damn-fool business: I should have fixed a sling there and I didn't. This time I will.'

Patiently, he led off again.

And Graeme found as he watched him, paying out the rope, that he was arguing in his head with Sean.

'Anyone can have the step break under his crampons on an ice slope of sixty degrees.'

'I dare say. But on this kind of stuff you've got to be that much better than anyone.'

'The piton held.'

'That was luck. By all the laws the three of us ought to be carved up like a dog's dinner at the bottom of the Wall.'

'I tell you anyone can have an accident. Hugh's at the very top of his class.'

'D'you think he's equal to this?'

'Of course.'

'In technique, perhaps. But in stamina?'

'I've already told you: yes.'

These words, he thought, spoke themselves in his head with the violence of one who protests too much. He remembered the occasion when Hugh had first suggested the climb, and he himself had argued against it. Through his argument, he saw Hugh get each moment a little sadder; there were long pauses while he blew small whistling dirges through his pipe. Finally he said, leaning forward and knocking the pipe against the fireplace (dear God, were there ever fires?), 'I'm quite equal to it, you know, Graeme. There's nothing on the

Heide's North Face that's too much for me, as far as climbing goes. I know all about the dangers—well, that's the luck of the draw: maybe you escape them, maybe you don't. . . . I want to go and see. . . . I know what my reputation is. I'm a good climber of the old school. In other words, I've had my day. Well, damn it, I haven't. I'm not a fool, an ageing *prima donna* who won't retire. In a few years I shall pack up the big stuff and run up and down nice little afternoon jobs at home. But before I do I want a few more great climbs to remember. And this is one of them.'

Difficult to argue any more.

But now? He watched Hugh climb on. Was he moving a little more slowly? He could hear the thought in Sean's head as clearly as if he'd spoken it, 'We've lost a lot of time.'

Time.

Its threat, he thought as he climbed farther himself, was everywhere: in the interminable stretch of ice, in the gnawing, strengthening ache of his ankles, in the sound of stone-fall, in the cold that bit through to his nerves, in the dull pain that ran from temple to jaw-bone, in the doubts springing in his mind. Behind each set-back was the certain knowledge: the longer you take, the less your chances.

Time. Stacking up against them like a snow-drift, silent, gaining by inches, but gaining hard. How many hours on the Ice-Field? The air seemed darker; there was no sun. Was it evening? A whole day gone? . . . No; storm. 'They've had bad luck with the weather.' An epitaph? It wouldn't be the first time.

Dear God in his glorious heaven: the end of the ice. The cloud-high, terrible rocks still above them, but the end of the Ice-Field. He felt a small lift of the heart, as if he'd escaped from some place of ill-omen. Exhausted, pressed close to Hugh, and hearing the noise of his own breathing, he watched Sean as he came over the last stretch of ice. He seemed sure and calm, moving with controlled haste.

'Thank God,' said Hugh, 'that it's behind us.'

'And the weather?'

He made a face. 'Another bloody storm.'

'We need to get higher than this.'

'We can climb to the foot of Steeple Crack. Tie on there for the night.'

'How many more nights?'

Hugh shrugged. 'One, after that.'

'Not more?'

'I hope not more.'

July 7th—Lundervald

Judith wrote to Stella:

> ... This evening I am going up to the hotel at Kleine Scheidegg, where I shall stay until they finish the climb. Martha's coming with me. Up there I shall be 3,000 feet higher, nearer to the mountain. This seems now a good idea.
>
> Everyone talks about the climb; it's rather like the war. People keep coming in with news that you'd rather not hear; this morning a little man with a fair moustache said that they'd been seen on the Ice-Field, and that their pace was dangerously slow. I don't know what that means. They all say the weather's been very bad; as I write the clouds are down over the whole Face.
>
> I should like to hear from you. Paris and our brief meetings seem very far off ....

She decided not to say anything about André Tévernin who had sat so immovably at the café table, asking so many questions. She was surprised how clear his face was in her mind; one would have thought in the last few days she would have forgotten him.

She scribbled also a card to Joseph, thanking him briefly and more than a week late, for his flowers, and went downstairs to the post. At the reception desk the young woman and the porter both gave her a sympathetic bow. She went out into the street. The air was warm and grey; to her left the huge swaddling cloud hung over the Face. Now and again people paused and looked towards it, then walked on.

And the whole of this, she thought, posting the letters, would be that much easier, were it not for Martha. Martha kept up a continuous flow of sympathy; this Judith parried with brief, antiseptic replies. Martha persevered, saying finally, 'I do think you're so brave, Judith,' when she had been particularly gruff and unresponsive. And now Martha was coming up to the Scheidegg.

'Oh honestly, Judith, I couldn't stay down here alone. It'd be so awful. And up there one's nearer to it; one will know more what's happening; I mean, I shall know what's happening to Sean. Rooms? . . . Oh, there won't be any trouble about rooms; if you're anything to do with the climb they *build* places for you. . . .'

Judith wandered down the street to the shop which sold, among other things, postcards, milk chocolate, cow-bells, Alpine hats and newspapers. The newspapers came in German, French and English; she bought an English one and walked slowly up the street, reading it. A photograph of the Heide, no more recognizable than a newspaper photograph of anyone. 'WILL THEY DO IT?' ran the headline: 'The three members of the British party which is making an attempt on the dreaded North Wall of the Heide (known as the killer mountain) have already run into trouble with the weather. Experts say the storms of the last two days have been the worst for many years, and any party meeting with such conditions would be well-advised to retreat. The climbers, however, are still on the Face. . . .' There followed some inaccurate information about Graeme, Sean and Hugh: their ages, their previous climbs; and the records of other men who had attempted the Heide and failed.

She walked farther down the street, the folded newspaper under her arm. In spite of exhaustion and anxiety it was possible to see the whole thing with detachment: it was something she was not prepared to undergo again. That, from the confusion of the last days, had come clear. The certainty of change which had struck her as she talked to Graeme on the terrace had grown stronger. She would see the climb through, to whatever end appointed. And then?

It was odd to be shivering in the warm street; she turned and walked quickly back to the hotel.

As she walked through the vestibule she was aware of a man sitting in one of the chairs shaped like a coolie hat. His head was down; he might, she thought, be a reporter. Safer not to look; she hurried on——

'I say——'

She turned.

'There's no need to look surprised,' said Joseph, getting to his feet. 'I said I'd see you soon.'

She stared at him. 'I think I'm too exhausted to be surprised at anything.'

'Yes, you look pretty done in. All this waiting about; I told you it wouldn't be any good.'

'I've just sent you a postcard.'

'You could have saved the stamp.'

'But where are you staying? Not here?'

'No; I'm staying, as you might have guessed, at the Altenhof, that great big vulgar place with a swimming pool. Nothing left but a great grand room with a bed big enough for four. So I've taken that.'

(Extraordinary whiff of another world; somehow Joseph's presence seemed to make the climb unreal; the dangers of ice and rock could, he seemed to suggest, be overcome by giving the right person a large enough tip.)

'But why've you come?'

'Let's say, curiosity. Even in Paris the papers are full of this damn' climb. And the English ones are plastered over with "Will our boys do it?"' He pointed to the newspaper in her hand. 'You've got one there. . . . I thought I'd come and see. After all, what's the good of having a lot of brass, if you can't go to places in a hurry when you want to?'

'I hope you've got a good ringside seat at the Altenhof.'

'There's no need to be angry. I'm not unsympathetic. Now I'm here, with the mountain knocking my elbow, I get the feel of it, same as anyone else; what it's like to wait about down below. . . . Where are you going?'

'Upstairs to pack. I'm taking the six o'clock train up to the Scheidegg, and staying at the hotel there until . . . until the climb's over.'

'I'll come and talk to you.'

In her room he sat on a small chair, and looked about him with interest while she put things impatiently into a suitcase. He said after some moments, calmly as though he made a diagnosis, 'You're not angry with me, you're angry because you've had such a hell of a time. . . . Is that all you're taking?'

'I'm keeping this room on, to come back to. I may need it.'

He was still looking at her. 'The trouble is you're very near the end of your tether.'

'No, I'm not; I'm the tough impervious type; I don't feel things. Ask Graeme. Ask Martha.'

'I'd rather ask you.'

She straightened her back and pushed her hair away from her face. Gentleness at this moment could trap her; she felt her throat tighten.

He leaned forward. 'In fact, that's one of the reasons why I've come. . . . No, don't look like that—unbelieving. I'm a kind-hearted sort of chap when I have time.'

'You mean you did that rather tiresome journey from Paris to Basle——'

'I flew to Zürich. And took a train——'

'Just to hold my hand?'

'And, let's say, to be around—to have you around, too. You're not the only one who needs comfort.'

Certainly, she thought, in these circumstances, one was tempted to feel so. She made an obedient effort. 'What's wrong?'

He shrugged. 'Have dinner with me, and I'll tell you. Take a later train up to the Scheidegg.'

She hesitated. Dinner with Joseph? . . . Somehow out of tune; not right for this moment. She said, 'No . . . sorry. I need to get there. Like an alarm being set to go off. And Martha's coming up with me.'

'Martha? The great girl? Aye, love, this trip's just about got everything, hasn't it?'

She shut her suitcase, looked absently round the room. Her mind had not quite caught up with Joseph being here; there was a feeling, since she wasn't giving him her full attention, he wasn't really there. She said, 'If it has, I asked for it. I chose to come.'

'Why?'

'I suppose because there comes a time when you have to go along and see. To be there and learn everything and not duck any of it. A time of certainty.'

He was frowning, as if he'd seen a fault in a column of figures. Then he said, 'Aye . . .' getting to his feet. 'I'll walk down to the station with you. . . . And what happens when you have learnt everything?'

She said, aware of a reluctance to tell him more, 'I don't know.'

As they walked together, she was again held by a sense of incongruity. This place with the chalets and the wood-carvings and the fear behind the cloud, had nothing to do with Joseph; he belonged to the life of cities which was in some sense bounded by reason, which the mountains defied. One has to learn, of course, she thought, that people spill over, out of their context; they are always a little larger and more unexpected than your conception of them.

Joseph glanced once or twice to the grey cloud which hid

the Heide, but made no comment. He walked in silence, looking a little uncomfortable, she thought, like an unbeliever caught up in the complexities of the Mass.

Martha was already on the platform. She wore a pale coloured raincoat with the collar up. She was standing with her hands in her pockets and her head down. Her face, turned from them, and unprepared for anyone, wore the look of sombre difference which each face wears when it is unguarded in thought. The truth of everyone is to be seen at times, Judith thought; and it is a sad truth.

Joseph waved good-bye to them as the train slid first down to Grund and the valley of the Lutschine, before climbing three thousand feet to the Scheidegg. She saw him turn away, a small stubby figure going quickly towards the luxury of the Altenhof. Alone and, he had said, in need of comfort. If she was going to feel sorry for both Martha and Joseph, this evening was going to be very odd indeed.

Now the train was beginning to climb away from the valley, travelling closer under the heights. Though these were hidden, their presence loaded the air like thunder. Voices in the carriage exclaimed as the train slid under the lower slopes of the Heide; she could hear German and Italian and English, all saying much the same thing: that the climbers had had bad luck with the weather. There was one voice— as there always is one voice—which had the whole thing summed up. '. . . not a hope of getting to the top. No, not a hope. I was talking to one of the guides this morning, and he was telling me that with weather like this they've no choice but to come down. If they can. Damn' fools, in my opinion, to go anywhere near the thing in the first place.'

The cloud seemed, if anything, deeper. It hung just above the skyline where the Scheidegg hotels stood out against a white storm light. From here, as the train climbed, it looked a lonely place; the last habitation before the rocks and snow. Now and again the train slid under tin-roofed shelters, built to protect it from the Heide's stonefall.

Martha said, 'It gets colder higher up. I've brought sweaters and things.'

Judith nodded. She had no memory of what she'd put in her suitcase. She said, 'If they do climb down, we might see them tomorrow.'

'By the evening, perhaps.'

'Yes, I meant the evening.'

In the carriage some people were standing up to get a better view of the Heide. The valley had dropped far below; evening sun had broken through, and the red-roofed chalets were held in rich, syrupy light. Here the hem of cloud had slipped a little farther down, and a wind came from the snows.

July 8th, 05.00 hours

Sean said, 'It's quieter.'

Stiffly Graeme made a movement. 'Yes. Soon all you'll be able to hear will be our teeth chattering—dear God! I've never been so cold.'

'Spent more comfortable nights, certainly,' said Hugh, taking food from his sack.

You can say that again, thought Graeme. A ledge no more than a boot's width across, the three of them tied to it, their clothing soaked and icy, and no room to brew coffee. And his jaw hurt. He said, 'But the cold! Dear God, the cold.'

'Yes.' The muscles of Sean's face were shivering like those of a boy who has stayed too long in the water. 'The sooner we get started again the better. No good changing into dry clothes here—we may need them later, and need them more. Higher up.'

And now, thought Graeme, for the argument.

Hugh munched in silence for a moment or two, swallowed his food and then said, 'I think we've got to take stock, you know. What d'you say, Graeme, eh?'

'From here,' said Graeme, trying to force his frozen un-willing hand into his sack to find food, 'we could retreat. It won't be pleasant, but it can be done.'

Sean said, 'So can the summit.'

Hugh, hunting through his sack, had found a rather grey-looking sausage. 'That depends on the weather.'

'But it's quieter!' said Sean again. 'And the mist is clearing.'

Hugh made a face. 'You'll have to admit we've been handed just about the bloodiest deal in weather that anyone could have.'

'Oh, f—— the weather,' said Sean.

'Precisely. But it's beyond our control. And it must have the last word.'

'I'm damned if I see why,' said Sean. 'We're four thousand feet up—more. Most of the bloody thing's done.'

Graeme felt a spasm of temper rise in him to answer Sean's. It was the wild, unreasoning irritation of extreme fatigue; one had to take care lest this got out of hand. He said as calmly as he could, 'Others have got as far as this and been forced to turn back.'

'All right. We've got just that much more guts.'

Hugh threw the remains of his sausage into the gradually clearing space below him; he didn't look as though he had enjoyed it. 'Guts aren't much good if a storm hits you on the Tightrope. Or, worse still, the Cradle. Bad conditions can mean a climb down. Any fool on any damned Face knows that. No dishonour, no cowardice, just sense.'

'One thing is clear,' Graeme said, 'if we go on we've got to be damn' near the summit before nightfall. As Hugh says we can't risk having to climb the Tightrope and the Cradle in storm.'

He glanced at Sean, who seemed to be thinking, Why did I get mixed up with these two old bastards who should be taking the waters or playing bowls. Sean said, 'Well, we shan't. The weather can't be against us all the way. We shall have it fine for the last stretch. . . . Why, look at the light!'

Indeed, thought Graeme, one could do nothing else. From their cold moist shadow, they looked out on to brilliance, a sudden flowing amber that stained the snow on the peaks about them, skimmed the ice of all shadow, sent colour streaming over the valley like a festival. His eyeballs were awash with light; light seemed to soak through his forehead to the bones.

'Curtain up,' said Sean. 'Act Three, conquest of the Pagan's North Wall. By us. What d'you say to that?'

Graeme looked at him. Soaked and shivering, his eyes bloodshot and his chin dirty with stubble, the triumphant ambition still glowed fiercely through. He still has, thought Graeme, that violent necessary urge to gain the top at all costs; and a man with that absolute determination has an engine of enormous power; in the end it's the head that matters; heart and lungs and strength come second. But for myself?

He thought that, in his heart, he would welcome a decision to retreat. Retreat would be hard enough. But it was familiar ground, and as each difficult stretch was negotiated, they would be nearer the valley, nearer home. The steep climbs above them—Steeple Crack, the Tightrope, the Cradle— were alien, more dangerous in his imagination, at their great height. If necessary he would try them. But he would be glad to turn back.

And Hugh? It would depend now on Hugh.

Sean was saying, 'I told you so! It's turned our way at last.'

Hugh grunted. 'For how long?'

'Long enough to make it.'

'Not before nightfall.'

'We can get high enough, tie on below the ice slope, and then tomorrow——'

Strange to hear the word tomorrow, as one used it about certainties, about a train journey or a dinner party.

'We haven't,' said Hugh, 'come to a final decision. There's still the prospect of going back.'

'Going *back*? *Now*, with that weather?' Sean was still shivering; his eyes were anguished, desperate. 'But that'd be . . . My God, we've nearly made it. Tomorrow we could be climbing down to the Scheidegg, with the thing done. *Done.* Finished. Our names'll be in all the papers——'

'Yes, our names'll be in the papers all right,' said Hugh. 'Question is, which column?'

'Men have spent days on this Face—*days*, and escaped alive.' He was driving his numbed hands together as if he slowly applauded the spectacle of the brilliant valley. 'We've got the whole thing—almost—in the bag. Fine weather——'

Graeme said, 'With a hell of a lot of loose snow and God knows what in the way of stonefall and avalanche——'

'We didn't come here for a joy-ride. Luck's been against us so far; now it's turned round. We can't throw that away.'

Hugh was silent. Graeme said, aware of Sean's eyes on him, 'At least one thing is clear: once we've climbed Steeple Crack our chances of getting down again are pretty slim. This is the point of no return.'

Sean said, 'Well, we've known that all along, haven't we?'

'It's one thing to know it in the valley, fed, warm and lousy with health——'

'Now shut up,' said Hugh amiably. 'We're all clear about everything: it's going to be bloody difficult, and we're all in varying degrees, bloody exhausted.'

'But we can *make* it!' It was almost a child's cry, desperate with frustration.

Hugh was silent, looking down into the sea of lighted space below him. His eyes were cloudy with thought. Did he see, perhaps, Graeme wondered, his fall on the Ice-Field? With Sean watching? (*'I'm a good climber of the old school. In other words, I've had my day. Well, damn it, I haven't.'*)

Hugh turned his head to look upwards. Graeme, following his glance, saw the rocks in their hard morning skin of ice, death-blue in their northern shadow, not yet touched by light. A small frown went over Hugh's face, like a word of doubt. The wind had dropped altogether; they waited in silence and cold, surrounded but not touched by the naked, clinical light.

128

Hugh said at last, 'I think we'd be justified in having a bash at the summit. Yes, I think so.' He was banging one hand against the rock to restore life to it. 'But it's for Graeme to say. He's the one that got that uppercut on the jaw.'

Graeme was in turn silent. He was, it seemed, the only one without the driving passion for the top, the desire that destroyed reason. No time now to examine this, to try to see the root of it. Just that the absurdity of death as it might come, within a few hours, was suddenly clear.

But this, he thought, was not such an argument as he could present on this ledge, at this time. He said, 'I'm all right. Let's try for the top.'

A grin of triumph and relief from Sean; a brief nod from Hugh. The fumbling preparations, their numbed hands disentangling the rope, were made in silence; we are bound, Graeme thought, by a current of excitement and fear and doubt, and of this there is nothing to say.

With Sean leading, himself second, and Hugh last, they began to climb once more.

July 8th—Kleine Scheidegg

It was possible from the terrace of the hotel to see the Face clearly. Here, six thousand feet below the summit of the Heide, it was hot and fine. The place was intensely crowded, not, Judith thought, with the casual crowds of summer, but with a multitude who all looked one way, who had a single question and waited for the answer. The telescope seemed embedded in the close, summer-dressed crowd who jostled for position at its end. It was trained like a gun on the Face. She made no attempt to go near it.

'Possibly this was not a good idea,' she said to herself. Certainly the close presence of the Face burned a hole in her attention; its clarity seemed too brilliant, like a carefully printed letter which one fears to read.

For the moment she sat alone, letting her eyes travel over

the crowd. Press photographers, reporters, tourists from Lundervald and Interlaken, Wengen and Lauterbrunnen. Voices in French, German, Italian, English and American, all exclaiming on the courage or the foolhardiness or the doom of the men who climbed; eyes turned to the Face, as if God had promised to make an appearance there.

Well, what did you expect? she asked herself. You can't seal the whole thing off and mark it Private, as you'd like to do. When things like this happen, the world comes in and watches and makes a noise and leaves its banana skins around. You can't fight that.

A blond young man, with one foot up on a bench, was playing an accordion. The sound, blending with the snows and the hot light, touched off a memory: the café on the Boulevard de la Madeleine where, penniless and in flight from Joseph, she had seen Graeme for the first time. From that moment to this. She looked up at the mountain. It seemed to make nothing of time, speaking of the long, empty ages of ice. . . .

All the same, she thought, I'm here, now. This is my point in time, however much comes before and after. And I find this unendurable. One will wait as best one can for a man who's gone to war, but this is exasperation as well as torment. I should have hung on to Joseph, accepted his offer, gone along with him——

(Should you? Stayed in some over-heated luxurious hotel like the Clarisse, where the news of the climb would filter through the warm, insulating comfort, through the defences of the waiters and the hall-porter and the expensive food, giving all these things the muffling feel of nightmare barriers between yourself and reality?)

No, perhaps not. But I don't do this any more. And God in His heaven knows, I don't do it with Martha.

She stood up and wandered away from the terrace. The voices thinned; she walked over the sunny slopes which formed the great ski-runs in winter. Now it was impossible not to look up at the Face, to stare until one's eyes ached at the dazzling terraces, to try to see——

'Hullo, Judith. I've brought the glasses. Do you want them?'

Martha. She herself had wandered away from the terrace in the hope of escaping Martha. But she was here, and offering glasses. In the midst of all this, it was necessary also to be polite.

She took the glasses. Nothing at first but the snow-rimmed rocks. . . . Then the figures. Small, dark, indistinguishable, yet somehow strangely human on the sterile width of ice. Three of them, scarcely, it seemed, moving at all. She handed the glasses back to Martha. 'Thanks. They make my eyes hurt.'

'Oh, me too.' Martha took the glasses and trained them on the Face. Anyone looking through binoculars, thought Judith, has an air of omniscience, of authority, but Martha especially so. 'It's marvellous about the weather, isn't it?' she said. 'But I heard them saying up at the hotel—I mean, you can't help hearing what they say, they talk about it all the time——'

'Yes, indeed.'

'They were saying that they're going too slowly; that they ought to be above the Cradle before another storm hits them.'

'Yes. Last night they were all quite certain that they'd come down. I just wish everyone'd shut up about it until it's done.'

'Oh but honestly, Judith, you can't blame people for talking; I mean they come here and watch it, they can't help having ideas about it, saying what they think, it's only——'

'I didn't say I blamed anybody. I said I just wished they'd shut up.'

'Oh well, yes. Yes, I suppose so. But you see when you know about climbing this sort of thing isn't only people, it's a kind of technical problem——'

'Martha, I'm terribly sorry, but I don't want to have anything explained to me.'

'Oh. Oh, I see. Well, I don't know why you should be cross with me; it seems a bit unfair——'

Judith put a hand through her hair. 'Does it? I suppose so. But understandable, surely?'

Martha was holding the glasses by the strap; she rubbed one bare arm with her hand. 'I don't quite know what you mean.'

'Not?'

'No—really. You were always much cleverer than I was——'

'Oh, strewth, this isn't anything to do with being clever. I ask a simple question.'

German voices of people climbing up the path. Martha said, 'I don't honestly——'

'There isn't any need to pretend, you know; not here.' She heard the impatience in her own voice. Later perhaps she would regret this; now the Face in its brilliant light with the small dark figures going so slowly over it seemed to make nonsense of all dissembling, to drive her to deal with truth.

Martha said, 'You talk as if—as if you knew.'

'Oh, grow up. Of course I knew.'

'How long for?' The voice was breathless, school-girlish and thin.

'Oh goodness, I don't know, I forget; what does how long matter, anyway.'

'A long time?'

'I suppose so.'

'Why haven't you done anything about it?'

'What d'you expect me to do?'

'Not to speak to me. Be very angry.'

Judith gave a small smile. 'That would have been tiring and awkward.'

Martha sat down suddenly on the grass, as if some strength had left her. There was cloud over to the west; Judith had her eye on it as she sat beside Martha. And all the time, she thought, the mountain makes this small; it dwarfs Martha and me as it dwarfs time.

Martha sat pulling at the grass. 'It was losing Bill. It was that that started it. Graeme was so—so kind to me that evening. I mean he sat and listened; let me pour everything out to him. And then after that he always seemed to be off climbing without you——'

'Yes.'

'And I thought you didn't mind. I really did. The first time I saw you after, well, after it had started, I expected to feel awful, but somehow I didn't. In a way I was shocked at not feeling awful, but there it was. And then it just got easy, because I have to make things easy for myself, I always do. Or try to. I shut away what I don't want to know. Anything's all right if I don't think about it, and I don't. I seem able not to.'

This seemed to Judith the most adult speech she had heard Martha make. She said, 'Well?' still keeping her eye on the cloud which was swimming outwards over the sky.

Martha was staring up at the mountain. 'I suppose this is a silly time to talk about it, anyway, waiting here——'

'No, I don't think so.'

'You see, I ought to have had children, and had a kind of *place* somewhere. I mean in an ordinary pattern. I ought to have married again, I suppose; people have asked me, but I never really wanted them when they wanted me. I remember one of them being very angry and saying I was one of those women who weren't happy unless they could find something to make them miserable, but honestly, I don't think it was that; it just seemed easier to go on seeing Graeme, when he could see me. I mean——'

'Yes,' said Judith. 'I can see what you mean.'

'And—I know I haven't any excuse, but you always seemed . . . well, so terribly independent. Sure of yourself. Different from me. I mean, you are, aren't you?'

'I expect you're right.'

Rapid, enormous and silent, the cloud streamed over the Face; on the slope where they sat the sun seemed to burn more hotly and to give more fierce a light.

'I hope I haven't said anything to make you cross; it was you who wanted to talk——'

'No, I'm not at all cross.' She looked at Martha as she sat beside her. Curious, but in spite of the guileless outpouring, she was aware of something baffling, unexplained. Surely she had gone on the assumption, all these years, that Martha had the readability of the innocent who practise deceit? Yet now, she thought, there is a cloud over her, as there is on the Heide.

She got to her feet, still looking at the mountain. The crowd wandered away from the telescope; a child swung it aimlessly towards the sky. Martha too scrambled to her feet and said, 'I hope I haven't——'

'It's all been very interesting.' The question, the sense of something having been withheld, still stayed in her mind. 'However, I think I'd like to go back to the hotel.'

Martha scrambled to her feet, and came quickly beyond her. The clear Alpine heat still stayed on the terrace, and the men and women in the sun still looked towards the Heide. But the cloud was increasing.

July 8th, 12.00 hours

Steeple Crack was behind them. And it had been, Graeme thought, the hardest stretch of all so far. Or did this new exhaustion spring from the fear that had been with him since morning? A different fear from any he'd known: it had little to do with the icy footholds or the dizzy height at which they were moving. It was a superstitious fear; a feeling that in spite of the clear light, all was not well with the day.

'And now,' said Sean, 'for the Tightrope.' Drenched and shivering, his bearded face lined with exhaustion, there still came from him a vibrant confidence; he was master of the snow and the steep ledges, and indeed of the mountain itself. I know how he feels, Graeme thought. I've felt it myself: the

swelling of elation in the chest; the trumpets of triumph
sounding so loudly that one doesn't feel fully the wet, the
cold nor perceive the danger.

No, he didn't feel like that now. Now the cold and the long
silent fall of air screamed along his nerves, he was jittery,
climbing silently on only because that was what he had to do.
His father, he remembered, had said once, 'Every climber
some time or other comes to the moment when he hasn't got
anything left. It's nothing to be ashamed of; it's no' but a
temporary thing; keep verra, verra calm, and it'll pass.'

No, thought Graeme, I'm not ashamed. I don't even feel
that this is a failure; somehow up here one sees oneself
clearly, and one accepts it all, the whole bloody lot, as one
accepts the calculation of one's weight from a weighing
machine: this is what one is. But I can understand those men
who've broken down in such places as this, wept and shouted
and had to be slapped back into sanity. Why am I afraid?
There seemed to be an answer pulling at his mind that he
had no time for now. . . . Nothing to do but to go on.

About an hour later, he saw the change in the sky. Of a
sudden the snowy heights about them were not brilliant,
only burning strongly in their own whiteness. The clouds
were as yet thin. They were still on the Tightrope. The
height was majestic, the dizzying air below their feet, Graeme
thought, a measure of their triumph—so far. It waited; it
could take them into death, and when their bodies had
fallen, scattered and bloody on the rocks, be as before, steep
and silent, unchanging except for the clouds. But now it was
theirs; for a little while they were in command.

But his fear grew. Sean was ahead on the Tightrope,
moving slowly but with confidence over the icy rocks. Five
thousand feet below were the thumb-nail chalets, the hair's-
width roads. The light was altering rapidly now; taller than
all the mountains, the clouds were grape-dark. The valley
still shone.

Graeme stood on what seemed to him an apology for a

ledge, paying out the rope. Sean was moving now very slowly; the rocks where he climbed diagonally upwards across the mountain from its east ridge to the west, slanted downwards, carrying the eye rapidly into space; they were glazed with ice. Graeme found himself swallowing, his ears drumming. That was the way he'd got to go, there wasn't any escape. And he was afraid. This was the authentic gust of fear, weakening limbs and bowels. . . . Nothing to do but let the fear go on, and obey some other part of the mind, as an adult pursues his way calmly with a screaming child.

Sean was now standing still. Ahead of him the rock, ice-covered, bulged out, so that in climbing it he would have to overhang the naked space. All about him were steep unclimbable walls. Above the overhang, the rocks grew easier, leading up to the Cradle, the wide steep gulf of snow which they had to cross. But the hanging bulge of rock had to be climbed first.

'The hell of it is,' called Sean, 'the pitons won't hold. The ice is too thin.' He felt tentatively for handholds; moved an inch or so to the right, then to the left. He made a little height on the bulge, and watching him Graeme felt the harder knock of his own heart. Then Sean climbed down again.

'Trouble ahead?' called Hugh.

'Not exactly a high road,' Graeme answered. He wondered if Hugh could hear, as he himself could, the flutter of fear in his voice.

'Have we climbed too far, perhaps? One should strike upwards from the Tightrope about two thirds of the way. . . .'

Graeme looked back over his shoulder. Nothing but steep unclimbable walls that sent the eye skidding helplessly down them. The sky had darkened altogether; they seemed to be standing in the depth of some grey November afternoon, a threatening roof of coloured weather above them. Cloud filled the steep air below; they were shut out from the world. Graeme saw again the baffled telescopes and binoculars; he thought, No one can see us now; what goes on is between ourselves.

Sean was still standing below the overhang. Graeme called, 'D'you think we've climbed too far?'

'No.' Sean's voice was sharp, the voice of a man who doesn't want to be asked questions.

'Werner and Klein did, d'you remember? They blamed the whole of their retreat on having climbed beyond the point where——'

'This is O.K.'

'Will it go?'

'It'll have to.'

But still his tentative reaching for hand- and foothold gave him nothing.

Graeme called, 'We could climb down a little way. I can see now what looks like a line of holds in the rock——'

'I'm not climbing down. Wastes too much time.'

'Wastes more,' said Graeme, 'if we stick here.' Standing so long on the Tightrope was increasing his fear; he was glad of the cloud which hid the great depth below him. 'And more still if——'

'*I tell you this will go.*'

An edge of temper on Sean's voice. Not a good thing to climb a pitch like that with anger disarranging the blood and the judgment. He said as calmly as he could, 'Very well. This is your party.'

Sean didn't answer but spent some moments more examining the rock above him. Then he said, 'I think I see it. There's a little flaw in the rock to the left. Not much, but it gives one a chance. You'll have to keep your eye on it.'

'Right.'

His own heart driving fast, Graeme watched him as he started to climb. Sean seemed to crouch, clinging to the rock by an effort of will that changed the laws of gravity. His movement seemed almost imperceptible, yet he was moving. . . . As he faltered for one moment, Graeme felt his hands

137

tighten on the rope, faster than thought. . . . No, he was climbing on.

The cloud was thicker now. He could hear the first lifting note of the wind, like a summons. A handful of snow scattered itself against his cheek. He wasn't seeing farther into the future than he could see into the cloud; he existed, minute by minute, watching Sean, while the wind stung his eyes with the increasing snow. . . . Yes, he can do it. He's opening a way up for us, up to the Cradle; one can hope again; it still might be done, we may still——

'*Hold me, Graeme!*'

The sting of panic on his nerves and the pain of the rushing rope through his hands.

Then he stood, tied to the rock, hearing the silence.

He called, '*Sean!*'

But it was Hugh's voice that answered him. 'He's badly hurt.'

Through the increasing snow Graeme could see him, some sixty feet below. He hung inert on the rope. Was he dead?

'Sean!' he called again. The cloud wrapped close. *Was* he dead? All that violent ambition suddenly quenched? 'Sean!'

Wind and snow; the vivid pain in his hands. Then, as he stared down he saw a little movement of Sean's head, a feeble lifting of one hand.

'Sean—can you climb back?'

'No.' Odd, even now, to hear Sean suddenly without his confidence and certainty. 'One arm's useless.'

'I'll try to pull you up.'

'It's not possible.'

He pulled savagely, but the rope, frozen and taut over the icy rocks, would not move. He realized for the first time the fullness of his exhaustion; his arms were like soft clay.

'There's a ledge below me.' Sean's voice was thinned with pain. 'About six feet down. Can you give me a little more rope? Better than hanging here like a turkey. . . .'

'Right.'

Not difficult to lower Sean on to the ledge, nor to secure his rope to a piton. But after that? There was no way down to him; above the ledge were the steep, unclimbable walls. He was half lying, huddled against the rock. Immobile as he was, the cold would soon eat its way through him. . . . How long could he survive there?

Graeme saw suddenly that Hugh, many feet below him, was untying his rope. He called, 'What the hell are you doing?'

'Climbing down.'

'*Down?*'

'It's the best thing. We've got to get help.'

'I'll get help.'

'That's out of the question. I'm the leader of this outfit, and I'm the only one who isn't wounded.'

'There's nothing wrong with me——'

'I'm sorry. I'm not having any argument. You're to stay with him, and I'll go down. A steel cable rescue from the summit's the only hope, and the sooner it gets started the better.'

Graeme said, 'You can't climb back, alone.' He saw the endless stretches of the Ice-Field; the Angel's Wing Traverse. 'It's crazy——'

'No, it's not.' Hugh's voice was crisp with command; somehow he kept weariness out of it. 'We prepared for this remember. There's a handrail on the Traverse, supplies at the Owl's Nest. With God's help I can do it.'

'Better to try for the summit——'

Hugh glanced briefly upward. 'I disagree. We don't know what's up there—except that it's the hardest of all. To cross the Cradle in this kind of weather's not much more than suicide.'

No time to argue more. Time, the continual enemy, now had a knife at their throats. . . . Already Hugh was moving, on his way back down the Tightrope. Graeme thought, We're here for the night, perhaps two. Perhaps more; this could be the end of it, the easy slide into frozen sleep. They say the last dreams of men who freeze to death are always of warmth and ease and rescue; you can tell by the look on their faces when you find them. . . .

Strange, but he did not feel sharply the fear of death. Perhaps they had been moving too close to it all the time; perhaps his brain was too fuddled with cold and exhaustion to take it in. But there was a fear, and it came sharply into his mind, defining what till now had accompanied him, obscurely, in shadow. He was afraid that he wouldn't see Judith again; that there would be no time to convey to her the truth of his love, the irrelevance of all else; how the division that lay between them irked and wounded him, and how here on the mountain, he had only one desire, to get back to her, to see her again, and destroy the fantasies and absurdities (for they could be nothing else) which had kept them apart. . . . The moment had a marvellous clarity; he was buoyed and heartened.

He called down to Sean, 'Are you all right?'

'Bloody cold.'

'Hugh's gone to get help.'

'Yes, I know.'

'Is your arm hurting?'

'Yes.' Through his voice came the bitterness of defeat.

Graeme on his narrow stance pulled the spare rope from his sack with one hand while with the other he held on to the rock. His hand was numbed and cold, and the thin nylon rope slid and knotted and would not uncoil. He heard himself swear. Clumsy as a maimed man, he secured two sweaters and let them down to Sean. He watched Sean's efforts, clumsy as his own, to disentangle the sweaters with one hand and pull them round him. Graeme said, hauling up the rope, 'Now food and medicine . . . can you reach any of your own?'

'No. My pack's lying under me.'

'Right. I'm giving you chocolate and dried fruit and biscuits. Benzedrine and Ronicol for frostbite.'

'You'll need that.'

'I can stamp my feet, bang my hands against the rock. . . . Here you are. A package deal.' He put the medicine in the food bag, tied it and let it down to Sean. He watched Sean's clumsy hand pull the package from the rope; he found he was tense, fearing that it would slip. . . . But now Sean had it safe, between his body and the rock. He made a little gesture of recognition.

Snow still scattered the Face, steadily but with a certain gentleness; the full force of the storm had not hit them. Cloud still kept them from sight, but the wind, Graeme thought, was quieter. He could see Hugh's figure, diminished now, climbing down slowly, but moving on. He began to have a little hope.

July 9th—Kleine Scheidegg

There was an even greater crowd round the telescope. The cloud had gone; the whole Face stood clear in a shadowless wash of light. It was—three? four? hours, Judith thought, since she had heard the first voice say, 'There is only one of them on the Face.'

She had swung the glasses up and down, altered the focus, as if clarity could become more than clarity; seen the snowy rocks blur and change. She could see one man, huddled on a ledge. Beyond this there was nothing but the empty crags and the snow.

Since the cloud cleared, a reconnaissance plane had flown several times close to the Face. The man on the ledge, it was said, had been seen to move; he was still alive. His face was turned towards the rock, and they did not know which of the three he was. Of the others, there seemed no trace.

Judith sat at a table, drinking black coffee. Martha sat with her, twisted round in her chair, looking, as everyone was, towards the Heide. She looked once or twice at Judith, and then said, 'I wish you'd let your little Jewish friend come up to lunch. I think it'd have been good for you. He sounded

141

awfully disappointed on the telephone when I gave him your message.'

'I'm sorry, but I really haven't anything to say at the moment that would amuse or interest Joseph.'

'I don't think he wanted to be amused or interested; I think he wanted to comfort you.'

'That wouldn't really have been any good either.'

'He's a bachelor, isn't he? Why hasn't he ever married?'

'Miss Right hasn't come along. Alternatively, he's been too busy making money.' She took pity on Martha's blunted and wounded look by saying, 'I'm afraid adversity makes me uncharitable. I'm fond of Joseph, but it wouldn't be a good idea to see him just now.'

Martha still looked vaguely wounded. Judith could see the words going up like figures on a cash register in Martha's mind: 'hard', 'tough', 'caustic', 'independent'. It was odd, she reflected how one spoke and behaved to people as they expected one to speak and behave. Martha said, 'Of course, you were always able to do without people. I think that's terribly grown-up. Somehow if anyone comes near me I have to see them and be nice to them; I can never say no; I don't want to lose anybody——' She broke off and looked again towards the Heide. 'Of course, I shouldn't have put it like that, should I? I mean about losing people; I say terrible things sometimes, but I don't mean them, honestly not.'

Judith was thinking, I'll give this five minutes, and then I'll get up and go for a walk. Alone, if I have to kill someone to do it—when she was aware of a shadow across the table, and a man's voice at her side.

'Madame! I have been searching for you everywhere.'

Cloudily, she looked up. The man's face confused her only because it did not belong to the Alpine sunlight and the high snows. She said, shielding her eyes against the sun, 'Where have I seen you before?'

'In Paris, madame. With your daughter. Stella,' he said,

as if perhaps she needed to be reminded of her daughter's name. He gave a small bow. 'André Tévernin.'

She was silent, looking at him. His light holiday clothes, she thought, did not suit him; he was a man who belonged to the city streets, to the crowded café bars, and the small furtive sanctuary of hotel rooms. Her profound depression at his arrival must, she thought, be due to the long hours of anxiety. For he was of himself of no importance.

'Yes,' she said at last, and added, 'How extraordinary.'

'Not at all, madame; I am *journaliste*. Perhaps this did not emerge at our meeting.'

If it had she had no memory of it. Nor any wish for him to linger here, as he was doing. He went on, 'I am covering the story for my newspaper.'

'I'm afraid I haven't got anything to say to the Press.'

'Absolutely not, madame, I understand perfectly. I am not here at your table as a reporter, I am here as a friend.'

That makes it difficult, Judith thought, not to ask him to sit down, nor to introduce him to Martha, who has taken her eyes off the mountain to look at him with surprising interest.

He bowed to Martha before accepting a chair. 'Enchanted, madame.' His eye, very clear and blue, stayed on her long enough to convey more than a formal interest, and he sat down with the rapid enthusiasm of a man joining friends. 'I wanted to express, madame, my deep feeling for the strain which you must be going through.'

Judith said, 'Thank you.' She would have liked to ask him about Stella, but something prevented her from allowing him a position of authority on Stella. She was waiting, she thought as she had done at the Deux Magots, for him to leave.

Two American children stood within earshot. 'Go ask Pop for the glasses; I wanna have a look.'

'You go ask him; Pop wants the glasses himself.'

André Tévernin said, 'To me all this is very terrible.'

Judith said, 'Yes, I don't exactly enjoy it.'

'I mean the attention of all these people. All these—I

143

believe the American term is rubber-necks. It is offensive to see—*pardon, mademoiselle*.' Making a gesture with one arm he had knocked the elbow of an elegant young woman in narrow black trousers. She gave him an unflawed smile of acknowledgement; he sat watching her with attention as she walked to the edge of the terrace and lifted binoculars; then said, turning back to the table, 'As I was saying, it is offensive to see their gloating interest; they are like the *tricoteuses* who sat round the guillotine—don't you agree?'

Martha said, 'Why *yes*,' in wonderment, as if this rather commonplace simile had struck her with force.

Judith moved in her chair. 'You're a reporter, you said?'

'I always feel the same disgust when I see any such exhibition. It offends something in my—I beg your pardon, madame?'

Judith repeated it.

'Yes. It is my job, I am compelled to go where there will be news. But I go to such—such desperate occasions as this with an attitude of reverence.'

Judith said, 'Oh, splendid.'

Martha said, 'I think that's rather wonderful.'

André Tévernin gave a separate glance, different in kind to each of them. 'It is possible to write of such things as this with true feeling and reverence, with a realization of all the human values involved, and at the same time to make the story readable and interesting to anyone who may not perhaps fully understand the importance of these climbs....'

She could see exactly the kind of story he would write, ringing with false grandeur and a kind of spurious solemnity. The idea of it seemed to tighten her nerves further, and before she could stop herself, 'You can count me as one of those.'

'So natural, madame, at this moment, that you——'

'Not only now.' She could feel the time slipping away, as it had slipped away with Stella; there was the same sensation of suppressed hysteria, of disaster waiting. 'I've never had any feeling for mountains, as Mrs. Farrer here, an expert climber herself, will tell you.' She put out a shaking hand for her coffee cup.

Martha was looking bewildered, like a head girl who has, in the midst of her end of term speech, heard an unambiguous raspberry. 'Oh, Judith! But you used to do such wonderful pictures of them——'

'So you are a climber?' André Tévernin was turned to Martha, the clear blue-eyed look became one of blinkered intensity.

Martha's colourless English voice seemed at odds with the increased colour in her cheeks. 'Yes, I climb. My cousin, Sean Randall, is on the North Face. At least—he was one of the party.'

'You have climbed with your cousin?'

'Oh, yes. Heaps of times.'

'This must, then, be a terrible ordeal for you, also.'

'Yes, it is,' said Martha.

Some form of silent communication seemed to pass between them; then he said, turning to Judith, 'Your daughter, of course, is also not interested in climbing.'

'As she has no doubt told you.'

He smiled down at the table, as if in understanding acceptance of her hostility. 'On occasions, yes.'

(And he has brought Stella vividly to my mind; I can see her bedroom with the oil painting of the fish, and the café table by St. Germain des Prés, where she seemed concerned with some problem of her own. . . . What is she doing now? Surely she has read about the climb? And yet she has said nothing.)

'So you know Stella,' Martha was saying. 'Pretty girl, isn't she?'

'Stella is beautiful, madame.'

More and more, Judith thought, she wished that Stella were there with her. She began to plan it in her mind, putting Stella beside her instead of Martha and André Tévernin. . . .

It was a pleasant diversion; better than listening to André Tévernin, or straining to see movement on the Heide. . . . She could feel Stella's presence, see the young aloof face softened in sympathy——

No. That was a dream. Nothing was real but the mountain and the question and the waiting. She took the glasses impatiently from the table, and looked towards the Face. The steep white empty rocks slid through the vision of the glasses as a ribbon slides through a bodkin. The man on the ledge did not move.

André Tévernin leaned forward and touched her arm. 'You must have courage, madame. I am sure he will return.'

July 8th, 02.00 hours

Now, Graeme thought as he watched Hugh climb farther down, one must come to terms with waiting. Concentrate on Sean; forget about the depth below you, and the hours you may have to stay here, on this narrow ledge. These are concepts of the mind only, after all. . . . The cold is another thing. He called to the huddled figure below him, 'I can let you down more food, when you want it.'

So long as he could think about Sean, he was himself less afraid. Indeed Sean on his ledge, deprived of the summit and in the unlikely company of the defeated, inspired an unexpected compassion.

He called again, 'Is there anything you want?'

A feeble movement of Sean's head.

'Hugh's on his way. We'll get help to you.'

He heard Sean's voice, savaged with weakness: 'How long?'

'As soon as we can.'

He could see Hugh's figure, dwarfed and vulnerable, moving on. Hope there. Small but alive. Rescue. Life. The world again; Oxford again; the sitting-room in the small house, the angle of sunlight on the bookcase on a summer afternoon. . . . And Judith again. (I shall see her and say it all to her, all the things that have been unsaid. . . .)

146

The sound at first did not trouble him. Here the peaks echoed and rumbled at each other; thunder stampeded in the distance, signifying nothing.

But the sound increased, coming with the gathering, panic speed of the express train which is passing through the station; it grew louder till the air roared with it and he heard himself shout, as if any shout could be heard, 'Hugh! Look out! Avalanche!'

Here it comes.

It was on and over him. It was like being pulled down by savage animals; he didn't know if he were still tied to the ledge or sliding down the Face in the thundering tunnel of snow. . . . Snow was in his mouth and eyes and ears; he could not breathe for snow; he had no strength, all the strength belonged to the snow. . . . Perhaps this was it. This, instead of the waiting and the cold and help coming too late.

He did not know how long the violence went on. As the pressure began to grow less, there came to him the idea that he had survived; that he was still tied to the ledge. . . . Wondering he felt for the piton. . . . Yes, firm in the rock. Himself standing there, not fallen, still there, gasping, snow in his eyes and mouth. And Sean, protected by an overhang of rock, still on his ledge——

He called, '*Hugh! Hugh!*'

But it was useless to call, for the rocks to a great depth were empty of the small vulnerable figure; the snow, stones and chips of ice were falling, far below. Beyond this, there was silence.

02.10 hours

The silence went on. It took time, Graeme thought, to absorb the fact of death. He could feel the fierce trembling of his limbs; his brain felt stunned and sick as though someone had cuffed him savagely on the head.

Hugh.

147

And Judith's voice from far back: '. . . someone you care for goes and smashes himself up at this filthy, foolish game. . . .'

He heard a kind of groan: perhaps from himself. Then Sean's voice, an urgency coming through the pain—'Graeme? Graeme, are you there?'

'Yes.'

'Hugh?'

'The avalanche flung him off.'

Silence from Sean. (And only the two of us here now, and though he doesn't say it and I don't say it, our chances of life small.)

'Dear God. Poor Hugh.' Sean's voice had a dry bitterness. 'Bloody avalanche.'

'He wasn't tied on. He didn't have a chance.'

'Poor bastard.'

Silence again. He could still feel the muffling, destroying weight of the avalanche as it went over him: the violent fact of Hugh's death was coming a little way into his mind and heart. ('*In a few years I shall pack up the big stuff and run up and down nice little afternoon jobs at home. . . .*')

No, one mustn't let the mind wander, or this heaviness in the breast sap one's will. Sean was still on his ledge: there was still some hope of saving him.

He said to himself, 'I shall have to go for help.'

'And leave Sean? There on the Face, in a terrible loneliness, colder and in pain?'

'But if I stay, help may not come. We're still hidden in cloud. We could wait until we die of exposure.'

He crouched down on his stance, to call more easily to Sean. 'I've been thinking it out. What's best to do. I shall have to go for help.'

Silence from Sean. Of agreement? Of opposition? Graeme went on, 'I've got to get help to you, as soon as I can——'

'They'll come anyway.'

'We can't be sure of that. I know it's going to be hell, alone on the Face——'

'Yes.' The short word was the more shaking for being colourless.

'But I must get help.'

Again a silence. Graeme said, 'Can you hear me?'

'Yes.'

'Do you agree?'

Another silence. Then—'You must do what you want.'

Graeme stared about him at the muffling cloud, the gently slipping snow. If the cloud were to lift, perhaps he could stay there, being certain that rescue would come. . . . (But one could be certain of nothing.) The cloud was thick and unmoving, and the colour of the day was the colour of the sea late on a winter's afternoon.

The moments passing, and time of such importance. Sean lying there, his eyes closed against the world . . . had Sean any hope for himself? Perhaps defeat in the climb loomed larger than the prospect of death. Perhaps pain and cold were larger than anything. . . .

He straightened himself. You had to take a decision; perhaps the shock of the avalanche and Hugh's death had disordered his judgment, but he could only do the best as he saw it, now, with time running out.

He called, 'I'm going to let you down another sweater——'

'You'll need it for yourself.'

'I have enough.' (Please God.) 'And I'll wrap some more food in it. Then I'm going to try for the summit.'

'The summit. . . .'

'Yes. I think it offers the best chance. And——'

'The summit. . . .' The word came up like a sigh from below.

'Better than climbing down. And it shouldn't be impossible.' (But he saw the high alien rocks above him, and the fear shook him.) He was preparing the sweater and the food for Sean. He called, 'Try not to lose heart. I believe I can get there and get help for you. Try to remember that, while you're alone.'

149

His only company now was the sound of his own breathing, the scatter of stones and ice, his voice as he swore or murmured to himself.

He was climbing upwards, towards the Cradle. He had retraced his way back down the Tightrope, since it would have been impossible to get over the bulge where Sean had fallen. He had found a flaw in the rock, a long crack which offered some hope.

He had made his decision. But doubt still persisted: now that he was climbing away from him, he felt Sean's loneliness on the ledge, in pain and cold, as the day grew darker and the night came. Should he have stayed? Would the comfort, the knowledge of another human being not far off, have given Sean the necessary hope and energy to hold on to life? He could not reach the summit before nightfall; Sean would have to spend a night alone on the ledge. Perhaps two. Knowing nothing of how Graeme fared, whether indeed he was alive or dead. As he paused to bang one numbed hand against the rock, he thought again of the cold. The terrible, unremitting, increasing enmity of the cold.

He climbed on. It was strangely silent. The wind was quiet; a little snow still drifted towards the Face, but the storm had passed. Cloud still hung there, as if to keep the chances of help away. . . . Concentration, passion and willpower, more than technical skill would get him to the summit. (The summit that Sean had so much hoped for.) Then down the easy West Face, to get help. There was a kind of comfort in the thought that he might save Sean's life. Because, he thought, saving life, any life now, is important: a blind giving out, a gesture in the face of Hugh's loss. . . .

How had it been for Hugh? In the sudden white anger of the avalanche? He saw again the small vulnerable figure, moving downwards with such care. . . . Had he tried desperately at the last moment to drive his axe into the ice? Hard to believe that he couldn't ask him; that he wouldn't hear Hugh say, 'Nothing to that. Kind of thing one's got to expect....'

But how was it with you?

A bit of a bastard. Didn't last long.

Was it worth it? All the long climbs in the mountains of the world, to find that moment of fear and pain at the end of them?

Oh yes. I've been lucky, after all. To others it's come sooner. Remember Lennox? He was only a boy. ... How's it for you, climbing alone?

Different. Silence, and the falling away of all companionship. And the rocks seem more alien and more terrible.

Are you afraid?

Yes.

Have you hope?

A little. Perhaps less than that.

The quiet deeper, the cold harder. Strange, but he felt a kind of satisfaction, a certainty, that triumphed over, as it included, the danger and the fear. Ambition was gone; indeed the striving egotist within him seemed to have gone, and this gave, even as he struggled against the icy rock, a sensation of peace.

He must get help for Sean, and see Judith again. That was all.

As he moved so slowly and with such care, the words went through his mind: 'Alone, at this great height.' He thrust them away; they sapped courage. He must make the top of the Cradle before nightfall; there was nowhere on the stretch of snow and ice where he could tie on for the night. Cold. And weariness. No snow, no wind. Only the cloud that hung at his back and hid him from the world.

07.00 hours

He was still climbing. Climbing not carefully but with desperate speed, his breath heavy and suffocating and his heart hammering fast. The steep snowy rocks of the Cradle stretched on for ever; he could not reach the end of them before nightfall. Here the rocks slid upwards

steeply and smooth, ice-covered. No handholds anywhere; he must dig
in with the claws of his crampons . . . but the ice is brittle and
cracks . . . is breaking as it broke on the Ice-Field, and this is falling,
this is death——

He woke, shivering. No, that was past. The long climb
through the Cradle was done, he was here, standing, tied to
the rock on a ledge not much wider than the width of his
hand. He forced his numbed limbs to move, kicked his feet
and banged his hands against the rock. Cold. Sinking
through his flesh to the bones, destroying energy and
thought. . . . But the night was gone. The long, strange
night: darkness and deeper cold and exhaustion after the
Cradle. . . . Sudden, feverish images that occasionally lost
themselves in a tunnel of dubious sleep. . . . Loud voices close
to him; a fury of urgent activity, the sense of some noisy
endeavour coming to its climax—then an end to it as he woke
and found the dark rocks again, the vast silence, and the
cold.

His stiffened incompetent fingers searched his sack for
food. Chocolate and raisins, tasteless in the extreme cold, yet
welcome. . . . He was here, still on the Face. He had survived
the night. And Sean?

He looked down the vertical snowy rocks until they were
lost in cloud. Had Sean too survived the night? He stood
motionless, almost as if he listened. . . . Yes, somehow he
thought Sean was still alive. It seemed as he stood there on
the ledge that there was a current in the air, assuring him of
Sean's life. . . . He said, No, I am not alone here: Sean is
somewhere below on his ledge, and I must get help for him.

The morning was grey and still; the snowy peaks about him
lifted from solid acres of cloud. So strange a place, he thought;
like an ante-chamber between life and death, not part of the
world. . . . And in his own head was a confusion born of
weariness and cold and the vast lonely silence. I have to
climb on, he said. He repeated it like a child, I have to
climb on. But a part of him, heavy, mindless, like an idiot,

did not want to move. It was content to stay here shivering against the rock; there was no energy in its body to make it go farther, and its mind was swaddled and dull. . . .

But I have to go on. Up those cracks in the rocks above me; up there, and on to the ice slope below the summit. (Six thousand feet above the meadows of Alpiglen, thirteen thousand feet above the valley. Hurdler and Meyer fell from the ice slope, so near victory.)

I have to go on.

Numbed with cold and without energy, you'll be certain to fail. Better to wait here, easier to wait; easier to slide into a frozen sleep. . . .

I have to go on. Hugh is dead, and I have to get help for Sean.

Slowly the stiff reluctant body obeyed the mind. His feeble hands untied the rope, began to search the rock above him. . . .

The ice slope. Driving in with the claws of his crampons, thrusting the pick end of his axe to keep his balance. Thrust with an arm not his own, that moved against the weights that dragged it down. The treble music of the ice chips as they fell; the rasp of his own breathing. . . . Beyond this, silence.

A difference in the air; the cloud below him glazed with light. Sun. And ice. And a fatigue like the end of the world, so that it seems impossible to move farther. Yet one does. He thought, Beyond everything, beyond hope and strength, there's still a bit left.

Three hours. Perhaps four. No, he thought, I don't know how many hours. But he was still on the ice slope, listening to a groaning sound, which seemed at last to be his own breathing. A great depth of brightness all about him; the cloud thinning. He was aware of it as, half-drugged in one's bed, one is aware of the weather outside. His thoughts swerved and skidded into absurdities: for a time he was having a long argument in his head with a spotty boy at school about cheating. Then he was mending a broken toy of Stella's, a farm wagon, much beloved, made of cheap wood that split. He could feel, closer than the North Wall, her anxiety at his elbow as he worked with glue and string. 'Yes, darling, it's all right. Look, I've mended it for you.' Snow. And ice. And the little wooden thing lost, in the years, in the depth of rock, quite gone now. . . . Himself here, climbing alone.

Yes, alone. And yet there was the sensation of someone behind him. Not speaking, making no sound, but climbing on. Someone he knew, someone he had loved, coming steadily behind him, keeping pace. Comfort, a kind of deep, sad comfort, knowing that Hugh followed. . . .

A wind now. Strange after the long silence. Why was there a wind? Cloud below him still, but here the sun, and his eye-balls aching with light; the brilliance banging about in his head like sound. . . . Was this falling? Death, perhaps? . . . No, he was on the ice slope; he was still climbing.

But the wind was stronger. Stronger and louder; great trumpets of sound in salute as he made one last, exhausted movement: a rushing, mighty wind. . . . *Dear God, this is it. This is the top. The end of it. Judith, I'm here. Judith darling, I'm here, not dead but alive, and there'll be help for Sean. None for Hugh, but for Sean. God willing. Judith, this is the summit, that blue there is the sky, and below me is the far distance of the southern side. This is the end of the North Wall. Judith, listen to me. I'm there.*

He had flung himself upon the snow, and lay there while the minutes passed and the exhaustion washed and soaked him, while the long noisy breaths gradually grew quieter. Slowly he lifted himself up, propped on one arm. He drew his hand over his face. Silence, but for the wind. Cold. The dazzling snow, the lonely kingdoms of sky and peak and sun. All his own, with the North Face climbed.

Slowly he got to his feet, and looked about him, swaying as he stood, pummelled by the wind. The summit of the Heide. The beginning so far off, with the three of them to-gether. . . . Now he stood alone.

Again he passed his hand over his face. No, not quite

alone; his numbed brain seemed aware of a shadow beside him, of a sense of companionship not quite lost.

Well, that's the lot, Graeme, old man. That's it. Done now. How's it feel to be there?

Lonely.

But you made it. A kind of triumph, surely?

I don't feel it yet.

It'll come. Down to the valley; they'll save Sean. It was well done.

Still he stood there, as if he awaited some enlightenment, as if there was something more to be done. . . . No, nothing now but the climb down the West Face. Life now, for himself, and for Sean, God willing.

He said, 'Hugh . . .' then turned with a shrug, a clumsy gesture of pain and acceptance, and began with staggering, exhausted steps, to walk on.

July 9th—Kleine Scheidegg

The crowd made raggedly the shape of a pennant whose apex was a boy in shorts and a checked shirt. In the brilliant light was the confusion of disaster and excitement, of gay clothes and holiday, courage and endurance; the plane that had been flying over the summit was back again; the photographers lifted their cameras, black against the sprawled snow.

Judith said aloud, 'Yes, it is Graeme,' though Martha was not near her. She went along with the crowd towards the man who was coming down from the West Ridge. She felt silly with weakness and relief, a little dazed in the hot sun, and by the brilliant colours of the crowd, stereoscopic in the Alpine air.

Graeme was walking with his head down, with the loose, unco-ordinated walk of the exhausted. His dark shapeless clothes, stained and here and there torn, contrasted strangely with the clothes of the crowd; he seemed to belong to some harsh and different world. After a while he lifted his head, seeming to become aware of the crowd; she saw in a change

TC–L

of movement his acknowledgement of the world again, of safety and the way the whole thing was different in the minds of the people coming to meet him, who had not been on the Face and saw only this, the moment of safety.

The whirr and click of cameras; the crowd driving towards him; the shrill German voice of the boy crying, 'You have climbed the Nordwand of the Heide?'

For a moment Graeme halted in his shambling walk, and stood there frowning in the sunlight with the flung cloak of snow behind him. His face, she could see now, was cracked with sun and cold and exhaustion, covered with a messy stubble of beard, the jaw bandaged and bloody, his eyes bloodshot and drunken with fatigue. The crowd pressed forward, questioning, trying to shake his hand. She stayed where she was and looked at him.

Odd that one could feel at once so much pity and love: and yet certainty of another kind too. For as she looked at him, so miraculously alive, she thought, Yes, this is the end of it. He's safe; and now I can go in peace.

Shaken by her own thought, she pushed her way through the crowd and went to him. As he embraced her, she heard the cameras turning. The hot light and the snow, the noisy crowd and the mountain behind him made this a curious moment of unspoken farewell.

He said, 'Is Martha there?'

'Yes.'

'It's Sean on the ledge. . . . Will you tell her that?'

'Yes.'

'They'll have to send a steel cable down from the summit.'

She could feel herself violently trembling. 'I didn't know what had happened. I thought perhaps you'd been killed.'

She could see now the heavy sadness on his face. 'No, it was Hugh.'

She said, 'Like Bill.'

He stared with his drunken eyes into her face, as if, through his exhaustion, he tried to perceive some meaning that escaped him. He said, 'He went down with the avalanche. But they will get Sean.'

She nodded, and gestured to the bandage on his jaw. 'Are you badly hurt?'

He shook his head. 'A stone . . . on the first day.'

She saw how long distant this seemed to him; that the days of the climb were a great tract of land which each of them had crossed, to arrive in new country. She thought he said, 'Judith . . .' but the crowd was surging round him, separating him from her.

She stood for a while, lost, until she felt a touch on her arm. André Tévernin, giving her a look of concentrated sympathy.

'I only wish to say, madame, how happy I am that your husband has had such a triumph.'

'Hardly a triumph. A man has been killed, after all.'

'Yes, that is true. One man has been killed, and one other remains to be rescued. But your husband at least has completed the climb to the summit.'

At the time she thought little of the words.

PART III

THE RETURN

CHAPTER ONE

SEAN turned his head. The movement was slow, seeming to require great effort. Strange images poured through his mind: changing lights, a gradual, suffocating darkness, pain and a driving endless cold.

A stormy half-sleep broke now and then to show the rock-face at his side, the traces of snow. Through sleep or waking the throbbing of his arm, grossly swollen now, persisted, never quite lost. Time had slipped into confusion; he could not remember how long it was since Graeme had climbed away from him. It seemed there had been only one night; that only once had he seen the strange gradual re-establishment of this lonely world of snow and rock, but he could not be sure.

Hope too was a confusion in his mind; there were hours when he had none, when he lay waiting to go into the dark tunnel of frozen sleep, waiting with a kind of powerless rage, while angry and bitter words seemed to be shouting themselves in his head. 'How oft when men are at the point of death have they been merry. . . .' No, there was nothing but anger here: a rage in the heart.

Sometimes hope was stronger; lying there, half-numbed, he saw, rather than thought of, images of rescue, of himself in comfort, in warmth, the pain eased by drugs, back in the easy places of the world, below the high rocks.

Then the images would fade, and the despairing anger would be back again.

He could hear the words in his head, fast, a streaming gabble like the words of a man in a fever: 'He shouldn't have gone. He should have stayed with me. If he'd stayed I'd have had some spirit to hold on. He climbed away and left me, to make the summit. The summit of the North Wall, that I dreamed and hoped for. . . . He should have stayed. He went on because he wanted to get to the top, to be the first Briton to climb the North Wall; that's why he went. He should have stayed. I want him here; the loneliness is intolerable; the throbbing in my arm is worse because of it; the cold is worse; you want a voice to call down, to say hang on, you'll be all right, to say anything, to shout words down these desolate rocks—any kind of words; you want a human voice. . . . Graeme's voice.

'Yes, I loved him. More than anyone, all my life. . . . And he never troubled to know, never cared a damn about it; he didn't even want to climb with me; I could see that, I've always seen it . . . if it had been Hugh on the ledge, wouldn't he have stayed?

'He went for the summit. Without me, leaving me here. Oh God, let the pain stop, let the cold stop, let the anger and rage stop. . . . Let me forget about him; let there be some peace.'

He turned his head again. The half-sleep was fading; vivid in his mind was a dream of Graeme: he had seen him climbing down, heard his voice shouting, heard the rattle of stones as his boots dislodged them. . . . Even as he woke there was a kind of cloudy joy in his head; through the pain and cold a sensation of peace. . . .

Gradually, moment by moment, it slid away. He was here, on the ledge. Weaker, sunk deeper in cold; a ravening thirst, only partially eased by snow scooped from the rock to his mouth; and, in spite of the medicine Graeme had given him, the fingers of his damaged arm seemingly dead, frighteningly wooden with cold. Now, without hope. Graeme was not there; he himself was alone on the Face, as he would be alone until consciousness slid finally away. . . .

Suddenly his eyes were open, fixed and open. The sound of his dream was there again, not in his dream (no surely his fuddled brain was awake) but real. The sound of stones and rubble falling; the sound growing louder; more than this, a voice, unseen, somewhere on the Face, shouting.

He could not hear the words. Only the voice coming through the terrible silence, coming through the wind and the fog in his own mind. The voice of the man who, lowered on a steel cable from the summit, was searching for him.

Then they had come. It was the end of loneliness, the loneliness to which Graeme had committed him. . . . He drew his breath painfully . . . shouted into the wind——

Or tried to shout. The effort was nightmarish, beyond his strength: the thread of voice could not be heard a yard from him. . . . Rage and weakness together were like a suffocation in his head; he heard the thread of voice in a kind of silent scream, saying, 'Graeme . . . if Graeme hadn't left me he could have answered—he could have answered him.'

The voice again. The silences between the shouts were longer, and the voice, when it came, fainter. Gradually, it was lost, and there was nothing but a long silence. He lay in increasing weakness, desperation and rage. The words now in his head were uncontrolled, spilling and seething: he thought he would be glad of death, because they were painful and it would stop them.

The men on the Heide's summit were stooped against the wind. The air was blackish, the noise so loud that their voices were torn away from them as they spoke. Slowly they wound the cable upwards and upwards, and on to the summit came their companion, the German, Friedlinger. He was a small man, rather ugly, with a bent nose and pale blue eyes. His face was drawn with cold, and for a few moments as he unstrapped the cable's harness, his companions helping him, he did not speak. Bulky and inhuman in his padded jacket and helmet, he stood bent against the violent wind. Then he said, 'That is a terrible place.'

'Did you see him?' they asked.

'No.'

'Hear him?'

'No. I shouted, but there was no reply.'

'Is he dead?—it is most likely he is dead. He has spent two nights now on the Face.'

Friedlinger shook his head. 'No. I do not believe he is dead. It is important to make another descent before nightfall.'

'The storm is getting worse.'

Friedlinger glanced about him. The snow was increasing: the wind plunging more fiercely. 'It is the more important to make another descent. He will not survive another night.'

'I do not believe he can be alive now. He appeared to be badly injured by the fall.'

'I feel somehow that he is alive. You will need to let me down farther to the west of the Face, directly below the Cradle and the Tightrope. I believe that way I cannot miss him.'

'You must be careful that you do not dislodge rocks and stones on to him——'

'I will shout to warn him.'

'Will he hear, in the wind?'

'One hopes he will hear.'

Sean with a feeble movement of his hand tried to pull the sweater more closely about him. The gesture was futile, the storm now being so loud with its wind and cold and dark air. Indeed, for much of the time now he seemed to be far off, all of it dulled, pain, cold, the rocks of the North Wall. Now and again clarity returned and he felt the force of the storm and the force of his bitterness again. Now he did not know whether he had truly heard a voice shouting. Now he hoped for nothing: only to lose sight and sound of the North Face; to drift finally from pain. . . .

Feebly, once more, he pulled at the sweater. He pulled it awkwardly, and it slid away from him, taken by the wind, down to the endless depths below him. Colder. And weaker.

The hand of his injured arm white, somehow obscene, flesh that did not belong to him. . . . No, they would not come. Graeme? Had he fallen? Or made the summit? He would not know.

When, through the muffling haze in his mind, he heard the stones again, he gave them no interest, did not even open his eyes. Part of the Heide's fire; part of the storm. . . .

There was a voice in the wind. Nothing strange in that; here in this half-sleep he could hear anything; the sounds of the Face were like the cries of men. . . .

But there was a voice. Becoming louder, through the wind. He could hear words now, words in a foreign voice, shouting in English. 'Beware! Beware the stonefall!'

The stones were coming faster now. Slowly, almost in a dream he turned his head, to keep it beneath the overhung rock. . . .

They had come. This wasn't the end. They had found him: those had been shouts he heard the first time. . . . Dear God, they had come back.

The man now level with him, at the end of his steel cable, his feet against the rock. Sean closed and opened his eyes; stared and stared. A man's face, blue-eyed and hollow with strain and cold. A face, smiling through the haze of snow. 'Greetings! You are alive!'

Faintly Sean smiled back, nodded his head.

'I have said so. We get you—like this'—he indicated the cable and the canvas sling at his back—'to the top. I do not speak great English. You have to sit here behind me, like a child. I make a signal—speak into the radio—and my good friends on the summit will wind us to the top.'

Sean looked at the cable, thin as string, vanishing into the storm.

The German said, 'You do not need to fear. It will be safe. I am afraid I shall have to give you pain, since I must get you on to the seat at my back. . . . I move closer to you and then I can help you to stand up. . . .'

165

The long effort, in exhaustion and pain, himself made more clumsy by this dream-fog in his mind. . . . And the strange knowledge coming through of companionship, of a man with him who promised life.

At last, spent with the effort, he sat in the canvas seat at the German's back. He heard brisk, German words spoken into the radio. A pause. . . . Then the cable began to vibrate and move, and slowly they began the haul upwards. The cable swung and swayed as they went, bringing away stones and rock. But it moved upwards. Upwards over the rocks where he had expected to die.

Drugged with relief and pain, he heard his own voice say feebly, 'Muir. Graeme Muir. What happened to him?'

'Your companion. Have no fear. He is alive and well.'

'Did he make it?'

'*Bitte?*'

'Did he get to the summit?'

'The summit? . . . *Ja*. He tells us where to look for you. He is alive and well.' He repeated the words as if he had learned them from a phrase-book.

Vaguely, somewhere behind his exhaustion and relief, was the thought that Graeme had made it, while *he* was dragged up the North Face, helpless at the end of a steel cable. . . .

From time to time the German spoke words of encouragement.

'Now you do not need to fear. The storm is less—listen! They will take care of you, at the top. You must have courage——'

'Yes.'

'Are you in great pain?'

'I don't know.'

'You are exhausted by the long wait. Two nights of waiting. That is terrible. At the summit there will be comfort for you.'

'Yes.'

Dimly he was aware of the lessening storm, and the rock

166

that splintered and fell as the crampons on the German's boots bit and cracked the ice. The blackish air was clearing and lightening, and high through cloud to the east there were other peaks, dark rock and snow leaning into the sky——

'*Siehe die Spitze!*'

A great joy in the German's voice. The movement of the cable faster now. . . . And then the dazzling snows of the summit, and the men in their hooded, padded clothes gathering round, and the noise of foreign voices loud about him. . . .

And the end of it. Gentle hands helping him from the seat: the German, free of his harness, suddenly huddled forward in exhaustion; a mug of warm liquid near his mouth; his own voice, as the German got slowly to his feet, saying, 'Thank you'; and other voices all about him, loud with relief and joy.

He was not part of it. Dimly through a sliding consciousness, he was aware of defeat. He lay there as they tended him; their voices were gentle as he murmured and moaned with pain. He closed his eyes so they would not expect him to answer them; would not expect him to share their joy.

CHAPTER TWO

JUDITH said to herself, 'Why am I afraid of him?'

The hospital bed was in a small wooden cubicle, thinly partitioned. There was a smell of antiseptic and a warmth too intense for comfort. Sean lay back on his pillows. His right arm, heavily bandaged, lay rigidly on the outside of the bed, as if it didn't belong to him. The swollen, blistered hand was naked. His face was thinned and shadowed. This, she thought, was to be expected, but not the curious sense that she faced a stranger; that there was a different intelligence behind the eyes, a different kind of vision making the set of the mouth.

She glanced at Graeme. He must surely feel, as she did, that they were doing no good here; that the sooner they left, the better?

He was leaning against the wall, an empty pipe in his hand, looking towards Sean. Graeme seemed, as far as she could tell, calm and serious, a man meeting a difficulty which he expected to overcome.

He said, 'The newspapers, of course, have made the usual messy sensation of the whole thing.'

'I suppose so. I've not seen them.'

'There's a lot about Hugh—photographs, stories of his past climbs—heavily written up, and much of it wrong. I'm afraid he'd have hated it.'

'I suppose he would. For myself, I'd like a bit of a flurry after my death, accurate or not. Better than being ignored. Have they found him?'

'No. A party went up as far as the Broken Finger yesterday, but they found nothing.'

Sean's eyes turned away. 'The Broken Finger . . . we were going well then.'

Graeme said, 'As soon as possible, we'll do a climb to-gether——'

'I shan't ever climb again.'

'Oh, nonsense——'

'I shan't. They haven't said as much, but you can read what they mean through all the jargon. I fractured this at the elbow, and the hand is frostbitten, you can see. They may have to amputate some of the fingers.'

'It may not come to that. I've known men who've re-covered from frostbite—even when they thought——'

'It's easier to talk like that when you've come through in one piece.'

Judith shut her hands on the bedrail. 'Graeme was able to tell the rescue party exactly where you were. They say it saved a lot of time in finding you——'

Sean closed his eyes; opened them again; did not look at her. Graeme said, 'No man who's been through what you have can see things straight. In a week or so's time the whole thing will look different; you'll find that you——'

'It really isn't any use, giving me that kind of bedside treatment, you know.' Sean's voice was tired and thin, his eyes turned away. On his face was an expression of boredom and disgust, like a man who has been forced to sit through some music-hall turn that offends him. 'I've got too old for it. I said as much to Martha when she came with that dread-fully boring man.'

'Man?' said Judith.

'Frenchman, some kind of journalist.'

'A man called Tévernin?'

'I don't remember names. . . . I told them both I hadn't time or energy for that kind of cotton-wool comfort.'

Graeme said, 'That wasn't what I was giving you.'

She saw Sean's weary eyes look into Graeme's face. There was a communication there, if only she could read it. Hostility in Sean's eyes, yet behind this a kind of bitter sad-ness. Again he was a stranger, and again she was afraid——

She made a movement away from the bed. 'We were asked only to stay with you a little while——'

Sean's mouth turned downwards. 'A merciful dispensation, isn't it? It was kind of you to come.'

Graeme said, 'You don't believe me, but next time I see you, you'll be feeling better. A little better. And then . . .' In the face of Sean's silence he made a small gesture with his hand, shrugged and said good-bye.

He walked away with his head down. Judith beside him could feel her heart beating, as if the encounter had been a noisy quarrel. And Graeme, she thought, was a little oppressed in spirit, as indeed he had been, ever since the climb. She was about to speak when, as they left the hospital, a small fair man sprang out at them like a wasp.

'Excuse me—Herr Muir? You have been visiting Herr Randall?'

She saw Graeme's effort at patience. 'Yes.'

'Have you anything you could tell my newspaper——'

'Absolutely nothing, I'm afraid.'

'Is it true Herr Randall is so badly injured that he will not be able to climb again? . . . You have no information? . . . He has said nothing to you?'

'I am sorry.'

'All newspapers, of course, have a great interest——'

'I know about the newspapers.'

'Your feelings, now, when you made the summit alone——'

'I am sorry. There is nothing I can tell you.'

On their return to the Scheidegg hotel, Judith went out on to the terrace, trying to ease her mind of the memory of Sean in the hospital bed. The Heide swarmed into mist; the air was cold. A boy swung the telescope towards the North Wall, then swung it back, baffled by cloud. Now there was nothing any more; the excitement had moved on; the climb was done.

She thought again of Sean, and of Graeme who since the

climb had seemed weary, disheartened, vulnerable, gentle with her. It was this, she thought, which had prevented her so far from telling him what she had decided. She still moved in the climate of her resolve; it was this perhaps that made the atmosphere between them transient and threatened, as if they had met at a railway station, one coming, one going.

When a little later they sat together at a table in the bar he said, as if his thoughts had been continually with Sean, 'I think he will climb again, you know. For the moment he's dispirited, weak, but in time . . . I think it'll be all right.'

She said, 'He worried me.' (Curious that her heart should still be knocking with a kind of apprehension.)

'Oh, well, the poor chap's been through a pretty bloody time. You can't expect him to sit up in bed and hand out charm.'

'He seemed cold. Hostile.'

'He isn't having much fun.'

'But he seemed to be hating us.'

'I don't think so. He was defeated. That's the hardest thing of all, for Sean.'

'He seemed to behave as if it were your fault.'

He shrugged. 'One needs to blame someone for one's failures.'

'But he was——' She broke off. Somehow, Graeme's stubborn defence of Sean was fraying her nerves. Better to leave it. She said, 'What are your plans now?'

She saw him glance at her and caught, as if in an echo, a strained formality in her own voice, 'Lundervald tomorrow. Then, when Sean's better, home. Via Paris, so we can see Stella. Has she written to you?'

'No.'

'Nothing about the climb?'

'No.'

He said, 'I don't understand that. No, I don't understand. I expect we'll hear.'

'I doubt it. Why must you wait here for Sean?'

'Why not?'

'You never cared for him. Just because he's fallen on a mountain, you're ready to throw everything on one side——'

A man at the bar turned his head, but he could not have heard; she was speaking quietly. And yet this was not what she had meant to say; the words sounded harsh and without sympathy. Graeme said, 'Judith darling, I haven't an idea what you're so cross about. Sean, poor devil, was climbing with me when he fell; of course I'm concerned for him; who wouldn't be? If you want to get back in a hurry, you can go home ahead of me——'

'Oh, fine, fine.' (How absurd for this to be happening here, where she had to speak quietly.) 'I can go home and wait for you to come back, as I waited for you to come down from that damned Face——'

'You're just not being reasonable——'

'Were you being reasonable when you climbed the North Wall, and risked all your lives, and lost Hugh's as you lost Bill's all those years ago?'

'D'you think I don't care about Hugh?'

'I don't know what you care about.' She moved an ashtray on the table, surprised to see how much her hand was trembling. 'I truly don't any more. Only mountains, I think, climbing or failing to climb them——' (But this is too harsh, too violent; none of these words are true, and yet they need to be said——)

'Judith darling, listen to me——'

'No, it's you who must listen.' (Pain on his face and the plaster stuck to the wound on his jaw; she mustn't look at these things.) 'Climbing is food and drink to you, and I can't take it any more. It's better said and understood; I've never said it before; perhaps I should have done, but I never did——'

'I knew you were impatient of it. That you had no sympathy——'

'None. None at all.' Harsh and untrue, but it had to be spoken. He looked as if she were punishing him, and she thought perhaps some part of her had wanted to punish him for a long time. 'When I knew you were safe, I made up my mind.'

His eyes were on her, absolutely attentive; they made her think of him when he was young. 'Well?'

'To part from you. No, don't try to argue. Or to look surprised——' (But he did neither.) 'It isn't any good; it hasn't been for a long time. I came here to find out, to get it clear. And I have. I can't join you in the thing you care about. Martha can: she's entirely with you, she knows how you feel; she——'

'Is this a quarrel about Martha?'

'This isn't a quarrel about anything. Or at least—yes, I suppose it is. It's about the whole of life, as quarrels always are; about all the things that have ever happened. And it's about Martha too, because that's gone on a long time, and I've been hurt and humiliated, and no woman in the world likes that, or if she does, name her to me.'

He had now, she thought, the drawn and haunted look of any man faced with a woman's anger. 'I thought you didn't mind.'

'That's what you told yourself for your comfort.'

'Oh God, listen to me.' He drew his hand across his forehead. 'On that climb—I thought of so much I wanted to say to you. Perhaps we've both left too many things unsaid. It was—oh, how can I describe it, make you understand—lonely up there; no, more than that.' His eyes were looking past her, seeing perhaps again the steep terraces of the Wall. 'One was without any prop, any sham of any kind; quite oneself—and I knew how much you meant to me. Knew it all the way down to my blood and bones. I've wanted to tell you, ever since I came back but somehow you made it difficult——'

'One feels these things under stress.'

'They were true.'

'Not true enough.'

'Oh, how can I convince you——'

'You can't. Not any more.' And this is like cutting loose one's mooring rope in the dark; sliding away, faster and faster. 'Because climbing is life and death to you; yes, I mean death; death as it came to Bill, and Hugh. And Martha is part of your life now——'

'No, that isn't so.'

'It's been so for a long time.'

'But this isn't possible. It doesn't make sense——'

'It makes sense to me.'

His eyes were raised to hers; she thought she saw a change in them. Perhaps exhaustion had reached its limit and he had no energy now but to accept. . . . Strange that this should convey a thrust of disappointment.

He said, his voice altered, 'We've dealt with Martha; has this got anything to do with Joseph?'

'No.'

'Martha told me he was here——'

'In Lundervald, yes.'

'Because women can sometimes deceive themselves——'

'I'm not deceiving anybody.'

'But he's never really left you alone, has he? He's kept cruising round, on and off, waving bank-notes at you, I suppose. Did he ask you to go to bed with him?'

'Once or twice.'

'Did you?'

'No.'

'Why not?'

'I can't think.'

The ashtray and the glasses on the table; the murmur of other voices at the bar. And a sense within her of violent things, of Hugh's death, and Sean, and this moment of parting——

'Pardon, m'sieur; I hope I am not intruding, but I should so much like to have a few words with you——'

She looked up, in a kind of enraged astonishment. André

174

Tévernin, leaning over the table, with a hand on the back of Graeme's chair.

Graeme, his face white, said, 'I beg your pardon?'

'My name is André Tévernin; I am a reporter; and I have already met your wife——'

'I'm sorry——'

'M'sieur, I shan't keep you long; after your terrible experience on the Face you must be unwilling to talk for a long time, but there are rumours going about and I felt it only right, in your own interest, that I should ask you one or two questions——'

Exhaustion and fury, she thought, made Graeme's face harshly new. He said, 'I haven't a single bloody word to say to anybody. Now will you kindly go away?'

André Tévernin stood still. His eyes rested on Graeme for a moment; his glance was secret, concentrated and hostile, as if he added up a long column of figures which he disliked. Then he turned abruptly, and walked to the bar.

Graeme said at last with a brief smile. 'That was rude. But understandable, I think.'

'He said something about rumours——'

'Oh, be damned to it; there are always rumours.' He sat back in his chair. 'Your plans, I suppose, are to leave at once?'

'Yes, I'm going down to Lundervald tonight.' She got to her feet. Graeme sat with his hands clasped on the table.

The things have been said, she thought. Now it is all changed.

She walked quickly away. André Tévernin turned his head as she passed, but made no sign that he knew her.

CHAPTER THREE

JOSEPH said, 'Eat your dinner. You look to me as though you need a good meal.'

'What I need is . . .' she began, but left it, since she had no idea. The surprise of sitting here in the dining-room of the Altenhof with Joseph was diminished by the drink which Joseph had already given her. There remained, however, the sense that all this was happening too suddenly: that the day which had included Sean in the hospital bed, the scene with Graeme, the return to Lundervald and the absence of any news from Stella, could not also include a long evening with Joseph.

'A gentleman has been telephoning you, madame,' the girl at the reception desk had said, after some suitable remarks about the climb, and the tragedy of Hugh's loss. 'He has telephoned several times, and we have told him you are expected tonight. Now he is waiting in the lounge.'

So now there was Joseph, and dinner at the Altenhof, not quite in focus. Beyond the blurred luxury lay tomorrow, full of harsh practicalities, since it was one thing to quarrel with Graeme and take the mountain train down to Lundervald; another to organize the journey home, and a life in which Graeme and Oxford played no part any more. So far she had not explained the position to Joseph, who was at this moment looking sombrely at her plate. The lines on his face suggested age, just as the sudden attentiveness in Graeme's eyes had suggested youth. She thought, We are none of us secure in the present, that's what makes it all so much more difficult, for one is touched both by Graeme young and Joseph old.

'Well, this has been a fine how-d'you-do, hasn't it?' he

said. 'Chaps being killed, chaps in hospital—what does Graeme say about it all now?'

'He doesn't say very much.' She wanted to avoid the thought of Graeme, sitting opposite her at the small table.

'I dare say not; not much to say, is there? . . . Now there's no need to look like that: it's all very grand and brave, I know, but it's ended up in a nasty mess, you can't deny that.'

'No, indeed.'

'Go on, eat your dinner. Whatever happens, you've got to eat; dying of starvation doesn't help anyone.' He poured more wine into her glass. 'You mustn't think I don't sympathize about the whole thing; I've seen a bit of trouble myself lately.'

The window of the dining-room looked towards the mountains, but they were hidden in the dark. 'Yes, you said something about it.'

'Aye.' He too gave a rapid glance towards the mountains, as if he feared they might interrupt him. 'Just before I left Paris, I was called to a nursing home. A friend of mine— woman I'd known years ago—pretty as paint, dark, with a fringe. Now she was dying. A few weeks more, the nurse told me.' He drank from his glass and looked round the dining-room; she could sense the faint pride of the man, generally protected from tragedy, who has seen it suddenly in focus. 'I talked to her for a bit but it wasn't much good. Then I came out into the street—nice, pretty, summer Paris street. And I felt lonely. A bit lost, and it's not like me to feel lost. Everything looked so damned unreliable, as if it could suddenly vanish. And I thought of you. You were the only person who could make sense of it all—people being young and pretty and having a fine time in bed, and then suddenly lonely and in pain and dying. I wanted you there, to sit and talk to me and make me feel better about it all. . . . You don't look as though you believe me.'

'Yes, I do.' Indeed, she could see clearly the violence of the last days: the unknown woman in the nursing home; the mist on the Heide's Face; Hugh's fall with the avalanche, and Sean in the hospital bed, changed and hostile. She knew what Joseph had felt in the Paris street; she felt it now herself. The uncertainty, the loneliness and the threat, all growing because one was oneself older; the need, in the face of this, to make a gesture of love that was, as far as it could be, total; to strain no more, merely to give and accept.

'So I came here,' Joseph went on, 'and then all this happens. . . . Seems to me we're both much in the same boat.'

'Yes, perhaps.' A little hazy with wine she looked beyond his shoulder. 'As far as I'm concerned, it's all at last making a shape.'

'What is?'

She said, 'Well, I suppose the whole of my life,' and giggled faintly. 'I've been keeping a stiff upper lip for years, and now it's fallen. Like arches.'

'Never had much time for stiff upper lips myself; they lead to a lot of silly misunderstanding. . . . What the hell are you talking about, love?'

'All the time I've been playing it as one kind of person, but there was another who couldn't take it. . . . Could I have some coffee?'

'You haven't had enough dinner.'

'Well, that's a matter of opinion; I think I have. You see, if I'd blown up about Martha or pulled her hair or wept on my pillow, I dare say it would have been all right, but I never did.'

'Lord save us——'

'But you can't pretend for ever; the real thing comes through in the end——'

'Stone the crows, love, are you telling me you've quarrelled with the climbing Don?'

'Yes.' (But now through the haze of the wine, it seems a little unreal, only making a dull bruise on the mind like an uncomfortable dream.)

'Have you left him?'

'Yes.'

Joseph put down his glass. 'I don't believe it. I honestly don't believe it.'

'Well, it's a very difficult thing to believe; I find it difficult myself, but it's true. . . . I should like some coffee; my dinner is now cold. It sounds like a foreign phrase-book.'

Joseph was looking as though he'd found a Cézanne in a dust-heap. 'When did this happen?'

'Just now at the Scheidegg.'

'What set it off?'

She found she couldn't remember. It seemed to have something to do with the visit to Sean, where threat still lingered. She said, 'Well, everything, I suppose. Martha being in Paris——'

'Aye, the great girl. I knew she was more of a bother than you told me——'

'She's always been everywhere, larger than life and four times as unwelcome. . . . I have no charity left, and that is a bad thing, but I can't help it.' (Yards and yards of self-revelation, coming out like stuff from a conjuror's hat.) 'I had an idea of myself as someone tough and grown-up and independent and I tried to live up to it. I was supposed to be the non-vulnerable type, unlike Martha, who can be seen publicly wincing from two to five any afternoon in Oxford Street. Well, hell to all that: I lived in dread and fury and jealousy, only I never let it out.'

'Never even,' said Joseph, 'came away with me for so much as a week-end.'

'That would have complicated things without making them any better.'

'You can't know. Any road, they've changed now.'

'Yes, they have.' (Graeme coming down from the Heide; Sean in the hospital bed; Hugh's room in the hotel, silent but for a clock ticking. . . .) 'Perhaps if he hadn't gone on this climb, it would have been all right; things would have gone on the same; it was this that broke it up, waiting for him to come back, with Martha there. . . . Golly, she's arrived again, like something with two heads. . . . Am I drunk, Joseph?'

Joseph roused himself from a state of brooding, sympathetic pleasure. 'Not so much that you can't take in what I'm going to say to you. I've got to leave here tomorrow evening. I'm going first to Paris for the night, and then to Amsterdam; there's a Vermeer for sale and I'm going to buy it.'

She cloudily, 'A Vermeer or the North Wall—men are all the same.'

'Aye, but you don't break your neck on a Vermeer. All you need to do is to go and pack your luggage and come back here tomorrow. I'll arrange all the rest. These things can always be done if you know how to do them, and I do. We can leave here together tomorrow evening. I'll book a room for you in Paris.' He was searching through his wallet, glancing at the times of trains, making calculations in his head.

She said, aware that all this was spinning too fast, 'But I shall have to go home. To Oxford. There are things to be done——'

'There always are, and they can always wait. Learning which top priority job can wait till next week's got me where I am. You've had a nasty little shake-up, and it's time someone took over——'

She said, making an effort to slow this skidding turn of events, 'I don't think I want to be taken over——'

'Yes, you do. And though I say it myself, I'm more use to you at this moment than that great climbing Don; he may be able to get up the North Face of the Heide, but he couldn't make you happy. . . . Now what's the matter, love?'

She said, 'They brought me a lot of beautiful hot coffee and I never drank it.'

'Well, there's no need to cry about that——'

'I can't help it. It won't stop. It really won't stop.'

'Aye, it's all been a bit too much. Come along, and I'll see you home. Then tomorrow we can get the hell out of here, and you need never see that damn' mountain again.'

She woke the next morning, hungover, emptied and calm. She had, she found, slept in her clothes. Hurriedly she bathed and dressed again. The self of this morning seemed to have the self of last night up before her desk.

'Well, that was a nice piece of behaviour, I must say.'

'I couldn't help it.'

'And where would the world be if we all said *that* every time there was trouble, I should like to know.'

'It hasn't happened before.'

'So I should hope. Clothes been slept in.'

'Yes, I know. That frock was said to be crease-resistant, but I'd say its resistance is low.'

'I don't find it funny.'

'Nor do I, ma'am.'

'Drunk too.'

She sat down on the edge of the bed. The bare room was silent except for the noisy self-confident tick of the alarm clock. (And I'm tired of hotel rooms: Paris, the Scheidegg, here. They are neutral and discouraging, like someone who is looking the other way and not listening: they do not receive one's anxiety and distress; it merely bounces back from the walls.) The sun was shining, but there seemed to be in her head a kind of grey weather, stretching indefinitely away. Finding herself in new territory, she must learn her way about. And this was new. This place of dead detachment where the sun intruded was new.

The uncomfortable days ahead had to be tied up and labelled; they would look better that way.

'What kind of future do you require, madam? We have one or two lines which might interest you——'

'Trouble is, nothing interests me.'

'Just allow me, madam. We have marriage with Joseph;

that would be very comfortable; really the best solution, one feels, in every way——'

'I don't see myself married to Joseph. When I try to, it looks like dressing up in a funny hat.'

'One mustn't be too particular, madam. We hesitate to mention it, but a woman of your age——'

'Oh, drains to that.'

'The only alternative is a rather solitary life, concentrating on your work. We don't really recommend——'

'I think it rather suits me.'

'It's up to you, of course, madam. Financial circumstances will be straitened——'

'They always are.'

'Your age is against you if you want regular employment—'

'For Pete's sake, will you shut up about my age? My only concern at the moment is that it isn't more, a whole lot more, let's say eighty-five.'

'Of course, if madam has a death-wish——'

'Look, I haven't any kind of wish: is that clear?'

'Solitary life has its problems, especially for those who have lived for years in the married state. There is of course the question of celibacy——'

'I get awfully tired of all this phallus-worship. I'm for getting through life in a single bed, the way some people don't eat meat.'

'This may be a result of emotional exhaustion: later on——'

'Later on can take care of itself. By some other means: sublimation or Swedish drill.'

'Of course, it's for you to make your own decision——'

'That's the trouble. I don't want to come to any decision.'

'I'm afraid you'll have to make up your mind, madam, we close at five.'

'It looks as though I shall have to settle for the solitary straitened circumstances and Swedish drill.'

'Very well, madam; I'll have it gift-wrapped for you——'

'No, hell, wait; I can't make a decision, not any decision.'

'We close at five——'

'All right, I'll go as far as Paris with Joseph. But after that . . . I can't answer for after that.'

'Certainly not, madam; we quite understand. That's all we want; just something to be going on with. If we may say so, we feel you're on the right lines. . . .'

But there remained a curious lack of energy and desire: she did not want to take the skin off this day and face the world, any world.

She went downstairs. Still no letter from Stella. More than ever a sense of drifting far off, of going out of earshot of familiar things. . . . She went out into the street.

Lundervald lay in morning quiet, a playground of long shadow and brilliant light, not yet inhabited. The postcard stands were out on the empty pavements; a man drove a herd of cows, their bells sounding a kind of emptiness too. She glanced once at the Heide; a marvellous confluence of snow, shadow and light, shining in the pale morning air. Well, today she would leave it and, please God, not see it again. (And this absurd desire to go back once more to Alpiglen, and look again for the last time at the high terraces must be the morbid activity of a mind fast losing control.)

When she came to the shop which sold newspapers and cow-bells, she paused. The rack of newspapers swung gently in the wind. The climb, now three days old, had slipped from the headlines; but on one French newspaper the word *Heide* caught her eye, and she drew the paper from the rack.

There was a picture taken with a telephoto lens from Kleine Scheidegg of Sean on the ledge. No difficulty in translating the firm black words below: '*The terrible North Wall: more revelations of great seriousness; Muir abandoned me to seek the summit for himself, says Randall.*'

CHAPTER FOUR

GRAEME felt the jab of the needle; his eyes were on the window of his room at the Scheidegg hotel, and he paid it little attention. The small Swiss doctor said, 'The pain of the needle is not so much; it is the stuff going in.'

'What we call in England a kind of double-take.'

The doctor smiled; it was impossible to tell whether he understood the word or not. He said, 'I doubt if any further injections will be necessary. But I am afraid that, since of course proper attention could not be given to it at first, it will leave a small permanent scar.'

'That really doesn't matter. My glamour days are past.'

The doctor gave another brief smile. 'It will not, I am sure, alter your wife's affection for you.'

'No,' said Graeme. 'It won't make any difference to her.'

'She was not at dinner last night?'

'No. She has to go home ahead of me.'

'Ah. So. I am sorry not to have said good-bye.'

Slight offence? Perhaps. Graeme said, 'She had to hurry to catch her train. We're both so grateful to you for attending to me while you were on holiday. Usually the last thing a doctor wants to do.'

The doctor shrugged. There still seemed a small brake on his friendliness. 'I always travel prepared. Often, in such a place as this one can be of much assistance. Besides, it is of course an honour to attend the . . . one would say, I suppose, the hero of such an undertaking.'

The voice a little flat, formal. Graeme looked up into his face, but the light was shining on the doctor's rimless glasses, and this gave him no expression at all.

Graeme said, 'Scarcely a hero. One who's lucky to be alive.'

184

'Ah . . . yes.' A kind of sigh. 'Your companion on the ledge . . . he is recovering?' Still the blank look, the light on the glasses.

Graeme said, 'Yes. But there seems to be some question whether he will be able to climb again.'

'Ah, so. Unhappy for him, no doubt, but a means perhaps of prolonging his life. . . .' He added thoughtfully, 'The cold on that ledge must have been very terrible.'

'Yes. His hand was frostbitten.'

Again a thoughtful nodding of the head; Graeme had the impression of a man considering evidence. 'Did he have no benzedrine or Ronicol?'

'Yes, but he couldn't get at his sack. I had to let them down to him.'

'Your own supply?'

'Yes.'

Faint surprise in the doctor's face? Graeme thought, I've had enough of this: the injection hurts, and I want him to go. The doctor said, 'How much longer will you be staying here?'

Graeme thrust himself to his feet. 'I go down to Lundervald today.'

The doctor nodded. 'I can understand. The Face, after all'—he nodded towards the window—'cannot hold for you very pleasant memories.'

Graeme looked at him. Still the light on the glasses. He said, 'No.'

'After the death of your friend. And of course the newspapers are so very . . . extravagant in what they write.'

'I've stopped reading the newspapers.'

'Yes.' A little hesitation—or perhaps the doctor was merely trying to think of his next words. 'I'm sure that is wise. . . . I hope I will see you, to say good-bye.'

'Of course. And thank you for being so kind.'

A small bow; nothing more; no handshake.

Alone, Graeme beat his fingers for a moment on the window ledge. The jab in his thigh was aching dully down his leg. The air smelt of antiseptic. He looked in the glass. A small permanent scar. . . .

'Well, to hell with that,' he said, and went out on to the terrace.

Many people there in the sun; he was used to the glances of interest and curiosity; if they seemed now to have a touch of unfriendliness, that was no doubt due to his own mood.

'That bloody quarrel with Judith. That damned bloody quarrel. It doesn't make sense——'

'Yes, it does. Look at the mountain there.' (A postcard picture: a tourist attraction, its fangs drawn.) 'You wanted it as you wanted Martha, unreasonably, having to suppress all the fears and doubts, being prepared, since possession mattered so much, to take the risks. This is the pay-off.'

'It can't be. Up there on that damned Face I was exhausted, frightened and cold. But I had a kind of peace, too. I saw the whole thing clear, Judith and myself——'

'And Martha?'

'She was someone I cared for, desired, could not quite bear to lose, did not love enough.'

'And now?'

His eye went up the steep terraces again. It had been lonely on the Ice-Field, lonely after Hugh's death, but the loneliness he felt now was more intense; it was the baffling loneliness brought on himself because where he loved he had been careless, and where he didn't love, he had, by desire and pity, bound himself too close.

He turned impatiently, walking between the chairs and tables on the terrace. A man was playing an accordion; there was an air of ease and holiday. He hurried to his room. One could at least pack and pay one's bill and go down to Lundervald. It wasn't the end of it yet.

CHAPTER FIVE

THE train for Interlaken didn't leave for half an hour. Judith walked up and down beside the railway lines. Tourists were filling the train going the other way, up to the Jungfraujoch. The sun promised well; the many tongues exclaimed in different languages that there would be a splendid view.

Unnecessary, of course, to be so early. She moved restlessly in the brilliant sun. She thought that the people of Lundervald, with the great mountains behind them, had the casual, modest pride of a hostess who has permanently in her house a celebrity of world renown. Turning her back on the mountains she saw on the other side of the road Ludwig Klein. He was sitting on a seat and smoking a pipe in the sun. The brown eagle-face under the white hair was placid; he seemed, looking towards the mountains, to be dreaming an old man's dreams. After a moment's hesitation she went across to him; he greeted her, she thought, with politeness and reserve.

She said at once, sitting beside him, 'Have you seen the papers?'

He shook his head, and looked down at his boots. '*Nein. I do not often read the papers.*'

'Do you know what they're saying—about Graeme?'

He shrugged. 'Newspaper reporters!'

'Yes—but you've heard what they're saying?'

'*Ja. Ja*, I have heard. It is the talk of all the guides this morning.'

'But they don't believe it? That he could have left Sean—left him, just to get to the top himself?'

The old man moved one boot as if he were trying out a foothold and said nothing.

'But they can't believe it——'

He shrugged. 'It is a story. An excitement. And I have told you, they do not care for the North Wall——'

'But you know. You know that he wouldn't do it.'

He kept his pipe in his mouth, still staring at the ground. The train for the Jungfraujoch had slid a little way on its journey before he answered. 'I have climbed often with Herr Muir. A man of courage and a fine mountaineer.' He sighed. 'But always this desire to climb the North Face, to be in the party which makes the first British ascent—this has been a kind of madness, an obsession. And a man obsessed is not himself. One cannot blame him for what he may do.'

'I don't care whether it was madness or not. *Graeme wouldn't leave someone in need of help if he could help him.* Can't someone say that to the guides, make them believe it, make everyone believe it?'

The train gave a twitch. No, it couldn't leave yet.

'It is possible of course that he makes a wrong decision. In good faith——'

'How could it be wrong, to go for help?'

'Some think help would have come. That he would have done more good to stay with the wounded man——'

'But can't you tell them——'

'They say that two men have been sacrificed on this climb. One is dead, the other badly wounded. Only one is safe, unharmed; able to claim the North Wall for himself and for the British.'

A curious sensation this: the nightmare one of shouting into a pillow. 'Has he talked like that? Has he waved any flags—is he that kind of person?'

'All the time I have known him, he has had this dream. This crazy dream. He brushes aside what I say of the climb, when I tell him the weather is not right. He becomes another person. A man for whom the summit of the Heide by the North Wall is everything. At whatever cost.'

'You mean you are sure?'

Ludwig drew on his pipe and looked up at the mountains, as if he felt happier with them than with women who pummelled him with questions. 'No. But I think the North Wall puts a spell on the men who attempt it. They are different, and afterwards nothing is the same.'

'And is there no one in the whole of Lundervald, no one who believes that he climbed on only to get help, for that and no other reason at all?'

A shrug. 'They argue. Some put forward this idea, some that.'

'But as a whole they think the worst? Oh, you don't have to tell me. People will always think the worst because it's more fun.'

He gave her a glance, as if recognizing her anger. 'Perhaps that is true.'

'I have to get my train.' She stood up. 'All I can tell you is I *know* that he didn't do it. I am sure. Can you understand that? I know all the things that are wrong with Graeme, but this he didn't do.'

'On the face of a mountain——'

'I tell you, I know.'

'How splendid is the devotion of a wife.'

She said, beginning to run, 'Oh hell, my train.' But the train stayed for a few moments longer, and through the window she could see Ludwig Klein sitting with his head down, in the sun. She wanted to shout across to him: 'It's nothing to do with devotion; I'm not, in my view, his wife any more; it's just something that I know and can't bear other people not to know.' She remained silent. The train with its empty wooden seats slid smoothly on.

In the small cubicle the heat, she thought, was more intense than the day before.

'I tell you,' Sean repeated, 'I said a lot of things.' He was pale, his eyes heavy and dull. 'I don't even remember them. The French chap kept asking me questions.'

'You mean he made it up? All this?'

He glanced to the newspaper on the bed, shrugged and was silent. It occurred to her how useless this visit must be, since one could not show one's anger to a man who lay as Sean did. She said quietly, 'Graeme went on to get help for you.' She seemed to have been saying that for days, weeks; saying it into a vacuum of disbelief. 'That you must know.'

He turned his head. 'I'm not sure of anything any more. You wouldn't be, if you'd spent two nights alone on the Face——'

'It must have been very terrible, but——'

'Words are easy. I expected to die there——'

'But help came!'

'Oh yes, it came.'

'And Graeme sent it, told them where to look for you——'

'I never said he didn't want me to live, didn't want me to be rescued. But he wanted more than anything to get to the top. If he'd stayed with me, he might have found some way of climbing down to me; he might have saved this hand. Now they don't think it can be saved.'

She stared at him, in pity and distress. 'He said it was impossible to climb down——'

'More impossible than it was to climb up?'

'He thought so. He truly thought so.'

He gave a small smile; on his face was the same bitterness she had seen before, with sadness behind it. 'He wouldn't have left Hugh.'

She was checked in a movement across the small space. 'What d'you mean?'

He met her glance; his eyes were a little brighter and his voice more vivid. 'It was Hugh who mattered, all the time. I saw that from the first. People give themselves away, they always do. You could see on his face how he felt when Hugh was climbing. It wasn't the same for me. . . . Would you pour me out some water? I'm clumsy with my left hand.'

As she poured the water, she heard the smooth sound of

rubber wheels as a trolley went past outside. She watched him as he drank. He had the naked, vulnerable look of anyone who has just revealed himself. Strange to find it here: the bitterness of despised affection.

He set the glass down shakily on the table beside him. 'You understand me?'

'Yes. Yes, I do. But not that you said what you did to this man, André Tévernin——'

'I didn't know he was going to go to town about it.'

'Once a thing like this gets started, it grows. It'll be in other papers soon. And gossip'll go way ahead of the papers, you know it will——'

'It'll pass. All of it'll pass. And Graeme will be able to go on climbing.' With his left hand he touched the rigid, bandaged arm. 'Not with the same companions, but with others.'

She took the paper from the bed. 'All I want you to do is to deny it—to tell them it wasn't true, that they misunderstood what you said. Someone from the hospital would do it——'

He was shaking his head. 'No. What would be the use?'

'It would be something. If you say you care for him, you don't want this story to spread everywhere. You don't want him to be hurt——'

He shifted himself against the pillows. 'Climbing the North Wall with Graeme was going to be such a splendid thing. I was very excited, you know. And it all began so well.' His eyes were adrift from her. 'I climbed quite a difficult stretch bringing two rucksacks with me; they were heavy, and I was proud of doing that. But then, as we climbed, something changed. You'd think you'd be very close to a man on a Face like that. But somehow Graeme wasn't with me, I could feel it, a kind of distance growing between us, all the time. . . . You look as though you understood that.'

'Perhaps I do. But——'

191

'He left me because I didn't matter enough. I've said what I think and that's the end of it.'

She stood looking at him, the folded paper in her hands, and then turned and went quickly from the room.

CHAPTER SIX

GRAEME sat on the bed of the Gletschergaten hotel in Lundervald. He had a tooth-mug of whisky in his hand, and a newspaper was spread out over the bed-cover. Of Judith's things there was no trace; the empty hangers rattled like bones in the wardrobe, and the table beside her bed was swept of all but an empty cigarette carton and a discarded envelope. The hotel porter, looking a little surprised, had said that madame had left this morning with her suitcase. No, there was no message.

He had on an impulse gone directly out into the street and walked a little way, as if in hope of finding her, but then the absurdity of this slowed his step, and he found himself standing still in front of a newspaper shop, like a man who has lost his memory. After a little while the photograph of the Heide made some impression on his mind, as a sound comes through sleep, and he drew the paper from the rack.

Now he turned to read it again. He found that the thought of Judith made a larger noise in his head, but the words in the paper had their own power. He was, he found, more than anything surprised, as if he had looked in the glass and seen some reflection other than his own. '. . . Sean Randall, who lies now in a hospital bed, with the pallor of one brought back from the very brink of death on the murderous North Wall, spoke of his friend who deserted him. . . . Muir himself has told our reporter: "I have nothing to say. . . ."' Graeme remembered the Frenchman at the Scheidegg hotel; the other reporters to whom he had given such brief replies. Well, they could get their own back now. He read on, 'It is understood that the North Face was beyond the strength of Hugh Ferris, the man who was killed, and that he was persuaded against his will to do the climb by Muir.'

He sat thoughtfully, taking occasional gulps at the whisky. Odd to be dangled before the public as the villain; to be lied about; to be so entirely misinterpreted. And yet some detachment of mind persisted; since the climb, he thought, the feverish egotist within him, who would have recoiled from this attack with hysterical violence, was quietened. He felt saddened, sombre, mostly concerned with Judith: would she believe it? So strange to be cut off from her, not to know. And Stella. . . . He saw her, sitting at a café table in Paris, reading the highly coloured French phrases. The image was painful; he wanted at once to cancel it by telephoning her, sending a telegram. . . .

He was not, he found, angry with Sean. He was angry with the French journalist, with the world of loud headlines and indifference to truth. For Sean, who had climbed with him and endured so long on the Face, and who had spoken in anguish and defeat, he could feel some pity.

He stood up and folded the paper between his hands. Some sort of protest was necessary; his mind began to form dignified phrases of denial, and then skidded off to show him Judith, already far off, no longer part of him. He went downstairs. Curious, there was a reluctance, now that this thing had been written and read, to go out into the street.

In the hall, sitting in one of the chairs shaped like a coolie hat, he found Martha. His immediate impulse, to go back quickly upstairs, caused him some shame. She was looking pretty, carefully dressed and serious, as if she were in church, and some part of him was quite at odds with her.

'Oh, Graeme! I'm so glad you're here. They said you'd be back this afternoon. Is Judith with you?'

He was not yet ready to tell her about Judith. 'No.'

'I wasn't sure. I wanted to see you because—oh, you've got it there——'

'The newspaper? Yes.'

'Graeme, isn't it *awful*? So absolutely beastly and terrible and unfair. I don't know how people can. It made me feel dreadful.'

He said with a slight smile, 'It's certainly a very great deal of nonsense,' finding the depth and solemnity of her sympathy somehow a little irksome.

'I've just been talking to André——'

'André?'

'André Tévernin, the journalist, the man who wrote it. You remember, I travelled back from the Scheidegg with him, and he drove me over to see Sean. I was . . . well, I mean, I was telling him how really ghastly I thought it was.'

'Then he's still here?'

'Oh yes, he's staying at the Schweitzerhof. Near the station——'

'Fine.' Graeme put the paper under his arm. 'I'll go and see him.'

'Oh, will you? Will you really? Yes, I suppose that'd be . . . I think I'd like, I mean, d'you mind if I come with you? Where's Judith?'

'She . . . she had to go home ahead of me.'

'Oh! Oh, I see. Did she? Well, I won't if you'd rather not, but I think it'd be a good thing if I came with you. You see, I mean, well, I know him. And actually, in spite of everything, of his being so awful, I mean, he's rather nice, in a way . . . sort of kind, sometimes. I thought perhaps if I was there . . .'

He was a little puzzled by all this. He said at last, 'Very well,' and they went out into the street, together.

André Tévernin lit himself a cigarette. He was, Graeme thought, quite at home in the bar of the Schweitzerhof whose noisy colours were muted by dim lights. They were sitting at a small table which got in the way of his knees; he thought he was tired of transient places, of hotel rooms and bars and dining-rooms; he wanted to be home. (And Judith . . . ?)

195

He said, 'If this were an English paper, I could get thousands on a libel action.'

Tévernin made a small movement with his shoulders. (Had not Judith said that he had been a friend of Stella's? The idea was unpalatable.) 'In France it is not so.'

'It was all the same a pretty damn-fool thing to print—the words of a man who'd waited two days on that Face for rescue——'

'His brain seemed quite clear——'

'If you'll believe that, you'll believe anything.'

'He was very . . . shall we say, persuasive. May I offer you a drink? . . . No? . . . And when I am told something of such interest, I naturally wish to give it to the readers of my newspaper——'

'Whether it's true or not?'

Tévernin moved his shoulders again. 'Oh . . . truth. I wrote what I heard from Monsieur Randall. If we wait to find out what is the truth we are writing a history book, not a newspaper.'

'It seems to me worth a try.'

'Yes,' said Martha, 'that's what I should have——'

'If you remember, monsieur, I made an attempt, up at the Scheidegg, to discover a little of the truth. You were not welcoming. I am doing a job. It is no worse than any other. I was prepared to listen to you, to hear your side of the story, but you were——'

'I was very rude to you, but that was due to circumstances outside my control. It doesn't seem to me a good enough reason for writing all this. And where did you get the idea that I persuaded Hugh Ferris against his will . . . ?'

Tévernin said with the small smile of a man who produces an unexpected trump, 'From your daughter, m'sieur. She has talked to me a great deal.'

'Ah. . . .' (Yes, there are things that can still hurt.) 'But the confidences of a girl half your age——'

'Nothing was said about confidence.'

No, he supposed it hadn't been; he could imagine how it had been said.

Martha was saying, 'I did try to say earlier, didn't I, that the whole thing was probably quite different——'

Graeme looked away from her. The whole of this encounter now depressed him; brief as it was, it had gone on too long. And Martha was, in some way, like a light shining too close to his eyes. He said to Tévernin, 'I don't know how many Press chaps there are left about, here in Lundervald——'

Tévernin shrugged. 'A few.'

'And I expect you know them all. I want you to round up as many as you can and bring them to my hotel about six o'clock. There'll be drinks, and I shan't keep them long. But I'm going to tell them what happened on that damned Face, and then they can make what they like out of it.'

Tévernin looked up quickly. 'Ah. Most certainly: that should be interesting.'

'Yes,' said Graeme. He got to his feet, and Martha rose too; he was aware that she was making the small useless movements of the insecure. He said to Tévernin, 'I shall expect you, then,' and walked with Martha beside him out into the street.

For some time he was silent. She glanced occasionally at him as they walked. Chiefly, he thought now, he felt sorry for her, and this would make the half-hour ahead the more difficult. But it had to be done now. He could see the Heide as they walked; it still kept him company. He touched Martha's arm, then let it fall.

She said, 'Are you going back to the hotel?'

The drift of nervousness through her voice touched him. He said, 'Not yet. I have to talk to you. Let's come this way, down towards the river. Somewhere where there aren't any reporters. Or newspapers. Or even people who read them.'

197

'Yes, I do see what you mean. . . . I do really . . . understand. . . .' Her voice trailed off. He walked down the quiet
path that led away from the main street. The sun was strong
and the tall rocks above them seemed in some way to command the humming, summer silence. He led her to a wooden
seat, placed to look towards the Heide. She sat, he thought,
rather primly, as if she were waiting for a bus.

He leaned forward uncomfortably, aware of the hard seat
and the too brilliant light. He remembered the beginning in
Skye, the oppressive heat of the valley after Pinnacle Ridge.
Now a different valley, a different time. He said again, 'I
have to talk to you. And may heaven help me.'

'I suppose you're going to be angry——'

'Oh my dear; no, no. . . . I'm long past being angry with
anyone. It's odd, like being sober at a party where everyone
else is drunk.' He gave her a smile to which she did not
respond at all; her face was closed, somehow on the defensive. This did not seem to concern him. He said, 'When I
told you just now that Judith had gone on ahead of me, that
wasn't the whole truth.'

'Oh well, no one says that, do they, ever? Or at any rate,
I don't expect them to.'

'We had a quarrel——'

'About me?'

'About——' he sighed. 'She said, The whole of life. And she
said she was going to leave me. When I got back to the hotel
today I found she'd packed everything and gone.'

'You mean really gone? Left Lundervald? But this morning she was with Sean——'

'*Sean?*'

'Yes, when I rang him up today to see how he was and
everything, he told me Judith had been there. Been to see
him——'

'Judith had?'

'Well, you see, she was angry about what he said, about
the newspaper——'

'You mean she didn't believe it?'

'Oh—no . . . no. . . . Well, nobody believes it really, do they? It was just Sean being upset. . . .' She paused, seeming to become aware of his silence. He looked at her, seeing her and not seeing her. He said again at last, 'She went to see him? All the way there? To the hospital? It would be the sort of thing she would hate.' He went on thinking about it, feeling the small lift of his spirit. Only after some moments did he hear Martha's voice again.

'. . . ought to have done something like that myself. Only you see it was difficult, Sean being my cousin.'

'Yes, of course.' He was not listening.

'And then André having been so kind to me. It made it difficult. He explained to me about it, about writing it up and everything. I always find it difficult, when people explain, not to understand. He liked me, and I like people to like me; it's all I want; I can't ever turn them away. I mean, it makes things easy; I don't know how to handle things, unless they're easy and people like me.'

All this blew past him, scarcely catching his attention. He shifted his position on the seat. 'What I have to say to you is this. I want any meetings we have from now on to be innocent.' It sounded like a pretty evasion, and he said more harshly, 'In other words, I want us to cease to be lovers.'

'Well, we haven't been very much, have we, I mean not lately.'

It wasn't the comment he had expected. Martha had stood so long in his mind, a figure accompanied by guilt, someone for whom he was responsible, to whose body his own responded with a kind of blinkered violence which for the moment obscured memory and loyalty and love. But how long since it had happened? He was still trying to remember when she said, 'In Paris . . . when you rang me up. . . . I told you they were all going out, and that I'd be alone all the afternoon. But when I met you for lunch, you told me Judith might be coming too.'

He was silent, looking at her. He tried to recall her voice over the telephone on that first evening in Paris, but there was only the feeling of guilt mixed with the excitement at the prospect of the climb.

She went on, the rapid colourless voice strengthened by grievance, 'Of course that made it all quite different; I mean, I couldn't go on and say any more about it when you'd said that, could I?'

Dimly he now remembered that during lunch at the Restaurant d'Alsace Martha had received his enthusiasm about the climb with unreceptive silences.

She said, 'You talked about the North Wall all the time, from the beginning to the end.'

'I'm sorry. I thought you'd be interested.'

'Well, of course I was; yes, I was; but I had told you about being alone: the house was quite empty, even the maid was going to be out. But you didn't say anything about it at all. Just that Judith might join us. You must see that it made it very difficult for me.'

'Yes, indeed.'

'Especially as I always thought that Judith didn't mind—that's what I always thought, and I said it to her——'

'To Judith?'

'Yes, well, we had a kind of talk, when you were on the climb. And it's no good being angry about that, because she started it——'

'My dear Martha, I'm not angry about anything.'

'I thought you must be, because of my being friendly with André. But I couldn't really help it, it's just that he's been helpful, nothing more; there isn't anything to be jealous about——'

'Jealous? Of that tiresome little journalist?'

'Well, I thought perhaps——'

He said, 'I am not jealous, nor angry. I'm not anything. You can say if you like that I've been humbled—by the climb, by Judith's going. By Stella saying nothing, not even writing to me. I am now quite . . . flat, I suppose the word is; without ambition and hope. Not without love: I love Judith and Stella; and you, in that I want to comfort and help you, if I could. But I shall no longer be any use to you as a lover.'

She was looking bewildered, as she had done once when he'd tried to explain some theory of philosophy. 'I don't think I ever expected you to say anything like this.'

'No. I'm sorry.'

'I often think out things in my head for other people to say, but when it comes to the point they never say them. It makes me feel I could have told you about the others——'

'The others?'

'Well, yes. I mean they weren't important, but sometimes there were other people, for me. After all, I was alone a lot of the time, and I'm not the sort of person to be alone really, I never have been.'

(All those years ago, after Bill's death, Martha saying, 'I don't think I know how to be alone.')

He gave a sigh, seeing it fall into shape; not a pleasant shape. 'Yes, I see.'

She said, 'I took such trouble to keep it all from you——'

'You were quite right.'

'I don't think I really understand. Not properly understand you. I mean, you're quite different, quite a different person——'

'That's what I've been trying to tell you.'

'You don't even *mind* that I——'

'Oh yes,' he said. 'Yes, I mind. Because any failure in loving is sad—mine or yours.'

When she began to cry, he said, 'I'm sorry. I didn't mean that to hurt you.'

She said at last, muffled with tears, 'I wish we'd never come here. I wish you'd never gone near that beastly mountain. It's caused nothing but trouble.'

He said, putting a hand on her shoulder, 'Trouble was there before.'

'It's changed everything.'

He didn't answer. Curious that he should feel at this moment of the end for himself and Martha only sadness that there had not been, for either of them, enough love.

CHAPTER SEVEN

JOSEPH said, 'We have an hour.'

Judith nodded. 'Everything is ready.'

They were sitting in the small dining-room at the Altenhof. Joseph was at once encouraging her to eat an omelette, and examining his tickets.

'Half past seven from here. I must say it does me good to see a job properly done. Sleepers for both of us from Basle: it's not every man who can get that in twenty-four hours.'

She thought he had slightly changed since yesterday: now that the decision was made, the tickets in his hand, he was a little less concerned with her.

Sleepers from Basle. She found that whenever she thought about the journey there was a pull in her mind, a little tug of urgency and unease. That could, of course, be hunger or exhaustion, or the failure of the encounter with Sean. She said, 'In an hour. I find it hard to believe.'

Joseph folded the tickets and thrust his wallet away inside his coat with an air of certainty like a zoo keeper with some small but precious animal that had to be handled firmly. 'Aye, I dare say. But it's settled now. And the best thing you can do is to eat that omelette; it isn't there as still-life. After that . . . well, half an hour or so with your feet up wouldn't do any harm.'

She thought, obediently digging her fork into the omelette, that it was like being told to put one's feet up when the house was on fire. Joseph went on, 'If you will go chasing off to Interlaken without any breakfast to see chaps in hospital—'

'It had to be done.'

'Well, you've done it.'

'I didn't get anywhere. It was a failure if ever there was one.'

Joseph shrugged. 'What d'you expect? People go on saying what they've said before; that's my experience.'

'You don't think it matters?'

'No. If we all got worked up over every piece of daft nonsense in the newspapers we should be spinning like bloody tops eighteen hours a day. A fine mess of words gets spilled over the morning news-sheets, about a third of them true and all of them forgotten by six o'clock.'

She said a little flatly, 'Yes, perhaps. But to me it seems . . . an untruth is an untruth . . . kind of Gertrude Stein. It needs to be put right. I have to do something about it.'

'Well, you've done it now.' He had put the whole thing away and shut the lid on it. 'When you've finished eating you can go up to my room and rest. Even go to sleep; you don't have to worry; I'll wake you in time to get the train.'

The train. The wheels beginning to turn, the hotel porter turning and walking away, all of it going, sliding back: the mountains and the North Face of the Heide and the chalets and the wood-carvings and the high sloping meadows above Alpiglen with the gentians in the grass; all of it discarded, lost as one loses the world in death, together with the people who still stayed there, with Graeme and the lie that was told of him——

'You're looking a bit on the pale side, love. The sooner you go upstairs and have a bit of rest——'

'No, I can't. Not yet.' Hands trembling and sweat on her forehead; galloping panic because she was leaving this place of ill-omen.

'Now don't be an ass.' Joseph's voice was patient. 'You've got a long journey ahead of you; I'll make it as comfortable as I can, but I can't change a *wagon-lit* chasing across France at sixty miles an hour into something that stands still. It's no good making a fuss now——'

'I can't help it. I'm sorry. I think you'd better cut loose from me, give me up as a bad job——'

'Lot of good saying that.' His crumpled face looked tiredly over the room. 'You know as well as I do, it's not all that easy as you get older to give people up as a bad job. The time ahead gets a bit shorter, and you want to spend it with someone who's been around for a long while and knows about you. I dare say that sounds a bit matter-of-fact, but there it is. Now come on, eat your food and let's just keep calm until the train goes. . . .'

She was looking at him, not clearly seeing him, hearing him say again, 'The time ahead gets a bit shorter. . . .' That, she thought, was why so many marriages unexpectedly survived: everything tolerated—drink, or ill-temper, or the occasional unexplained week-end; the rags of emotion held on to because of the threat, because there wasn't all the time in the world, only a little time, only a few people that could in the end sit close about the dwindling fire, be there when one woke in the dark. . . .

She said, 'I'm sorry. But I shall have to go back to the hotel. Before we leave.'

He looked at her thoughtfully, as if he were making a calculation in his head. 'To see Graeme?'

'At least to see that everything's all right.'

He gave a short laugh. 'You'll wait a long time to see that. Better to stay here.'

The sense of urgency had increased; the dining-room now had the look of a place where one has stayed in ease, forgetting an appointment. She said, 'I really must go back——'

'There's not time.'

'Yes there is; there must be; you said we had an hour——'

'Quite a bit of that's gone——'

'Then I must go now. At once——' She pushed back her chair, began to rise a little clumsily to her feet. Joseph was looking at her with attention, a mixture of sadness and anger. 'If you've got any sense, you'll stay here.'

'I'm sorry.'

He said at last, 'Very well. But I'd like you to promise to come back.'

'Yes.'

'And quickly.'

She said, 'Yes.' There was still some food on her plate. All this was hazy, hurried, necessary, somehow desperate. 'I'll come back as soon as I can.'

Walking up the sunny street she found that the sense of urgency was eased; this was a respite, a breathing space. There wasn't much time, but this was necessary, and it wouldn't take long.

CHAPTER EIGHT

THE room was painted grey; there was, surprisingly, a small bar at one end under a striped awning; and behind the counter a bored young man in a white coat who occasionally bit his nails. There was about the place a feeling of hurried, makeshift activity mixed with dust and long emptiness, as if the chairs had only just been brought up from a basement, and the few bottles on the bar counter diverted from some larger and more permanent store.

'A disused bar,' the hotel proprietor had said, 'where Herr Muir can see the gentlemen in private.'

Private, Graeme thought, was not quite the word; through some confusion there was at the far end of the room, sitting below a large mural of an Arab woman dressed in purple, a group of men and women from the north of England who were eating sandwiches and anxious about their coach. Occasionally their anxiety grew loud and penetrated to the small group of journalists who lingered uneasily near the bar.

Rather like an occasion in the church hall, Graeme thought, on a night so wet that only a fraction of those expected have arrived. Had it been possible, he would have moved elsewhere, but the barman and the bottles had been put there for his especial benefit, and it seemed ungracious not to make use of them. And he had the feeling that, incongruous though this place appeared, it was the one that had been appointed: that some few last words had to be said, and since they must sum up an enterprise that had contained so much violence and confusion, they might as well be said here as anywhere else.

Among the few journalists he saw André Tévernin, the young man who had greeted Hugh and himself on their arrival in Lundervald, and one whom he vaguely remembered as having spoken to him outside the hospital in Interlaken. It had been no part of his plan, he thought, that Martha should be there, but she had arrived, silently, and looking a little tearful. She touched him on the arm and said, 'I just had to be here. No one must take any notice of me,' and sat down on a hard red chair whose back showed a light film of dust.

He began to talk. He told the story of the climb in dry sentences that nevertheless brought the taste and smell of it back: the rocks and the fear and Hugh's close company: Sean full of ambition and life. Martha seemed to be listening with a placid, somehow shallow attention. He could see Judith very clearly in his mind. As he talked he was occasionally thrown off course by the voices of the north-country men and women who were by now certain, many of them said, that something had gone wrong. He was also aware of coming and going in the dusky hall which led from this room: his back was turned to it, but he could feel the pressure of people who occasionally paused to listen, to see what was going on.

He said, 'There's one other point.' He drank from his glass and glanced round at them: they were all, he thought, politely attentive, yet in some way not concerned; he wondered whether anything he had said would do the least good, and had a sudden sense of isolation. He went on, 'I got to the top but at a terrible cost. And as far as the Press is concerned disaster has to be someone's fault: it has to have behind it a murky tangle of ignoble motives——'

He paused as a voice cut clearly through from the end of the room: 'A great thing like a bus can't go and lose itself, not in these mountains: it's daft; it can't climb. Henry, go and find someone who knows something . . .'

He went on, 'Had we all made the summit, you'd have dressed the whole thing up in gold braid; you'd have put us along with Mallory and Irvine, Mummery and Whymper.

You'd have brought out your adjectives, talked about courage and adventure——'

André Tévernin said, 'If you had all succeeded, the whole thing would have been very different. Hugh Ferris would still be alive; Randall would not now be in hospital——'

'But we would all have been the same. The same men, the same motives——'

'And who,' asked the blond young man who had first greeted them in Lundervald, 'do you blame for the disaster?'

'No one,' he said. 'Conditions were bad.'

'We understood that Randall fell while attempting a severe iced pitch. You do not feel, perhaps, that he was careless——'

'No,' he said, maintaining patience. 'It was no one's fault.'

'It has been said that Hugh Ferris was too old for the climb; that he was persuaded against his will——'

'No one persuaded him. It was what he wanted to do. And he climbed magnificently.' Very clearly now he saw Hugh; heard the crisp, familiar voice; felt the pounding and destroying weight of the avalanche. He said, 'We did our best. All of us. You will have to take my word for that.'

'And you, Herr Muir, did more than your best: you conquered the North Face——'

Here, unexpectedly, an English voice came from a hitherto silent gentleman in a grey suit: 'And a bloody fine job it was. It's no good saying I'm not proud of it because I am.'

('He must be somewhere; a bus driver doesn't go suddenly daft——' 'I don't see why not: bus drivers can go mad just like the rest of us, I would have thought——')

He said, 'Yes, I made it. But like everyone else who's done it, I shall never attempt it again. What's more, it's the last big climb I shall do.' The words seemed to have spoken themselves. A little surprised at them, he went on, 'I'm not a young man any more. I've had a good run, and I've been lucky. Luckier than some of the others. I'm prepared to settle for the easier jobs at home.'

He thought at first that this had commanded their silence. Then he saw that their eyes were not on him, but on a point beyond his shoulder. He glanced irritably behind him.

And then the whole thing changed.

He said, '*Stella*.'

More dishevelled than usual, dressed in trousers and carrying a canvas bag. With something in her face that, because of the confusion, the weariness and the hope in his mind, he could not read.

'*Stella*.'

'Hullo, Pa.' She kissed his cheek. She was pale, a little awkward, and glanced at the group of men who surrounded him. 'Am I interrupting something? I'm afraid this must be one hell of a surprise and I'm sorry for it. I got a plane from Paris to Basle, and if you get a plane you're there before you're ready. It cost a fabulous amount; I've only got twenty-five francs left.' Her glance went in the direction of André Tévernin, then came back again. 'I came to say I'm glad you made it. I'm glad you were all right.'

He smiled, shaken by pleasure so unexpected, so out of tune with this dingy hour in the bar. 'All the way from Paris, my dear, just to say that?'

'No.' She put down the canvas bag and thrust her hands into her trousers pockets. 'I came to apologize. And to tell you that I know all this stuff about leaving Sean on the ledge is a lot of bloody lies. Foul, bloody lies.'

And happiness, he thought, can knock you as silly as surprise or three strong drinks. He said, 'Apologize?'

She looked again towards André Tévernin. 'Yes. I've made an ass of myself.' He thought the small downward smile on her face made her look both more adult and less sure. A large woman from the party at the other end of the room went up to Martha and asked in a clear whisper where the toilet was. Tévernin, he noticed, had a look on his face of controlled impatience; the other journalists were looking a little cynical, as if they suspected a put-up job. The blond young man said, 'This we understand, is your daughter——'

'These are gentlemen of the Press, darling,' said Graeme. Happiness kept swimming towards him, dissolving the room and the weariness of the past hour.

'Yes,' said Stella. 'One of them I know.' She said to André Tévernin, 'You made the most of everything I said, didn't you? The very most.'

Tévernin shrugged. 'I write what will interest my readers. It is unnecessary to talk to me about honour and confidences——'

'Be fair,' said Stella. 'I wasn't such a dope as to mention either.' Graeme saw that her hand was trembling. 'When I got here a little while ago, I went first to your hotel. I thought I'd say all the things I had to say first, before I went on to find Pa. But I dare say it's better this way.'

'It is remarkable,' said Tévernin, 'how your attitude has changed towards this climb——'

'Yes, isn't it,' said Stella. She sounded angry, Graeme thought, but there was also a little enjoyment there too: of using the whip on Tévernin, of the attention of the small circle of men who listened. 'I read about the climb after you'd gone. I read about Father having got there, and Hugh being killed—and I was with it, part of it, I couldn't help being; shaken and proud as well. And then I read your stuff. With a lot of the things I'd said, dished up to look worse. And that hit me just about here'—she put one fist on her midriff— 'the feeling of "please make it so I haven't done it: yes but I have". So I packed this rather grubby canvas bag, got a cancellation on a flight to Basle this morning. It's surprising how much you|can get done in how little time, once you try.'

Yes, Graeme thought, bless her, she's enjoyed this almost as much as I have. Fun to take the stage, and at the same time to make anyone as happy as she's made me. Just for a little, it even obscured Judith.

The journalists, he noticed, were drifting away, with something of the air of those who have been promised more lavish entertainment than has been provided. He bade them farewell, indifferent to them now. Tévernin was the last to go, and Martha, something to Graeme's surprise, went with him. Stella's glance followed him until he was out of sight. She made a small grimace when he had gone and said, ' "So quick, so clean an ending, Oh that was right, lad, that was brave." Quoting is allowed when one's young and always putting on a bit of an act whatever happens, wouldn't you say? . . . And he seems to have got a new chum now; Martha, of all people; what d'you know?'

He said, the idea only just at this moment coming into his mind, 'Were you in love with him?'

She said, carrying off the hurt with a slight swagger, 'Oh yes. But you'll be glad to hear, I expect—parents being what they are—that I didn't sleep with him. Saved by the gong really—or rather, him coming here to Lundervald. So there's no need for me to have myself a glorious *crise de nerfs* now he's gone. All the same . . .' She looked after the way he had gone, shrugged and took out a cigarette. 'Well, there it is.' She smiled at him over the cigarette. 'I've made such an ass of myself. But I'm sorry.'

He said, 'Listen, darling. The whole of this has been . . . an unhappy thing. The climb; the accidents; the things that were said. And I dare say a lot more'll be said; this kind of rumour's hard to quench, once it's started. But seeing you just now was a lifeline; that God-given thing that one scarcely dare hope for, but which happens . . . now and again.'

'Oh, fine. Fine, I'm glad of that.' She pushed her fringe back from her forehead. 'Rather like that for me too. Comforting to be here. And to be forgiven.'

'Forgiven?'

'Not a thing one expects when one's young . . . perhaps because one isn't all that good at forgiving, oneself. One has to learn, I suppose.'

He went on looking at her. It couldn't go on being as good as this; she would return to Paris, and the differences between them would slowly emerge again. Yet this would remain, and nothing would be quite the same because of it.

He put an arm across her shoulders. 'Come along and let's find you a room.' It was not time yet, he thought, to say anything about Judith. For the moment he would evade Stella's questions. He began to think of what he could say.

Judith saw that a large blue coach was parked outside the Gletschergaten; men and women were coming down the steps towards it and exclaiming loudly in annoyance and relief. 'I told you,' one woman was saying as she passed her, 'you can't lose a great thing like a coach. . . .' 'All the same, I don't like it. A bus driver going to sleep in the sun; it doesn't seem right. . . .'

The hotel itself as she entered it seemed held in a curious silence; the chairs like coolie hats were empty; no one sat at the reception desk. This was not unusual, but for the moment everything seemed strange, as if she were under the influence of some mild drug. All of it deeply familiar, as though the few days she had spent here had multiplied in memory. As she went through the hall she noticed automatically the difference between this and the four-star Altenhof. Joseph seemed suddenly far distant, like someone to whom she had already said good-bye.

The odd silence endured. Within it she heard the flat vowels of Joseph's voice: 'I'd like you to promise to come back.' She heard also the far clamour of her first arrival here with Graeme and Hugh. . . . There was a smell of cooking; movement somewhere upstairs.

She saw Joseph in his room at the Altenhof, shutting his suitcase, gradually becoming restless as the clock hands slid round, but all the time, in spite of her, sure of himself, of the train, of the Vermeer in Amsterdam. He wouldn't wait, she thought, beyond the appointed time; he would fling his coat over his arm and make for the train, in company with an anger and disappointment which would gradually fade, eased by the luxury of first-class travel and the best of the wine. . . . But she saw the sad Jewish eyes, and the stubby figure as he walked quickly and alone the few yards to the station. She remembered the young man who had walked beside her along the Boulevard de la Madeleine, deprived of his week-end. *Plus ça change*.

Now it seemed she had known for a long time that she wouldn't go with him. Perhaps when she had spoken this morning to Ludwig Klein, or in the hospital with Sean, or from that first moment when she had stood in the street with the newspaper in her hands. ('. . . promise to come back.') Guilt was submerged by the sudden beating of her heart as she began to climb the stairs.

As she hesitated on the first landing, a bedroom door opened and Stella came out wearing the dressing-gown she had worn in the Paris room.

Judith was suddenly still. She said nothing at all. It occurred to her after a few moments that her mouth was open. Before she could speak Stella flung her towel over her shoulder and said, 'Well, hi. Been wondering where you were. I'm afraid I'm a terrible shock, but that's not entirely my fault. I'll explain, but not now because there's a bath running——'

Judith savoured the young face which was changed from the face she remembered: an authority there, mixed with friendliness. She said, 'Stella, darling, I'm so terribly glad to see you.'

She hugged her, and Stella emerged from the embrace, rubbing her fringe. 'Well . . . gosh . . . isn't that fine. I seem to have got it right this time. After all, whatever one thinks about mountains, and personally they give me the creeps, one couldn't let all that nonsense get said about Pa without a shot fired, now could one?' She grinned and backed a little way away; she was abashed, Judith thought, like a delinquent child caught out in a good turn. 'Going to be gorgeous tonight; food *and* wine, Pa says. . . . My *bath.*'

Judith said, still a little hazy with surprise, 'Where's Graeme?'

'In his room—isn't that where you'd expect him to be?' Over her shoulder, a little surprised, flying towards the bathroom.

Judith climbed to the next landing, Stella vivid in her mind. She hesitated again before she opened the door. English voices of new arrivals in the hall, exclaiming on the beauty of the view.

One had to go in.

He had his back to her; he was apparently searching in a drawer for a tie. A moment's shock in this: the somehow surprising knowledge that life would go on for him, whether she was there or not. He turned at once, and she thought he had been expecting Stella, for a smile on his face faded.

She said quickly, a little breathless, 'I've seen Stella. It was wonderful that she came.'

He nodded. His face did not change. He had removed the plaster from the cut on his jaw, and the wound showed clear, reddish and uneven, giving him a look of difference. He said, 'Is Joseph waiting for you?'

She shook her head. 'No. He will go on his own.'

'To wait for you somewhere else?'

'No.'

'Why not?'

She smiled, as if the sternness of his questions were a little too much for her. 'Because I had to come back. There wasn't anything else to do.'

'Come back to me?'

'Yes.'

Curious to feel his arms suddenly about her, to feel the forceful certainty of his embrace, hear his voice saying, 'Nothing made any sense without you, nothing at all . . .' as if from now on everything was going to go well, as if Sean

215

did not lie in a hospital bed, nor Hugh in the Heide's snows; as if trouble wouldn't come back. . . . Well, for the moment let it seem so.

The noon sun was brilliant; the meadows above Alpiglen shone with heat and the ink-stamp blue of the flowers. The Heide's North Face was beginning to emerge from shadow: the immense tower of rock and snow was coming slowly into its brief tenancy of light. Now and again there sounded the distant crack of stonefall, the tuneless drone of flies, the sweet empty clang of a cow-bell. Beyond this, there was silence.

Graeme stood, looking at the Face through binoculars, with Judith beside him. He said, 'What weather! If we'd only had it like this. . . .'

He moved the glasses slowly upward, and she said, 'Can you see any sign of him?'

'No. . . . I suppose there's not much hope. The guides searched again yesterday; they climbed more than two thousand feet. . . . They found no sign of a body.'

In the warmth, she felt the cold touch her. She said, 'If you see him?'

'Then I can tell them, and, if it's possible, they will bring him down.'

She stood there beside him in the hot sunlight, feeling the beginning of fear again. He looked at her. 'I've promised. None of the big stuff any more——'

'I'm still afraid.'

She scarcely listened to the passionate words of his answer. For it no longer seemed to matter, what he could say or promise; she was bound with him, joined by the tough fibres of marriage, until death broke them. What came, she would try to accept. Conflict, at least, had ended; she felt weakly convalescent, recognizing the return of lost appetites and desires and courage.

He said, 'I'm going to have one more look for him,' and moved closer to the Face, lifting the glasses again.

She watched him as he stood, a small figure below the towering, snow-stained rocks. He had said, 'Nothing like this'; but, she thought, you couldn't be sure. . . . She went on looking until her eyes ached with the smallness of his figure and the brightness of the snows.

Then he turned and came towards her, the glasses in his hand. She remembered that he had climbed the great Wall behind him, and she felt within her a twist of fear and pride, like the first thrust of desire.

He said, 'No, I can't see any trace of him. Other climbers will find him, please God. I would like him to be found.'